Praise for *Where the Road Bends*

"With her signature heartwarming style, Rachel Fordham takes us on an emotional, restorative journey in *Where the Road Bends*. This book is a heart-tugging story of choices and second chances, and these deftly woven characters will linger in your thoughts long after the last poignant page."

Laura Frantz, Christy Award–winning author
of *A Heart Adrift*

"A thoroughly engaging romance! Once again, author Rachel Fordham will delight readers with this poignantly romantic tale of hope. Against a backdrop of the American Midwest in 1880, the story captures the spirit of Jane Austen's *Persuasion*, as Quincy Barnes and Norah King are like star-crossed lovers, each scarred by the past and mourning a love too easily surrendered. Yet as fate has drawn the two apart, only Providence can reunite them in this compelling and often emotionally gripping novel of faith, forgiveness, and a second chance at happiness. Christian historical fiction fans are sure to love *Where the Road Bends*!"

Kate Breslin, bestselling author of *As Dawn Breaks*

"*Where the Road Bends* is the perfect romance, with a twist or two so there's no predicting how the story will play out. It's perfect because of snappy dialogue, three-dimensional characters who make mistakes and have to recover from them, and side plots that support the theme of telling the truth and doing the right thing. Rachel Fordham's novels always engage me, and this one didn't let me skip to find out how it ended! A joy to read all the way to the end."

**Jane Kirkp̶_____ ̶___rd-winning author
of ̶

T0204529

Praise for *A Lady in Attendance*

"Fordham balances historical touchstones of chivalry and chaperones with the modern appeal of a story about choices and consequence. . . . Fordham brings new depth to her signature charm as her characters grapple with questions of self-worth, accountability, and justice."

Booklist

"Such a great historical fiction story that had me laughing as much as researching! . . . I learned so much through this book."

Write-Read-Life

"A beautiful tale of romance, danger, and possibilities! I highly recommend it!"

Interviews and Reviews

"Rachel Fordham's *A Lady in Attendance* draws you in from the first page and leaves you captivated until the oh-so-romantic conclusion. A poignant and beautifully written story of faith, forgiveness, and the healing power of love."

Mimi Matthews, *USA Today* bestselling author

where the
ROAD BENDS

Books by Rachel Fordham

The Hope of Azure Springs
Yours Truly, Thomas
A Life Once Dreamed
A Lady in Attendance

where the

ROAD BENDS

RACHEL FORDHAM

Revell

a division of Baker Publishing Group
Grand Rapids, Michigan

© 2022 by Rachel Fordham

Published by Revell
a division of Baker Publishing Group
PO Box 6287, Grand Rapids, MI 49516-6287
www.revellbooks.com

Printed in the United States of America

Library of Congress Cataloging-in-Publication Data
Names: Fordham, Rachel, 1984– author.
Title: Where the road bends / Rachel Fordham.
Description: Grand Rapids, MI : Revell, a division of Baker Publishing Group, [2022] |
Identifiers: LCCN 2021041401 | ISBN 9780800739744 (paperback) | ISBN 9780800741549 (casebound) | ISBN 9781493436309 (ebook)
Subjects: GSAFD: Love stories.
Classification: LCC PS3606.O747335 W48 2022 | DDC 813/.6—dc23
LC record available at https://lccn.loc.gov/2021041401

This is a work of historical reconstruction; the appearances of certain historical figures are therefore inevitable. All other characters, however, are products of the author's imagination, and any resemblance to actual persons, living or dead, is coincidental.

Baker Publishing Group publications use paper produced from sustainable forestry practices and post-consumer waste whenever possible.

22 23 24 25 26 27 28   7 6 5 4 3 2 1

For the "other" Rachel,
who is brave and fearless
no matter the bends in the road.

"You pierce my soul. I am half agony, half hope . . . I have loved none but you."

—Jane Austen, *Persuasion*

_1_

BLACKWELL, IOWA, 1880

The small band on her ring finger glistened in the sunlight as Norah King walked the family land she had nearly lost. This land, her father had said before he died, was their legacy. It was the backdrop of their story—their wrestle and toil—and their love.

She lifted her hand in front of her and sighed. She'd told Jake she didn't need a ring, but he wouldn't have it any other way, claiming that his bride would be up on all the latest fashions. In two weeks' time, she would be married, and the thought made her heart beat unevenly. But there was no turning back, no other way. He'd come courting the very week the banker had threatened to call in her loan. Jake had come to rescue her, and she would be thankful.

"Norah Granger," she said. It sounded strange to her ears, but with time, she assured herself, it would become who she was. Jake wasn't the romantic suitor she'd pictured marrying, but now at twenty-two years old and short on money, she was willing to let her former idealistic notions go. Jake was an able-bodied man, and though older than she was, he was willing to rescue her in her time of need—that counted for something. That was enough, was it not?

Norah stopped walking when she reached the creek that ran through her land and couldn't help but smile when she heard its familiar burbling. A bench her father had gifted her on her tenth birthday beckoned her to enjoy a moment's respite.

The gentle rolling of the creek mesmerized her as it had always done, soothing the restlessness inside her. She removed her boots and stockings and gathered her skirts in her hands. Jake had agreed to live on this land when they married. Her family deed would soon be in his name, but this creek and this bench would always be hers.

Her spine stiffened. Jake wouldn't care that she found the water delightful and sloshed around in it, would he? She laughed. What a ridiculous fear. Jake farmed. Surely he appreciated and enjoyed the land and water. He wouldn't fault her for wanting to cool her feet in the summer heat. Besides, she would work long hours to make up for any time lost. Shirking was not in her nature—she'd show him that.

She waded deeper into the water, letting the delicious freshness lap against her calves, and for one blissful moment she had no worries. Gone were her money troubles, her marriage fears, and her loneliness—washed away with the current.

Two vultures circling not far off caught her eye. Around and around they went, swooping lower with each loop, readying, no doubt, to land by some poor creature that had lost its life to the elements. Their circling motions interrupted her calm. Her heart beat faster and worry crept in, causing her to drop her skirts and run toward the birds and what they had found.

She rushed from the creek as quick as a fox from a henhouse. Her hogs and cattle were profit animals. She couldn't lose them. Her finances were already precarious. Her land was prime, that was true, but a loan came with it. Evidence of the year she'd struggled to farm on her own while wading through the unfamiliar waters of grief.

Her bare feet and wet hem tried to slow her advance on the circling birds, but she refused to be hindered. She pushed hard and fast, her feet crying out when they landed on a rock, but still she pressed on, unwilling to slow her pace. Her focus jumped from the yellow plants around her to the carnivores above. What did they see?

To her right, her small herd of cattle grazed, unaffected by the birds above them. Nothing seemed amiss, so she slowed her pace. Perhaps she had been too rash with her worry. Clinging to that thought, she nearly laughed. Her nerves had her frantic, but all was well.

Norah raised a hand to her brow, blocking the sun, and sighed as she admired her endless fields dancing to the rhythm of the wind. Ignoring the birds above, she turned back toward the creek and her abandoned shoes. Two steps were all she took before stopping again. A patch of crushed wheat and . . . a trail of red. Her fear returned. Something *was* hurt—or dead. She forced her breath to come slow and quiet as she followed the path of blood. Her hands shook, and she forced them into fists. This was her farm. Until Jake moved onto it, she had to take care of the animals and keep them safe from predators.

The amount of blood increased as she went on. She braced

herself to see a mauled animal, a sight she was certain would turn her stomach. The trail veered left, so she veered with it and then froze.

A head. Full of matted hair. It was . . .

Her skin tingled. A man? She didn't understand. She had feared a cow or a hog but had never once imagined the birds were circling above a man. Inhaling deeply and letting her breath out slowly, she forced herself to stay present despite wanting to run and hide and pretend the wretched image away. This man, whoever he was, needed her. There was no one else.

"Sir?"

He didn't move. Norah clung to her meager courage and knelt beside him. Her hand trembled as she reached toward him, only to pull back and clutch it to her chest. Death was not new to her. The cows and hogs and, of course, chickens were all butchered, but suddenly an image of her parents overpowered her. Her mother's sallow, sickly face before illness took her, and her father, bloodied and broken after he'd fallen from his favorite horse. She pressed her eyes closed and searched for the strength and fortitude she wanted to believe she possessed—that she needed to possess in this moment.

"Are you alive?" She forced her still-weak hand to the man's chest and held her breath, focusing on him. A slight rise and fall.

"You're alive!" She let the air out of her chest, instantly relieved and less afraid.

His dark, shaggy hair lay matted against his scalp, and his face was badly swollen from bruises that gave him an allover purple hue. His nose appeared badly broken. It did not take much imagination to believe that the rest of him was equally battered. It was difficult to know what this man would look like if he were in good health. He could be anyone. Perhaps he was even someone she'd seen before. Questions swirled in her mind, but she couldn't dwell on them, not when his heart beat so weakly.

The vultures and hot afternoon sun were worrisome, as were his injuries. His survival, she feared, teetered on her ability to care for him. Norah stood on her bare feet and looked around, desperate for a solution. She feared leaving him, afraid the birds would grow daring enough to land and add their own injuries. If she could rouse him, maybe he could limp beside her back to the house. With uncharacteristic boldness, she lifted his arm, put it over her shoulder, and tried to pry him from the ground. He groaned, then fell limp again.

Certain she could not carry him all the way to the house, she grabbed a rock from the ground and threw it toward the birds.

"Go away!" she shouted. They mocked her and continued their circling.

She could do little about the birds, other than hurry, but she could be of some help in protecting the man against the sun. She tore the wet hem of her skirt and pressed the damp fabric to his forehead.

"I'll come back," she said before running toward her house in a reckless sprint.

It took her longer than she wanted to get home, hitch a horse and makeshift pallet, and get back to him. She kept her eye on the birds as she returned. Only one circled now. Was the other on the ground? Her stomach tightened and her hand went to the pistol in her bag. "Come on," she urged the horse. "No lollygagging."

He nickered his resistance but increased his pace.

"He's just ahead," she said to the horse. "Faster."

Once she was close enough, the second bird came into view. Large and malicious, it stood near the injured stranger. She leapt from the horse, spread her arms wide, and growled at the large bird. It hopped a few feet back but didn't fly away. Norah pointed her pistol at the bird, pulled the trigger back, and fired. She missed, but the sound of the shot sent the bird soaring high into the air. There was no time to gloat over her victory, so she shoved the gun back into the saddlebag and turned her attention to the desperate man.

"Let him live," she whispered before once again placing her hand on the man's chest. A steady thudding confirmed he was alive. His eyes popped open and his hand came up and grasped her own, making her recoil in fear.

"Water," he said, before his hand fell and his swollen eyes closed.

He said no more, but his words had struck their mark. A fierce determination burned inside her. No matter their difference in size or the distance they had to cross, she would get this man water and aid him however possible.

Sweat ran down her forehead as she dragged his large, broken body to the pallet. Whenever she felt unequipped for the task, she shouted again at the worthless birds and told them they couldn't have him.

"Go find another meal," she yelled when her muscles threatened to give up on her. She was strong thanks to years of plowing, hauling water, and chopping wood, but even with years of farm muscle on her small but sturdy frame, the task of moving this giant of a man was difficult.

"I'm taking him home. You can't have him!" she shouted to

the sky. She stood near the man's head, put her hands under his shoulders, and pulled with all her might. Her muscles screamed in agony and her back ached, but she did not stop.

Only when the man was secured on the pallet did she relax and acknowledge what a feat she'd accomplished. He was twice her size, if not more, and all muscle. She blushed and pushed the observation away. She certainly hadn't saved his life yet, but she'd saved him from the birds and that alone brought a smile to her face.

"Getting you back to the house will be bumpy," she said over her shoulder as she led the horse away from the field. "Once we're there, I'll clean you up and go for the doctor. You smell like a rotten carcass." She wiped her brow with the back of her hand. "I shouldn't say that. That's terribly rude even if it is true."

Being mindful of his situation, she chose instead to fill the air with lighthearted conversation. She occasionally glanced over her shoulder and tried to deduce what she could about the man.

"Where are you from?" she asked, not truly expecting a response. "I've lived on this farm my whole life. If you were feeling better, you'd see how beautiful it is. The crops blow in the wind like a wave on the sea. I've never seen the sea, but I can imagine it. Can you?"

He, of course, made no answer, but she pretended he did. His large stature led her to believe he had a deep voice, so she imagined he told her about the hue of the ocean and the sound it made when it crashed against the shore.

"It must be beautiful," she said while leading the horse around a rut. "But I don't believe it's more beautiful than King land."

He didn't utter a sound, leaving her to wonder if he even heard her chatter.

"We're eight miles from town. Are you from our town? Or maybe you traveled from somewhere else? Azure Springs or another place to the east? I suppose you'll tell me when you're able."

She rambled on and on, never slowing her pace or her talking. "Sometimes I imagine I'm young again and this farm is run by my father, and my mother is inside the house. It was all so much easier when my father was alive." She bit her lip, frustrated that she'd led the conversation back to the dead. "We have cattle and hogs. And we grow wheat and corn."

She sighed. "That's what we always had and we did so well, except when my father gambled. Don't judge him too harshly. He still managed to keep this place going. With him gone, I'm the one who's failed this place. But . . . but Jake's going to fix everything." He'd blown into her life like the dust on the wind—seemingly small but capable of overtaking everything. "He's got to."

She led the horse the rest of the way to the house in silence, mindful of her charge but also deep in thought. So much had happened in such a short amount of time, she could hardly keep up. She looked back at the man on the pallet, another unexpected happening. And now he was going to be in her home, under her care. She cringed, thinking how that would sound to the already less-than-cordial neighbors. Come what may, he was here and she would not leave him to the birds.

Getting him inside the house was far from graceful, and she couldn't help but hope he didn't remember a moment of it. She dragged him by his arms, rolled him across the floor, and even attempted to push him by his feet. Several times she had to stop and catch her breath but always went back to her task, refusing to forsake him. More pushing and pulling and at last he was securely inside.

"You're a brute, too big for your own good," she snapped at him when his head bumped into the wall. Remorse followed, and in a gentler voice, she said, "I will choose to believe you would help me if you could. Since you're not up for talking, I'm going to assume you are the victim of an atrocious crime and in desperate need of kindness." She laughed at her own absurdity. "Whatever you are, you showed up on my land."

Rather than attempt to lift him onto a bed, she pulled the mattress from her parents' room, laid it on the floor of the parlor, and rolled him onto it. Sweat ran in streams down her face when she at last had him settled.

She groaned when she thought of all she still had to do today. Everything in her wanted to collapse, curl up, and sleep for hours, but animals needed feeding, her garden ought to be weeded, and her stomach hadn't been filled since daybreak. But first she had to see to the stranger's wounds. A squeamish fear niggled its way into her mind, attempting to steal her resolve. Cleaning him would require her to see more of this man than she wanted to see. Perhaps if she went for the doctor, he'd not only see to any wounds but also wash this poor man's stench away.

Unsure what to do, she looked out the window at the sun, low in the sky. Fetching a doctor would take time, so she'd have to travel in the dark. She scowled, knowing her situation was less than ideal, but what options did she have? Leave him and ride into the night or stay beside him and hope her mediocre doctoring skills would suffice. She felt ill-equipped to make such a decision. At last she decided to first inspect his wounds and see how severe they appeared. At the very least, she knew how to feed a convalescing invalid—nursing her sickly mother had given her plenty of experience.

Still stalling, she offered the man water, only to have it run down his cheek. She put the water aside and braced herself for the inevitable. With fresh rags and soap in hand, she set to work cleaning the caked-on mud and blood from his skin. The bruises could not be so easily washed away, but with time the swelling and color would dissipate. When she was bruised or scratched, her mama never fetched a doctor. Granted, this man had a great many more such injuries than she'd ever had, but they still did not seem so bad that a doctor needed to be summoned in the night. She took a deep breath, knowing his internal injuries could be worse than those on his purple face.

His shirt was tattered. Rather than save it, she cut it off and washed his arms and chest. *It's merely doctoring*, she reassured herself when she felt her pulse jump with each stroke of the rag against his flesh. Two gashes in his upper chest required bandaging, and when she touched his ribs, he jerked to the side. Poor man—his ribs were so tender, likely broken or badly bruised. Once finished with his upper body, she covered him with a sheet and stepped away to catch her breath and prepare herself for what she must do next.

Many years ago, her mama ran out to help a field hand who'd been injured. He'd cut his leg awful bad and she'd slit his trousers up to his thigh without even batting an eye and stitched him up like his leg was nothing more than a seam to be sewn.

Just doctoring, Norah reminded herself before returning to her patient. Shoulders squared, she attempted to display the same body language she'd seen in her mama all those years before. With forced confidence, she cut his already torn trousers from his ankles up to his thighs and inspected him for injuries. Though she tried to think of nothing but chores and how many hogs she ought to sell when the time came, she couldn't help but notice that this man was muscular and clearly worked hard for his daily bread.

"Who hurt you?" she asked aloud before tackling any more of the much-needed cleaning.

He rolled his head toward her. She gasped and flung the sheet over his body before dashing a few steps away.

"You're injured. That's all this is. I was just trying to help." Her words were true, but she still felt guilty for the skin she'd seen.

"Where?" His voice was hoarse and uneven.

"You have some gashes on your head and a broken nose. I believe your ribs may be broken, and well, you have bruises everywhere. Though I . . . I haven't inspected *all* of you."

"Where"—he tried to clear his throat—"where am I?"

"The King farm just outside of Blackwell, Iowa." She swished her rag absently in her bowl of water, now darkened by the blood she'd washed from his skin. "If you think you'll be all right while I'm gone, I can fetch a doctor. It would take some time, but I'd ride fast. I'd go for a neighbor to help, but . . . well, there's no one very close, and most wouldn't want to help. Or I don't think they would, but I could ask."

"No. Don't go." He tried unsuccessfully to prop himself up. "Where am I?"

"Blackwell, Iowa." She said the name slowly, putting emphasis on each syllable. Perhaps she should check again for head injuries.

"No." His head rolled to the side as though it were too heavy to control. "I can't be in Iowa."

"Unless everyone I know has been lying to me for my entire life, then this is assuredly Blackwell, Iowa."

He groaned.

"We're small, but we have a doctor. You needn't worry."

"No doctor," he said. With his right hand, he patted his chest. "Where's my shirt? Give me my clothes and I'll go."

Heat rushed up Norah's neck all the way to her ears. "I cut your shirt and . . . and your pants. They were torn, and I ha-had to see if you were injured. I did not expect you to wake. I can only guess that getting you out of the sun has helped." She grabbed the soiled shirt and held it out to him. "Here. But you won't be able to wear it. I'll get you clothes of my father's when you're ready to be on your way."

His weak hands reached for the shirt before falling to his side. "Money? Was there money in my shirt, in my jacket?"

Norah shook her head. "You didn't have a jacket, and I didn't go through your pockets." She put a hand on his arm. "Don't agitate yourself. I'm sure whatever is wrong can be set right. If you'll trust me, I'll help you." She looked away when she said it. So many things were impossible to set right and she knew it, but she couldn't help but hope his problems could be resolved. "I'll get you feeling better. Let me get your water."

She reached for the cup she'd brought earlier, only to see it overturned. As she headed to the kitchen, away from him, the reality of her situation settled on her. *He could be bad*, she thought. She knew nothing about him, not even his name. Without getting his water, she darted back to the parlor. "What's your name?"

His eyes had been closed, but he opened them when she spoke. "Quincy Barnes."

For no reason at all, she felt herself relax. Apparently, it was more comfortable being under the same roof with a man whose name she knew. "Mr. Barnes, I'm Norah King."

"Call me Quincy."

"If you insist." She pivoted away from him. "I'll fetch you your water now."

When she returned, she sat on the floor beside Quincy and fidgeted, unsure what to do next. He drank a few sips and then fell asleep, shifting and moaning from pain. When he cried out or winced in his sleep, she put a hand to his shoulder and he settled.

When he woke again, she propped him up long enough for him to drink more water and tried to comfort him with her words. "Would it help to talk about whatever it was that brought you to my land?"

A crease formed between his dark brows. "I don't know how exactly I came to be here."

"I told you all about my land and even about my problems. You may not have been awake for it all, but I did an awful lot of prattling as I struggled to get you under my roof. Seems if I'm to sit beside you and bring you water and soup and nurse you back to health, you ought to tell me about yourself. What if you're some awful villain and I don't know it?"

The corner of his mouth pulled upward, and her fidgeting hands stilled at the sight of it. With his injuries so fresh and plentiful, she didn't dare call him handsome, but there was something enticing about his faint smile that intrigued her. "If I were a villain, do you think I'd tell you?"

"You've a point. I suppose I'll have to heave you back

outside and let the vultures have you. It's a shame though. You were ever so much work to drag inside."

He laughed, then grimaced. His hand went to his side as he fought to catch his breath. "I woke up out there once, and I saw the birds." He shuddered. "You saved my life. I'm indebted to you."

Norah brushed her hands on her skirts, smoothing nonexistent wrinkles. "No, I did what anyone would do. You were in need, and so I helped."

"You're alone here?" He attempted to look around her parlor, only to give up before much of an appraisal. Norah observed it even if he could not. It was a pretty room but with sparse furnishings since she'd sold so many of the family's pieces when money got tight. Still, it remained warm and inviting, with rich wallpaper, a dark wood floor, and large windows along the front. She frowned. Her fine house kept her safe from wind and hail, but it'd not been enough to save her family's reputation.

"I'm sorry it was your land I ended up on."

"Don't be. I've not had many guests lately, so in a way, you're a welcome surprise." She blinked quickly, fighting off the ache of loneliness that had so often blanketed her since her father's death. "It can be quiet out here, and there's always so much work. Nursing you back to health will be a diversion and a reason to work faster." Her engagement ring caught her attention. An odd impulse nearly caused her to tuck her hand away. Instead, she said, "I am to be married soon. My home will not be this quiet for long. And on Monday a few field hands will be stopping by to help. They aren't much for conversation, at least not with me, but I feel less alone when they're here."

"Engaged." His voice grew soft. Was it from his pain or something else? His eyes moved slowly to her hand. "I was in love once. Well, I thought I was at least, but"—he winced again—"love is a farce."

"Oh, I'm not in— I mean, you think it's a farce?" Her hand flew to her mouth, shocked by the confession she'd nearly made. She didn't love Jake, not yet anyway, but she was grateful for him. "I have animals to feed. It's already late. They've been neglected." She spoke fast and frantically, ashamed of her verbal misstep. "I think you should rest. If you wake and need something and I'm not here, there's water in the cup beside you and"—she cleared her throat—"there's a chamber pot if you can manage and a bowl with a rag and water. And there's soap. I didn't . . . there are parts of you that still need cleaning. I won't be long. I know you're weak, so don't overwork yourself."

"Norah."

"Yes?" She flinched at his informal address, but the sincerity in his eyes kept her from making a fuss.

"I won't hurt you."

For a long moment, they stared at one another. "I believe you." She smiled, knowing that despite the odd circumstances and his massive size, she did believe him. Perhaps it was his injuries and helpless demeanor that evoked her trust. Or was it something else . . . something she couldn't pinpoint but that she could feel? She shrugged and said, "I don't think you could if you wanted to."

He raised a weak hand and let it fall. "You're right. I'm useless."

"You'll be on your feet soon enough." The swiftly setting sun cast long shadows over the room. If she didn't hurry, it

23

would be dark before she was done for the night. "I have to go. I have chores, and I left my boots by the creek."

Quincy opened his eyes again, wider this time. "Your feet have blood on them."

She reached for the door. "It's nothing. Minor scratches. Don't waste your energy worrying about me. Just rest."

"I'm going to pay you back," he said before closing his eyes again. "Someday, I will."

2

*Q*uincy dodged left, then right. He brought his fist up to guard his face. When his opponent moved close enough, he jabbed quickly then pulled back. His heart beat faster, every muscle tense despite the sickening repulsion that twisted inside his gut. He hated the ring and the rabid onlookers. All around him drunken men cheered, shouting louder with each jab. He was a spectacle, something to bet on, to jeer at and then forget.

To his surprise, he saw her there. He stopped mid-swing. Time stood still as his eyes roamed across Norah King's face, taking in her large blue eyes. They had questions in them, and sadness, as though she were disappointed with what he was doing. Something about the way she looked at him was different from the rest of the crowd. She seemed to truly see him. He wanted to run to her, to look at her face and understand her, but he couldn't. The blows kept coming.

A fist hit him square in the jaw. His head jerked left. He staggered and then braced himself for defeat. He cried out, begging them to stop the fight, but the crowd enjoyed his *pain. Blow after blow came. He covered his face, trying to protect himself, but he couldn't thwart the punches.*

"Quincy? You're dreaming. I heard you crying out," a voice, her voice, said, rousing him.

"I'm sorry," he said, embarrassed and weak. "I didn't mean to wake you."

Norah sat beside him on the floor. He could only see the outline of her small figure, but he felt her nearness. And then he felt her touch. Her small hand pressed gently against his shoulder. "I can fetch a light. Would that help?"

"It's not the dark that torments me."

"That's a shame." She moved her hand, but he could still feel her eyes on him. "The dark is easier to cure than other fears."

"Is it?"

"Much easier. Without fail, if you add light, the dark dies. It's a tried-and-true remedy." He heard her shift before saying, "If it's not the dark that makes you restless, what is it?"

"You wouldn't understand," he said, still trying to make out her face in the darkness. "My life, it's not been easy. There's no remedy."

She was holding a cup of water as she helped him sit up enough to drink. "I'd listen."

The water ran down his parched throat, calming the drought he'd only moments before suffered from. A new stiffness had settled over him as he slept, making each movement excruciatingly painful and difficult. The last thing he wanted was to voice the ugly memories of his past and add the pain of reminiscing to his physical agony.

When he did not speak, she moved to stand. "You should sleep. It was wrong of me to pry."

He grabbed her hand and stopped her. When her fingers tightened around his own, he lost his boldness and wanted to simply savor the feel of human kindness. Her touch was brief but powerful, and it chipped at the wall around his aching heart. "Tomorrow?"

"If you are well enough and willing." She didn't leave. "I'll sit beside you in case you need something."

Quincy closed his eyes. "Who takes care of you?"

"I take care of myself." A sadness crept into her tone. "I have for a long time now, but soon, I'll have family again and will not be alone. I want the walls of this house to be filled with children laughing, and I want to go to sleep knowing I don't have to face the next day in solitude."

"It's a good aspiration." He'd never lived in a loving home. The longing in her voice roused something in him. He shifted and turned away from her.

"Is something wrong?" she asked, watching his movements. "I've talked too much. I should let you rest."

"It's not you," he whispered into the darkness. "I've got my own worries, that's all."

She leaned in close. "Go to sleep for now but don't decide already that tomorrow will be troublesome." She smiled. "It may very well prove to be full of surprises."

"Is that what you do? Smile through your troubles, hoping they'll vanish in the night?"

"I try to remind myself that I don't know what's ahead. It's hardly a flawless plan, as I still have many lonely days, but it does help."

"I can't see that it'd hurt." Or could it?

"No." She stood and moved toward the door. "It never hurts to hope."

He didn't say anything or try to stop her when she left the room. Arguing with her and telling her that life had shown him again and again that every new tomorrow was as bad as the last seemed pointless. Besides, he liked the picture she painted with her brushstrokes of hope.

Someday soon he'd walk away from her and she'd forget his name. He sighed. But for tomorrow, he'd enjoy having someone care for him, someone to talk to, and someone to glean a bit of human compassion from.

Norah paced back and forth in her bedroom as she wrestled with what to do next. Whatever had happened to him still haunted him. She knew about fear. Her own fears and worries had increased since her father's death. But she wasn't afraid of Quincy.

I ought not to trust him, she admitted to herself, aware that a man didn't end up in his condition by happenstance. She kept a pistol near her bed she could use if circumstances required it, but she felt no pending dread.

She stopped walking and plopped on the window seat her father had built her when she was a child so she could look out at their land and see the stars at night.

"There's a big world out there, Norah girl, but nothing beats the view you've got right here," her father said when he showed her the seat. As a little girl, she'd played with her dolls in this nook. As a schoolgirl, she'd cried from this perch when Jacqueline Draleau told her she didn't want to be her friend. And it was also here in this room where she'd written love letters to Phineas Stevens when she was eighteen. She pressed a hand to her chest as she remembered the embarrassment she endured when he wrote her back, telling her he would never marry into a family like hers. For two days she holed herself up in this room and sobbed, wondering what was wrong with her and if she'd ever find love. She'd been right to worry. The years that followed were filled with familial love but void of romance and friendship.

Soon she would marry Jake, and they would share the bed in her parents' old room. What would this room become? Change was coming. It was brewing like an unstoppable storm. Her throat tightened and her chest ached. So much depended on Jake and his willingness to take on her debt and give her his name. He was all that stood between her and desperation, yet she still felt the heaviness in the air like the wind before an Iowa storm. She shook her head, trying to will away the eeriness that loomed heavy on her mind. Grasping for the hope she'd spoken of to Quincy, she thought of the children who would come and the sound of small feet on the old wood floors and not of Jake or what would happen if he changed his mind.

When she saw Jake next, she would tell him about Quincy and how he came to be under her roof. It was the right thing to do, of course it was.

"There's a man in the parlor," she practiced in a soft whisper. "I found him hurt and brought him back to tend to him."

What would he say? She closed her eyes and imagined Jake's face, with its sharp angles and commanding brow. Speaking to Jake always felt like asking her elders for permission rather than speaking to an equal in love. But he was levelheaded and would understand that compassion spurred her actions. Surely he would not have wanted her to leave an injured man to the birds.

Quincy had tried to sleep, but between the pain that raced through his troubled body and the thoughts that assaulted his mind, he'd had little success. His dreams were always there to remind him of what his life had been—throwing punches so he could eat for a week until he threw punches again. Nothing about his life had been fulfilling. Nothing had been wholesome or good. But he wanted it to be. Here in this home full of kindness, he felt a yearning for it.

"It's not even been twenty-four hours and already you're looking improved." Norah watched him from the kitchen. "I thought broth might settle well in your stomach. Will you drink some if I prepare it?"

He gawked, unable to pry his eyes off her. With the early morning light playing against her fair skin and golden hair, he felt as though he were looking at an angel. He forced his gaze away. "I'd drink it."

"Very good." She moved to the stove and rekindled the fire in it. "I hope you slept. My parents always told me to sleep when I was unwell."

"The pain kept me up some." He pushed his palms into the mattress and forced himself to a sitting position. His back leaned heavily against the wall, but at least he did not feel so vulnerable as he did while flat on his back. Boxing had taught him to be on guard. He could not see his opponent while on his back, though nothing about Norah was threatening—at least not in the usual way. "You asked me last night about my injuries."

"I did." She stopped working. "My ears are itching to hear your tale."

"It's normal for me to have a bruise or two. I fight at least once a week." He waited, expecting to hear a reaction, but she said nothing. "I didn't plan on becoming a fighter." He felt heat rise to his face. Did she want to know all this? "It started by accident."

"Go on," Norah said. He heard her put something into a pot. "What did you plan to become?"

"I, well, I . . . I wanted to . . ." He tried to remember. What had he longed for as a boy? "I don't know, but it wasn't taking blows from a stranger. I was desperate when I took my first fight. I'd been on the streets, and it'd not been easy. When I won, people started betting money on me. It's a filthy way of living. You wouldn't understand. It's a dark world back there."

"All night I'd wondered what your story was, and not once did I consider you were a man who used his fists or lived a back-alley life." She returned from the stove and sat beside him. "The broth needs to simmer for a while. I woke early and tended to the animals so I'd be able to sit with you and listen. Talking with you will help fill the silence."

"You don't like the quiet?"

"I've had too much quiet this last year. But now here you are and"—she looked at him with twinkling eyes—"you are not busy, so I've vowed to do everything in haste so I'll have time to sit and talk. The time will pass far quicker with someone to share it with."

"You eager to marry? Is that why you're wanting time to pass?" he asked, immediately regretting his words. Her getting married had nothing to do with him. "I imagine it's a good sign, being anxious to wed."

The sparkle left her eyes. "I suppose I am eager, in a way.

In two more weeks, I'll not have to worry so much about money and losing this land. I better stir your broth." She stepped back to the stove. He heard the spoon rhythmically tapping the pot. *Clink, clink, clink.* When she returned, he could tell she'd schooled her feelings. She even offered him a smile. Her teeth were straight, except for an obstinate one on the right side that had turned its own way. "You aren't from around here, are you?"

"No."

"And you don't plan to stay?"

"No." He wasn't sure where this line of questioning was leading. "I never meant to come here."

She scooted close to him again, and with hands wrung together, she said, "I don't want to start off my marriage with rumors that my feet are cold. I don't have parents to talk to or anyone but God, and I've been talking to him, but I think I need another person to speak to. It's probably wrong of me to say so much, but, well, I am getting married, and I know I'm supposed to be nothing but excited—"

"But you're not. And since I'm not going to gossip, you're going to tell me your woes."

"Not woes, not exactly . . . I don't know what it is I'm feeling."

He nodded. The least he could do was listen. "Why aren't you an eager bride?"

"I suppose it could be because it has all happened so quickly. The bank told me it was going to take my farm if I did not make payments toward my loan. Jake showed up out of nowhere, and only days later he asked me to be his bride. I have had little time to think through my choice." She shook her head. "We didn't even court. A few walks around the land, an inspection of the barn, and suddenly we're to spend our lives together. Do you think a marriage that begins for practical reasons can become a love match?" Her gaze went to a portrait on her mantel. Two people stood side by side. Her parents, he presumed. "I believe Jake is a good man. He seems to be a God-fearing, hardworking farmer, and he's willing to keep my land in good order. My father knew him and never said a bad word about him."

"He was your father's friend?"

"Not a close friend. Jake is forty-two, so a few years younger than my father, but what difference does age make when both parties are grown?"

"I hardly know," he confessed. His dabbling in romance had been misguided, and even his parents' union had been hostile. He was the last person she should consult for advice, yet he wished to offer her comforting words. "Seems to me two people with similar goals ought to be able to make a life together, if they are devoted to their promises."

"Yes." She brightened. "That is what I keep telling myself. Two people together with the Lord can have a good life." She paused and pursed her lips a moment. "But I do wonder if there might be a man out there somewhere with whom it'd be *easier* to make a life."

"Easier?"

"I was thinking the other day how some women are easy for me to talk to and others are not. With some people, friendship is so natural. It's effortless. I'm making a mess of this. My thoughts are so jumbled." She laughed, and he found himself smiling despite his pain. Her flushed face and rambling words were endearing in their own way. "I had a friend named Emily Humphries when I was young who would make me laugh whenever we were together. What I'm trying to say is, she was easy for me to be friends with."

"Are you saying you want a man like Emily?" He brought his brows together as he tried to follow her line of thinking.

"No! Of course not. But if some friendships are more natural than others, then I wonder if there are men who'd be easier to be married to as well. Is there a man out there who I could converse with effortlessly? A man who I might laugh with and feel confident around." She paused, her lips turned down at the sides. "I don't want marriage to be hard like it is for me to be friends with the women in town."

"And Jake is like those women?" He fought off a chuckle at the unflattering image she painted of her intended.

She laughed and covered her mouth with her hand. "He's not like them at all. But when Jake comes to call, we'll go walking, and the entire time I have to work to think of things to say. And when I do speak, I feel like a child trying to pretend I'm a woman. I wonder, Will it always be that way?"

"I would hope not. I only just met you and we're conversing easily enough, and I find it quite obvious you are a full-grown woman."

Norah blushed, but her eyes held his. He found himself wanting to hold her gaze as long as she was willing.

When she looked away, he tried to bring Opal's face to his mind. What had they talked about all those years ago? All he could remember was the wild way his heart raced when he was near her. He had no advice to offer. What he'd thought was love had turned out to be a selfish illusion—the opposite of what Norah wanted. "Perhaps he's shy because he's so smitten by your pretty face."

"He's never mentioned if he finds me pretty, and I don't believe him to be a shy man."

"He's getting married and has never told you how lovely a face you have? He's a fool. You ought to tell him off and find a better man."

"I can't tell him off. Fool or not, he's to be my husband." She paused for a moment. "I've always longed for a brother to talk to, but my brothers died as babies."

"I'm sorry," he managed to say.

"You're here now, so I suppose you'll have to fill that role."

"Of a brother?" He flinched. It wasn't a role he'd ever excelled at. His older siblings had taken off like he had, and he figured the younger ones had by now too. Their bond had been weak at best, and now distance and time separated them.

"Yes, of brother, or confidant. Call it what you like. Will you be my listening ear?"

He cleared his throat, stalling. "I need to pass the time somehow, but I'm not sure I'll be much help to you."

Norah stood and clapped her hands together. "I am certain you will be a great deal of help. I knew when I found you that you were here for a reason. With someone to talk to, I'm certain I can calm my jitters."

An argument jumped to the tip of his tongue—if she knew the sort of man he was, she'd know there was nothing providential about his arrival. She knew he boxed, but she didn't know how crude and shallow his world was or how every moment of every day had been about survival, and that decent living was a far-off dream for him.

Norah moved across the wide-planked floor toward the door. "But you mustn't tell me to shoo Jake away. I've already agreed to be his wife. And once I've talked out my troubles, you will tell me exactly how you ended up fighting for a living. I'm twenty-two, have lived on the same land my entire life, and have never seen a fight, but I might have some advice for you."

The set of her jaw and the intensity in her gaze told him they would share secrets when she returned from her chores, whether he wanted to or not. He leaned heavily against the pillow and sighed. Being trapped with a friendly, beautiful woman and convalescing under her care did not seem overly daunting. In fact, it felt rather like a gift.

He allowed his stricken body to relax, only to be startled by the opening of the door and the rush of Norah's feet. "I forgot your broth." She dashed to the kitchen, filled a cup with the warm liquid, and brought it to him. "It's hot."

"It'll cool." When he took it from her, their hands brushed together. He didn't know her, not really, but he felt something in her touch and in the way she looked at him with such concern. He was twenty-five years old and too hardened to believe the tightening in his chest meant anything, yet it all felt significant. He looked at the steaming broth, then back at her hand, and managed a throaty, "Thank you."

"What else can I do for you?" she asked, lingering.

He raised his cup of broth toward her with his shaky hand. "This, my new friend, is more than I deserve. Your kindness and contagious hope in tomorrow is good medicine."

She studied him from near the door. An understanding seemed to pass between them. They were strangers, but life had brought them together and they were now friends. Before leaving, she said, "You are a very easy patient to tend."

He stared after her as she walked out the front door, skirts swaying around her. She neglected to close the door, but he didn't mind. The warm breeze was fresh and welcoming, and the sunlight rejuvenating. He let his head sink into the pillow, and with tears welling in his eyes, he realized that this was what a home should feel like.

3

A firm peck to his nose startled him from his rest. His eyes flew open. A rooster, red and large, hovered above him. It drew its wings back and puffed itself up as it strutted near Quincy's makeshift bed on the floor.

"Go away!" he yelled, trying to make himself appear as large as he could despite being bedridden. He waved an arm in the bird's direction in hopes it would flee, but it didn't back away. It attacked Quincy's hand, flying up and scratching its claws across his skin.

Quincy let a string of curses fly in the bird's direction. To his chagrin, the bird seemed unimpressed by his verbal bashing and only strutted around with more confidence. Quincy tried to smack at the bird with his hand, but he only clucked, swaggered, and attacked him with more force. Every effort to get away from the rooster was in vain. He was too weak and injured. He cried out instead for Norah, all while batting frantically at the vicious bird.

When the match was about to be called in favor of the bird, Norah darted into the house. She dashed across the floor and grabbed the beast by the legs, swung it upside down, and ran outside and tossed the wretched animal back where it belonged. "Get back with the hens!"

"Close the door," he said as soon as she returned, in a voice much higher than he intended. "Quick."

Norah slammed the door shut, leaned against it, and burst into a fit of giggles. "I'm sorry. It's not funny."

"It's not!"

"But . . . you're a giant, and it's just a rooster. You could break its neck with one hand if you wished." Her laughter, like a joyful chorus, filled the air. "I'm sorry," she said again. "I haven't laughed like this in so long, but if you'd seen yourself or heard your voice . . ."

Feeling safe from the murderous bird, he now saw the humor in it all. "That rooster was ready to eat me alive. Had I not been bedridden, I would have crushed it."

"You looked awfully scared of it." She shook her head and turned back toward the door. "I better get back to work. I'll make sure to close the door behind me this time."

"Before that devil bird came in, I was actually thinking what a nice place you have here."

"Forget the bird, and believe me when I say it's a good place." She grinned, and his heart skipped a beat. She was lovely, with her gentle features and bright, dancing eyes. "Thank you, Quincy. My ears might be scarred from that dreadful language, but I needed a good laugh. It's been a long time."

He rolled onto his side. "Glad I could oblige."

When she left again, he thought over the whole ridiculous scene and laughed until the pain in his aching body forced him to contain himself. He hadn't confessed it to her, but it'd been an awful long time since he'd had a good, hard laugh too. The scratches from the bird were a small price to pay for such a moment.

———————|———————

Norah worked quickly, pulling weeds and watering her rows of plants, chuckling under her breath at the image of Quincy swatting at the angry rooster. There was more work she ought to do on her farm, but the rest could wait. She found herself eager to get back to Quincy. When she did, she changed his bandages and begged him again to let her fetch a doctor. He assured her that his ribs would heal, as would the bruises and gashes.

They talked while she shelled garden peas. He dozed off for a bit, but when awake, he seemed content listening as she talked and talked about her farm, the creek, and her childhood.

"It rained last night. I could smell it in the air," Norah said before popping one of the freshly shelled peas into her mouth.

"I smelled it too, when you left the door open."

She smirked. "I'm sorry about that."

"Once the rooster came in, all I could think about was not being pecked to death." He strained, pulling himself to a partially sitting position, only to fall back down and seemingly accept his vulnerable situation. "That rooster is as bad as the vultures."

"I had no idea that a man who fights grown men for a living would fear a little chicken."

"He's no little chicken. He's a regular devil rooster."

"That's rather harsh." She laughed, delighted with her guest.

Their easy conversation meandered from weather to land and then to music. His unpolished ways charmed her, evoking more laughter and smiles than she'd known in a very long time.

"What will you do with the peas?" he asked when she had filled her bowl.

"I'll eat them, of course. I like them raw, but my favorite is to make them into pea soup in the cold of winter. A bowl of thick pea soup is like a bit of heaven."

He turned up his nose. "Pea soup should never be compared to heaven. It puts a damper on the whole idea."

"I'll make a pea soup so savory and warm, you'll change your mind."

"For you, I'd pretend to like it," he replied. "But I hope heaven, if I get there, is much more satisfying."

"You'd pretend?" She almost swatted his arm, only stopping at the last moment when she thought of his bruises.

"You've pretended I'm not a burden. The least I could do is pretend to like your warm, comforting pea soup, when in fact I think it tastes worse than spoiled milk."

"I don't find you burdensome. I do find you shocking at times. And terribly irreverent."

"I'm not the one who compared green mush to heaven. I think you might be the irreverent one."

"Last night you cursed in your sleep, and you said the most atrocious things to my beloved rooster. There is no denying that you are a little unrefined," she said, consumed by their playful exchange. "And when I first got you into the house and I had to be your nurse, you were alarmingly battered. It was all very shocking."

He smirked. "You mean when you cut the clothes off my back? Had I been more awake, I might have been the shocked one."

"I was tending your wounds." She put her hands on her cheeks, and they were burning hot. Never in her whole life had she jested and laughed in such a way. "I shouldn't have mentioned such things. I was flustered then, and I feel flustered again thinking of—"

"You're thinking of me without my shirt on." He feigned surprise. "Norah King! Is that how you'll always see me in your mind?"

"I wasn't thinking of you like that, not like you're making it sound." This entire conversation was utterly appalling and all too entertaining. "I don't know what it is about you that makes me talk so freely and laugh at such horrible things. Well, I suppose if I did have living brothers, we'd talk openly too. Don't you think?"

"I don't know," he grumbled, his eyes losing their humor.

Unsure what had changed his mood, she tried to be more careful and speak only of proper things, but that was difficult to do when he had the power to loosen her tongue. Like a bee to honey, she kept rushing back for more.

"I am grateful," he said in a softer, more serious voice. "Being here, away from the city, with you. I find a growing desire to live . . . differently than I had been living. I want to look forward to tomorrow and whatever is down the road. I'm grateful you scared them birds away."

"I think you should hold on to that desire and follow where the road bends. You can have a different life."

"What of you? What do you desire for your future?"

All she'd dreamed about since her parents' deaths were large harvests and financial freedom. "I used to dream of little things, like being on the arm of a handsome man for a dance. I was never the girl who drew attention. I was always the one on the edge of the crowd wondering if anyone would ever ask me to dance. It's silly, isn't it? To hope for such things."

"It's not silly." He shook his head, defying her words. "What else? Tell me more."

She looked out the window at her endless land and thought of the work that waited for her. It never ended. "For one week, I'd love to have no chores and to sit inside or perhaps on the porch with a whole stack of books. I'd read and read and not feel bad for neglecting my chores. I think it'd be blissful."

"What stories would you read?"

"Adventure stories and romance. I may be marrying for convenience, but I believe in love matches—at least I think I do." Surprised by her boldness, she looked down at her bowl of shelled peas. "I have a heart full of little fancies that may never happen." With the peas shelled, she no longer had a proper excuse for sitting and lollygagging. But there was so much she wanted to know. "Quincy?"

"Yes."

"How did you end up here? We've avoided it all morning, but I would like to know. I won't judge you, even if it's not a pleasant tale." Her father had often gambled, a weakness he battled his whole life. It was never so much that they were destitute, but their coffers were never as full as they ought to have been. She knew good men struggled under the powerful grip of the vice. Bad men, she'd decided, were those who gave up the fight, not those who fought until the end. "I'd like to know."

His face grimaced with a new pain.

"I told you of my wedding worries and all my secret dreams." She inched closer, hoping he would feel as safe talking to her as she had felt sharing with him. "I'd like to think I am not the only one speaking openly."

He shifted on the mattress before saying, "I threw a fight. I'd hoped to make enough money that I could leave that life behind and start over. I wanted to get away from the drunken crowds and the spectacle, but I didn't know any way to, unless I had money in my pockets."

"You lost on purpose." She closed her eyes and tried to imagine the scene. This man who laughed about dances and teased about peas had swung at another man and taken blows. He was so large, massively large, and yet he'd fallen on purpose. "I'm sorry."

"Sorry?"

"It must have been a horrible life you were leading if you risked the vengeance of the crowd to get away. You may have been wrong to do it, and I'm rather ignorant of betting sports, but I'm glad you are now free of it."

His voice cracked when he spoke. "I can only blame myself for the life I led, but you are right—it was a terrible way to live."

"Your injuries are from your loss?"

"Not all of them. After I lost, I was dragged from the ring and Lloyd, that's the man's name who ran the bets, confronted me. He said he knew I'd thrown it." Quincy's breathing came quick and shallow. "He had a couple of men take me behind the building. I can fight in a ring with rules and one opponent, but I had no chance with all these men coming after me. I'd been selfish, like everyone there. When I lost, I was only thinking about myself, and they made sure I knew the consequences of what I'd done."

"They beat you?"

He looked away, and his expression darkened. "I thought they'd kill me. I was certain I'd never open my eyes again. It's not like here, with farmland and rules and manners. It's a rough place, a rough world. I fought behind saloons and in abandoned factories. They must have stolen what money I had and thrown me on a train, thinking that was what I was due." He recalled the story with little emotion in his voice, but she saw the pain in his eyes. His world may not have been a pretty one, but it had still given up on him and discarded him like she cast off the shells of her peas. He asked, "Are we near the tracks?"

"I found you not far from them. A quarter mile perhaps."

"It's all fuzzy, but I imagine an angry conductor pushed me from the train and then I staggered around for a while trying to find a place to collapse and be done." He met her gaze. "I'm sorry it wasn't the providential arrival you'd wanted. The truth is, I am, in many ways, the villain you feared."

"No." She grabbed his hand with startling urgency. "I believe in a God who can use the worst of circumstances for our good if we're willing. You can have a better life. Both of us, we have good things ahead." Surely Jake was sent to turn her life around for the better. And now that Quincy was away from the fighting, he could change his course. "I think you ought to have your fresh start. You may have come about it in an uncanny way, but you still ought to seize it."

"I'm penniless, far from anything I know." He rubbed his swollen face. "It's no concern of yours though."

"No, I suppose it's not." She stood and went to the window, unsure why she felt drawn to his problems, why she wanted to solve them for him or, rather, with him. "Don't you think it's better having someone else cheering you on? It may not be my problem, but I am here and willing to root for you."

"The only people who've ever cheered for me have been people with money at stake."

"Then it's time you had someone rooting for you simply because we are both lost souls trying to find our footing in this troubled world." A rustling sound stole her attention. "I think I hear someone coming."

"One of your hands?"

"It's Jake." She spotted him out the window, then looked around her, pausing on Quincy. "I'll be back," she said before rushing from the house. She closed the door behind her in time to see Jake slide from his horse. His silver hair bounced when his feet hit the ground. He wasn't an unattractive man—lean, well-dressed, and with manners.

"I thought I'd see if my future bride would go for a walk with me."

"I have some time." She forced herself to smile up at him. "I'll have to tend the animals later, and I planned to pull some weeds."

He offered his arm, and she took it. "Soon your list of chores won't be nearly as long. I'll hire more hands and get things running how they ought to around here."

"I'll be grateful for it," she said, wondering if she'd always feel she owed him a debt of gratitude for saving her farm.

Certainly, her land and her hardworking ways were worth
something, as was her honest nature. She flinched, aware that
until she spoke Quincy's name to Jake, she could not call herself honest. "There's something I'd like to discuss with you."

"If it's about the bank, I've already talked to them." He
looked hungrily at her land and kept talking. "Your father
never worked these fields to their full potential. I'll lease my
land out, and that'll bring in more money." He spoke with
such confidence, so much authority. In one sense, it eased
her mind knowing her land would be in capable hands, and
at the same time it scared her. Would she have any say over
the land she loved?

With the conversation turned to the farm, she addressed a
different idea and decided to discuss Quincy later. "I thought
if we were to keep the hogs this year and breed a few more
of them, that'd be a wise investment." Practice, she hoped,
would make conversing with Jake easier.

"Leave all that up to me. There's no need for you to think
about the hogs, not anymore." He put his arm around her
shoulder and pulled her closer. "I'll take care of every decision that needs making, and you can tend to the house and
the garden and the nursery when the time comes. You've
been doing a man's work for too long."

Despite the many rebuttals she could have offered, she
forced her posture to remain poised under his touch and
latched on to the one thing she yearned for. "I do look forward to motherhood."

"We'll start a family right away." He ran his hand slowly
up her arm, letting his fingers graze across the fabric of her
sleeve and then to the skin at her neck. No pleasure came,
only a shiver. "I thought I'd hire some men to start bringing

my belongings to the house so it's all set up before the wedding." His hand wandered south from her shoulder to her waist. "I don't want to worry about such things after the wedding."

"Could I have a few days?" She stepped backward, giving herself room to think. "I need to go through all my parents' belongings so there's room for yours."

"Of course." He moved closer, reeling her back in. "You've made me a very happy man." He lowered his head and pressed his lips to hers. She responded the best she could but felt nothing. No tingling warmth, no excitement. "I'll let you tend to the rest of the chores. I'm headed into town to pick up your wedding gift."

"A gift? You don't have to—"

"I know." He patted her cheek. "But I want to. A girl ought to feel like a queen on her wedding day. Besides, the house needs a new stove. The modern ones are the talk of the town. We won't be the only family without one."

A new stove had been on her mind for years, and soon she'd have one. "That's very kind of you."

"I'll get the place put back in order. You'll see."

He was rescuing her—saving her from financial ruin and now offering her a gift. A useful, generous gift. And still, the thought of being tied to him held no romantic appeal. Love could grow, she had to believe it could. Real life, after all, did not look like it did in dime novels. Their union would begin with practical roots but blossom. Hard work and loyalty, not butterflies and rapidly beating hearts, would be the soil they'd build upon.

"I have to tell you something," she said, wanting to do her part to grow their union.

"Can it wait?" He looked off at the horizon. "I've got lots to do yet. Even coming out here has taken more time than I should have spared, but with us getting married soon, I knew I should come see you. I wouldn't want the town talking about my neglect."

"No . . . we wouldn't want the town to talk. I . . . I suppose what I have to say can wait." She squeezed his arm. "I'll see you sometime soon. We'll talk then."

He bid her a good day, promising to stop by sometime next week. She quickly finished her most urgent chores, all the while wondering how she was going to tell her fiancé that there was a man sleeping in her house.

Quincy woke the next morning to the sounds of Norah working in the kitchen. He closed his eyes and let his imagination wander. What would it be like if this were his farm and Norah his wife? If the sounds of pots clanging and fires being rekindled were the sounds of his everyday life? He smiled large enough that it hurt his aching face. He couldn't help it, the thought of knowing her every look and gesture was appealing. Out of reach but an enticing thought.

"You're awake," Norah said when she stepped into the parlor. She blushed, like she always did before she asked if the chamber pot needed to be emptied. "Do you . . . may I empty the pot?"

He'd never wished to use an outhouse so badly as he had since entering the King home. But alas, even using the chamber pot took an enormous amount of energy. "Thank you," he said as she took it out back.

When she returned, she sat beside him, fidgeting with the

cuff of her dress. "If you were getting married, what would you want for a gift? I have little time to figure it out, and I don't have much money."

He gaped at her, saying nothing until she looked up and met his gaze, her eyes pleading for an answer. He wet his dry lips, stalling for words. "I suppose I'd want something that testified of my intended's love and devotion. I don't imagine a wedding gift from a bride to a groom is supposed to be practical, is it?"

"I don't know. I've never been married before, and I don't know what sort of gift Jake would like, but I want to start this marriage off right. I know he is buying me a new stove." She furrowed her brow. "I thought maybe I could have my father's watch polished and cleaned, but he has one and it's nicer than my father's. Try to imagine that you were marrying me. What would you want?"

Quincy closed his eyes again. "Make him a list."

"A list? Of what?"

"Of your dreams. Tell him about wanting to waltz and wanting to read for a week straight. He ought to want to know it all." He swallowed, surprised by the tightness of his throat. "If I were marrying you, I would. Knowing what's in your heart, that's more valuable than any tangible gift, don't you think?"

Norah didn't reply, not for a long time. Afraid he'd spoken out of turn, he waited nervously, clenching and unclenching his hand. At last, she raised her head high enough that he could see tears pooled in her eyes.

"Someday," she whispered in a voice that made his heart pound wildly in his chest, "when you're reformed and your nose is healed and your ribs are done aching and you have your new life, promise me you'll ask a girl what her dreams are. Make them come true."

He held her gaze, surprised to see longing in it. "I promise," he said, his voice still weak but full of conviction stronger than he'd ever felt. "I promise to lead a different life. I'll be the sort of man a wife would want beside her, and I'll do everything I can to make her smile."

"Good." She bent down, surprising him, and kissed his cheek. It was quick and brief but enough to steal his breath and seal his promise. "If you can, will you write me and tell me of your good fortune? I love happy endings."

"Happy endings?" he repeated, still trying to grasp what was happening.

"Where a man and a woman defy their circumstances and come together." Her face took on a faraway look. "I don't think it happens often enough, but for you, I believe it will. I want it for you. In fact, I will pray for it."

"You have my word that if my life ends up blissfully happy, I'll find a way to tell you. Do you think old Jake will mind if I show up and sit on your front porch and tell you all about it?" He cleared his persistently dry throat. "I better just write a letter."

She twisted the small engagement band on her finger. "I don't think he'd deny me a letter from a friend, but I can't say for certain. Forget I said anything. I only hope for good things for you. That is all I meant to imply."

"And what of your happy endings? Will I ever hear about them?"

She threw her hands out to her sides. "This is my happy ending. I've been given a way to keep my farm. I have a man willing to work beside me, and someday I'll sit by my creek with a child at my side." She shrugged. "There isn't any mystery in how that will unfold."

A child, a beautiful farm . . . He'd likely never have such bounty, yet she did not look like a woman about to live her dreams. He wanted to reach for her hand and let his fingers slide across her skin. The urge was strong and powerful. He clasped his hands together, fighting the impulse. "This land is beautiful, and you . . . you will be a good mother."

New tears glistened in the corners of her eyes. "Thank you," she whispered. "I have more to get done. You should rest."

"I'll help you. I'm well enough." Without thinking, he sprang from the ground too quickly. He swayed. She tried to catch him, but he was so large. He collapsed, hitting his head as he went down.

4

Norah paced the hallway of her home while she waited for the doctor to finish his appraisal of Quincy's health. She berated herself for not fetching the doctor the day she'd found Quincy. What if it was too late and Quincy had internal injuries so severe, he'd never recover? He'd only just entered her life, yet she could not bear the thought of him dying. She rubbed her forehead as she waited, but there was no soothing her worries.

"Miss King," the doctor said when at last he approached.

"Yes."

"It seems our patient, Mr. Barnes, has endured a brutal beating." She tried not to show her impatience for news she did not already know. "He has three broken ribs, bruising, and a broken nose."

"I know all that. He also has a large welt on his hand from my rooster. What I don't understand is how he went from doing so well to being unconscious on the floor. Something must be wrong beyond gashes and ribs."

"Calm yourself," he said. "You've done a fine job nursing him. I believe Mr. Barnes stood up too quickly and collapsed because of weakness, and now he has a bump on his head to go with his other injuries. Rest, proper nutrition, and close observation are all he needs. A week of bed rest, and I'd expect him to be on his feet, ready to add activity back to his life."

"Activity? You're saying he'll be alright?" Relief, sweet and powerful, washed over her, making her knees sway. She put a hand on the wall. "He won't die."

"No. I don't believe so." He paused near the door. "I don't think moving him is advisable, at least not yet." He cleared his throat. "How does Jake feel about him being here?"

"Jake?" She took a half step backward. "I haven't told him yet. I had planned to . . . I do plan to."

He studied her before saying, "I'll keep this between you and me until you get a chance to speak to him."

"I appreciate that. I'm sure he'll understand."

"An engaged man will never understand why a stranger is sleeping in his intended's home." In a fatherly way, he added, "This town has long frowned on your family. You know I don't feel as they do, but, well, be careful not to lose Jake. You're a wise girl and well aware of the gossips in town. Handle this swiftly and subtly. You don't want your charity to become a scandal. As for your safety, Quincy is in poor condition and doesn't seem to be a threat, but you'd best speak to Jake."

"I'll discuss the matter when I see him next." Norah opened the door and thanked the doctor again for coming. With him gone, she gave herself a moment to find her composure. The doctor's words gave her much hope for Quincy's recovery, but his warning alarmed her. It took her several minutes to calm her nerves by reassuring herself that caring for an invalid, no matter their gender, was an act of compassion and not improper. The Lord himself spoke of offering aid to those in need. Feeling better about her choices, she stepped into her parents' old bedroom where, thanks to the doctor, Quincy now rested.

"You scared me," she said in a hushed voice. When he collapsed on the floor, she checked for a pulse before riding hard and fast for the doctor. It'd been hours now since she'd seen the whites of his eyes and the curve of his smile.

"I'm sorry," he said, his voice quiet and weak.

She sat in a chair next to the bed and took his hand, grateful he was alive. "You shouldn't have gotten up. I never said you could. You weren't well enough."

"I've never had someone care." He chuckled and put a hand to the bump on his head. "I didn't think to ask permission."

"You must have had a mother who cared?"

"No, I can't say that I did. Don't look so distraught. I brought most of my troubles on myself."

"But you're done with all that, remember. You're starting over. You promised me. I've no doubt that you'll begin again, and you'll have the finest home and family a man could wish for."

"I promised, and I'll keep my word." The swelling in his face had subsided enough that she could see his hazel eyes and the dimple in his cheek. He cleared his throat. "I heard the doctor."

"You did?"

"You haven't told your man yet," he said matter-of-factly. "Why not? You think he'll throw me out and accuse me of being the lowlife I am?"

"No, I—"

"You've sworn me to a life of honesty. Tell me the truth."

"I thought he'd make you leave, and you're not well enough to travel." She swallowed, knowing there was more. She felt an irrational bond with Quincy. Why, she was not sure. Perhaps because he seemed to understand her loneliness or because he listened when she spoke. "I didn't want you to leave." She stood and moved away from the bed. It was nonsense, all this talk that could amount to nothing. Even if she wished it, he was a penniless stranger who would soon be on his way. "I do plan to tell Jake when I see him next. I did start to tell him, but I . . . well, I should have insisted he listen to me. I'm not very good at that yet."

Quincy's eyes followed her around the room. She could feel them on her, but she did not mind his scrutiny.

"I don't know what kind of a wife I'll make. I've always been honest before." She rubbed her forearms as she struggled to put words to all she felt. "I don't know what's come over me. It was wrong of me not to tell him about you."

"Your pacing is making my head spin. Won't you stop and just talk to me?" Quincy said in a low voice. "Don't fret. I've no doubt your Jake will forgive you. It's a fairly minor indiscretion—"

"For you, perhaps." She gasped and covered her mouth. "I only mean that it is not in my nature to conceal things from others. It may not be a love match, but I will do what I can to make it an honorable marriage and be a good wife to him." She plopped back down hard into the chair and put her head in her hands. "Do you think he'll forgive me?"

"Forgive you for caring for an invalid? For taking in a man near death? You didn't ask for me to come." He gently put a hand on her head. "If he doesn't understand, he's not worthy of you. He'd be a fool. But you wouldn't marry a fool, would you?"

"I'd marry any decent man who could save my farm and keep me from the streets." She looked up, and for one brief second his hand slipped to her cheek. His fingertips grazing her skin before falling away. She tried to ignore the warmth that zipped through her but found it impossible. "I shouldn't have said that. Wedding nerves have me worried."

"It is the wedding night I'm told most women have jitters over, not the marriage."

"Oh my." She covered her flushed cheeks. "I'll never get used to your blunt ways. I don't even let myself think about the wedding night. I want children, so all that is inevitable, but I don't dwell on it. I'd rather not."

"If you want children, then you're right—it is inevitable." He chuckled softly. "With the right man, I would assume it'd even be exciting. But your nerves, you say, are not for the wedding night. That's a shame, because you could overcome such nerves. Some matronly woman could give you advice and ease your fears."

She stood and moved for the door. This line of talk would lead her nowhere. "You should sleep."

"Any man?" he said before she made it from the room.

"Excuse me?"

"You said you'd marry any man who could help you keep your land. Why not be particular?" He had such an unfamiliar way about him. His words weren't brash or unkind. They were straightforward and challenging but spoken with concern. "Norah." He sucked in his bottom lip before saying, "I don't know you well, but what I know is that you are a woman many men would want by their side. Look how you've cared for me—fighting off the birds, dragging my heavy hide inside, sitting beside me, filling the room with pleasant conversation. And your heart is full of hope. Why not find a man you care about? One with pockets full of money who can save your farm, of course."

"I don't have that luxury. I was wrong to ever belittle Jake. I should have kept my doubts to myself." She put her hand on the doorknob. "You say that I am a woman many would desire, but you're wrong. You see something in me that others do not, perhaps because you hit your head so hard. I don't have a line of waiting suitors I can pick from. I am nothing more than a lonely, desperate farm girl."

"No." He looked ready to jump from the bed and rush to her. "You are more than that."

"Enough of this," she barked at him. "I have Jake and no time to seek anyone else for help. No one wanted me before Jake, and I cannot gamble my farm and my security on the hope that someone will want me down the road. Let's not speak of my marriage again."

⸻

Quincy hated seeing her leave. Every time she entered his room, his heart leapt. And every time she left, he was reminded of how little he could fix. If only he could move around and take life into his hands and control it, but he could not. He'd been living only to survive since he left home at fourteen to escape his drunken father and neglectful mother. In all those years since, he'd been busy, always struggling to make ends meet and never sitting back and doing nothing. Granted, much of what he filled his time with was unsavory, but nonetheless, he was active.

What am I to do next? he'd asked countless times since being sentenced to bed by the doctor. At first he questioned only himself, and then he tried asking a higher power. *I want a new, changed life away from the fights and the lying. But how?*

There'd been no sure answer, but he'd felt a measure of peace, enough that he believed an answer could come. Maybe there was work for him in Blackwell. He was strong. Surely someone could use his muscle to work their land. He'd never considered farming, but he was willing to try it. He pushed the idea from his mind. He couldn't stay in Blackwell, not when his thoughts were so full of Norah. Even when he dreamed, he saw her angelic face. Living here, so near her, watching her life unfold with Jake—there was no appeal, and there was no way to keep Norah from Jake. With no money and no home, he was not the hero she needed. He'd have to get away from here so he could clear his head and forget her. It wouldn't be easy, not with the way his heart beat faster when she entered the room or the way her laughter filled his ears with delightful music. But he would go and hold on to the promises he'd made to her to change the course of his life.

Mere days together should not have been enough to affect him, but he feared himself besotted. Love wasn't something he understood. During his time with Opal, he'd believed he knew what it entailed, but he had been wrong and had lost all faith in the idea until now. What he felt for Norah, he could not help but believe to be the seeds of love.

Three days after the doctor's visit, Norah came into the room after emptying his chamber pot. "Jake sent word with one of the farmhands. He's coming by today. I plan to bring him in to meet you. I want him to know for himself that you're a good man who happened to need shelter under my roof."

"Norah"—he pulled the blue patchwork quilt off his body and swung his legs off the side of the bed—"I'm well enough to go. I'll leave, and then my presence will never matter. I shouldn't be here. You're getting married in just over a week. I'm in the way."

"The doctor said a week in bed, and it's only been three days." A look of panic like he'd never seen filled her every feature. "You could get hurt out there."

"I've been hurt plenty of times. I know my body, and it's well enough for me to leave." He wore her father's old nightshirt. If he were more properly dressed, he might have left already. "You said once that I could have a pair of your father's britches."

"You're really leaving?" Her voice rose, and his pulse with it. "What about your promises to start over? What about all our talks about dreams and finding out what you were meant to do next? You can't figure that out if you're dead on the side of the road. You need to recover."

"Stop worrying about me. I'm not your husband. I'm nothing to you." He glared, not at her but at the mess his life was and the fact that no matter how badly he wanted to be the one to save Norah's land and make promises to her, he could not. "It's a waste, you worrying over me when you have so much else to concern yourself with."

"Don't tell me how to feel or what to worry over." She reached into an armoire and pulled out a pair of trousers and shoved them at him, knocking him back onto the bed. "I'm a grown woman who can think for herself, and I think you're being a fool. Running off like this when your face isn't even done being purple, it's impulsive, it's . . ."

He stood up quickly and held out his arms, knowing her anger was not all it seemed. She fell into his open arms, buried her face in his chest, and wept. Grateful for his returning strength, he used it now to console her. His arms encircled her, tucking her away from her fears and whatever else plagued her.

"I promised you I'd start over, and I meant it. And you have your plans to marry. It's time I leave," he said, his voice cracking. "But I will remember everything you told me. I'll go somewhere, and I'll make a good and honest name for myself. I promise you that."

Without leaving his embrace, she whispered back, "And you'll find a girl whose dreams you can make come true."

"I promise." His insides twisted. He had a girl in his arms, and he didn't want any other. He wanted this woman. This bold, beautiful woman who treated him as an equal when he knew she was far his superior. He didn't want to let her go, but he wouldn't let his presence hurt her. Leaving was inevitable. He pressed his lips to her hair, kissing the top of her head and memorizing the softness of it. She'd rescued him in more ways than one when she scared off those vultures. No gesture, no words would ever fully capture his gratitude. Leaving now was the only gift he could give.

She didn't move from his touch. Instead, she sighed. "Quincy, what if—"

"I have to go." Guilt nagged him. Norah wasn't his woman, no matter how much he wanted her to be. Unwilling to hear a plea for help that he could not answer, he moved his lips to her forehead and let them linger there for only one intoxicating moment before saying, "I'll be forever grateful."

He pulled away enough that he could see her face. Her cheeks were rosy, her eyes glistening with tears, and her lips inviting. He swallowed. Lips were not something he ought to be noticing now. He would not indulge himself, nor ask it of her, when he knew the damage it could do. "I have to go. You've put my needs above yours since I came. It's my turn to think about you, and going now before I say or do something that can't be undone is best."

"But . . ." She reached out and put her hands on his chest as though she wanted to pull him closer. Her touch lasted seconds, then she stepped back. "I understand. You're right and . . . I should thank you."

His heart thumped quickly, silently begging her to come back to his arms but at the same time telling him to leave.

"I'll dress and be on my way," he said, hoping if he said it aloud, he'd follow through. He'd promised to be a man of integrity and to change his old ways. He'd promised her, and from his sickbed, he'd promised God. This was his first test and quite possibly the hardest there was—to walk away.

"I'll pack some supplies." She busied herself pulling out some of her father's clothes from the armoire and stuffing them into a carpetbag. Her hands trembled, but she didn't stop. "I need to clear this room out anyway. Take all of this. My father was a large man, not as big as you, but I think they'll fit until you can get other clothes."

He watched her pull a shirt from a drawer, press it to her face, breathe its scent, then pack it in the bag.

"I don't have to take—"

"I want you to," she said with force. "He would have liked

62

you and wanted you to have these to wear. He was a good man, despite his weaknesses. I know he'd give you even more if he could."

"I'll try to make him proud."

Not ten minutes later he had a bulging carpetbag under his arm and terribly ill-fitting clothes on his back and was walking away from the warmest roof he'd ever resided under. He'd asked Norah twice before leaving if she was certain she'd be alright, and both times she said yes. A quiet sob that penetrated his very core was the last sound he heard before stepping away, knowing he'd never come back.

Soon she would be another man's wife. It was as good as done. There was nothing else for him to do except promise once again to repay her kindness someway, somehow.

Two Years Later

5

Quincy set his account books aside when Sam Landon entered the small hotel office. His businesses were doing better than he could have hoped for, that much he knew, and the rest could wait until after his meeting.

Sam, the town's carpenter, was a quiet man with a hardworking disposition that Quincy admired. "I have the furniture you ordered."

Quincy stood, crossed the room, and shook his friend's hand. "Good. I'm eager to get those upper rooms in working order. It's hard to ask a guest to pay for a room that doesn't have a bed in it."

"I never thought this town would be busy enough to fill a hotel." Sam stepped toward the door. "I brought Clifford to help. Do you remember him?"

"Of course. He's learning the trade from you. What is he? Sixteen or so?"

"Seventeen. He thinks very highly of you. I'm training him to be a carpenter, but it won't surprise me if he decides to be a businessman."

"Tell him I hope he becomes a better man than me, whatever his profession." He shifted, uncomfortable under the praise. There were pieces of the past Quincy had never mentioned to Sam because he saw no benefit in dredging up what had already come and gone.

"I'll tell him." He laughed good-naturedly. "We can have those rooms furnished in no time. With a little luck, you could have them filled tonight."

Quincy took off his jacket and laid it across one of the office chairs. Sam had built the dark wood furniture in this room too, complete with elaborate trim and perfect symmetry. It was during that first interaction that they'd become friends. Perhaps it was Sam's down-to-earth ways that made him so agreeable. Whatever it was, Quincy found himself at ease in his presence. "I'll help you carry up the furniture."

The two men went out the hotel's back doors to the alley, where Clifford waited near the wagon loaded with finely crafted dressers, bed frames, and an elegant armoire.

"Excellent." Quincy walked around the wagon, appraising the load. "It's hard to believe you've only been at this a couple of years."

"When I was logging in the Dakota territory, I made some rough furniture in my spare time." Sam handed his young associate a headboard and directed him where to take it. "What about you? What did you do before buying up half the town? All you've told me is you came into some money and invested it."

"I don't own half the town." Quincy's chest grew tight. Would he ever feel at peace about how he'd gotten his fresh start? Likely not. "I lived back east and was always fighting to get by." *Quite literally*, he thought to himself. "But it

wasn't until I came farther west that I found my footing."
He shrugged. They were friends. Surely he could tell him
more, but what purpose would it serve? "Longfield is where
it all began."

As soon as the words were out, he knew they were false.
His fresh start had come the day Norah King discovered him
half dead. She was Norah Granger now, and bringing her up
with Sam would only make it harder to shake the image of
her beautiful face from his mind or the burden of regret from
his heart. Besides, he'd sound ridiculous, like a starry-eyed
schoolboy pining over a girl he'd barely known.

Thankfully, Sam wasn't one to pry. He nodded, accepting
Quincy's story, then together they heaved a large dresser
from the back of the wagon and carried it to the third floor of
Quincy's building, the Mission Hotel. When he bought the
hotel, it was only partially finished and ill cared for. He was
cautious with his money, working in stages, making improvements to the main floor and lobby first and then the larger
second-story rooms. Every penny felt like a gift, sometimes
a burden, but always something to be treated with care.

They pushed the dresser against the sidewall of an upper
bedroom, then stood back. Quincy smiled. The room was
coming together nicely.

"Will this complete it?" Sam asked as the two headed back
down the steep stairway that was used only by staff. "Will
all the rooms be ready for guests?"

"The rooms I plan to rent will all be complete, but don't
worry, I have lots more work for you, if you're willing. I want
to redo the counter in the old store. It's got damage from a
roof leak, and the café needs all kinds of carpentry work."

"I'd be glad to do it." Sam looked at the door that led

down to the lower level of the hotel. "If I remember right, when Ernest owned this place, there were a couple of rooms on the lower level. I went down there once with a school friend when he hired us to haul supplies for him."

"Yes," Quincy said slowly. This building was old. He couldn't pretend the rooms weren't there, even if he wished he could. "I don't plan to rent them, not yet anyway."

They stepped back outside into the late summer sunshine that made them squint under its brightness. With the three of them working, it didn't take long to unload the wagon. The once-empty rooms soon boasted finely crafted furniture that his housekeeper would make up with mattresses and wonderfully stitched quilts. They were just rooms, but he couldn't help but feel proud of his efforts in revitalizing the once-neglected hotel.

With the job done, Quincy pulled Sam into his office, unlocked the bottom drawer of his desk, counted out crisp dollar bills, and handed them to Sam. While Quincy entered the amount in his ledger, they talked. It'd become a habit, and even Clifford joked that he'd take a nap in the wagon while he waited for the two friends to finish talking.

"You plan on buying any other businesses around the town?" Sam leaned back in the leather chair across the desk from Quincy. "I heard the livery may be in need of a new owner if Ray really moves farther west."

"I never planned to own all I do." Quincy scratched the back of his neck. He missed the loose clothes he used to wear, but he was grateful for the life he had in Longfield. "I think the hotel, store, and café are enough to fill my time. My cooks keep getting married and running off on me. It's a busy job keeping everything running."

"That last one wasn't much of a cook." Sam laughed. "I don't think she put salt in anything."

Quincy had fretted over what to do when he began losing customers over her bland cooking. Matrimony in that instance was a godsend. "Her poor husband."

"They seemed happy enough. And it worked out well for you. I was in yesterday, and the new cook seems to know what she's doing." Sam rubbed his stomach. "It was good eatin'."

Quincy wasn't an expert at reading emotions, and certainly not those of a quiet man like Sam, but something about his expression gave him pause. Had Quincy's new cook caught his eye? "Her name's Alice. She was working here at the hotel, but when the cook left, she begged me for the job."

"I thought she looked familiar."

"She's been in the area six months or so." He ran his hand along the smooth wood of his desk. He could still remember the night Alice arrived at the hotel. Sickly, dirty, and distraught but fiercely determined to make something of her life. "You'll have to frequent the café and get to know her better."

"Well, my cooking's not worth bragging about, so maybe I will." Sam stood and moved for the door. "I got another order to deliver today. I'll come by soon and get measurements for the counter in the store."

"I appreciate that. Don't forget I need repairs done at the café too. We could meet there, and you could sample more of Alice's food."

"Don't go playing matchmaker on me. I have rotten luck with women."

"Nonsense—"

"You know I do. Every girl I've ever cared about picked someone else over me."

Quincy wasn't sure how to console his friend. He'd heard the story from Sam himself. Sam had left home when he was still a young man, engaged to a girl he'd loved for years. He worked the railroad line, and then logged, saving every penny he made so he'd have enough to come back and marry his sweetheart. But before he could return and claim her hand, she wrote him, turning him down. There'd been another woman too, before he came back to Iowa.

Sam shrugged and said, "I think I'll just eat Alice's food and make your repairs. Besides, you wouldn't want me courting your cook. If by chance I was able to woo her, I'd leave you shorthanded again."

"Excellent point. I take back what I said. Don't even look at her. Let her stay my cook forever."

"What about you? You are Longfield's most sought-after bachelor. Do you have your eye on someone? You like Alice's cooking. Have you thought of courting her?"

Quincy shoved his hands into his pockets and shook his head. Not once had he considered anything but a working relationship with Alice or any other woman in town. No woman since Norah had caught his eye.

"I haven't made time for courting." The old twinge of guilt bristled inside, reminding him that he'd promised Norah he would find a lady and make her dreams come true. Of all the promises he'd made, that was the hardest one for him to keep. He knew Norah was married, settled, and leading a life without him, but his life was still deeply altered by her lingering memory. "One day I'll find time."

"You could stop working so much or try lingering a little

after church. Or there's the baseball games you're committed to. You might meet a woman there. You hit a couple balls off the field and the ladies will all be swooning. I know my sisters would be impressed." Sam's family, made up of ever so many sisters, was always dragging him to every town event there was. He'd groaned about their persistent matchmaking schemes ever since Quincy had met him. The last thing he needed was to be pulled in as well.

"I'll be at the game. I can't make any promises about the rest." Quincy felt more comfortable tackling business matters than he did dressing up and trying to convince everyone he was the well-to-do bachelor they believed him to be. His businesses were successful. They were thriving thanks to his hard work, but no matter how well he was doing, he could not shake the nagging feeling that he was a fraud. "Thanks again for getting me that furniture so quick."

Quincy looked at his watch after saying goodbye to Sam and decided to sneak off to his room before he was due to meet with the café staff. When he first bought the Mission Hotel, he planned to live in it only temporarily, but in those early months he ended up working in every position of the hotel just to keep it afloat. He brought everyone's bags to their rooms, changed bedding, and checked guests in and out. Living in the hotel was easier, and now he was accustomed to the noisy, ever-changing atmosphere.

His room was small but his belongings were few, so he had little need for more space. A Bible beside his bed testified of the man he sought to become. Clothes of a businessman hung in the armoire, and stacks of books lined the far wall. In one drawer he had the ill-fitting clothes he'd worn while walking away from Norah. He pulled them out now, like he had so many times before, and let himself remember all that had transpired since he left her.

His heart had been heavy as he turned his back on Norah and forced his legs to take him away. He'd wanted to stay, to save her from a marriage of convenience and somehow promise to love and care for her, but he couldn't. How could he, a displaced man, ask a woman to rely on him anyway? He'd done the one noble thing he could do—he left so she could be safe, so she could have her farm and go on with her life.

There had not been one morning since walking away from her that he had woken up and not thought of his promise to make a new life for himself. When he'd begun reading his Bible, it'd been to try to become the man she believed him capable of being. Only, once he read it, he discovered the comfort to be found within its pages—such solace and direction. Even with his newfound comfort in God's Word, he still felt an ache knowing he'd been incapable of helping the woman who'd helped him.

He grabbed the faded shirt, wadded it into a ball, and threw it on the floor. Doing the right thing was supposed to be easy. He'd walked away and never looked back—shouldn't she be gone from his head by now?

For the first ten days after he left Blackwell, he wandered aimlessly, doing odd jobs, sleeping in barns, and waking up to do it all again. And then an old man took him in and insisted he bathe and clean up before sleeping in his home. Quincy complied, eager to wash off the travel grime and ready to change into unsoiled clothes. Once clean, he opened the bag Norah had hastily packed for him.

Inside the pocket of a pair of her father's trousers, he discovered a folded stack of bills. Hundreds of dollars. At first, he stared. Dumbfounded. And then he sank to the floor, sobbing. Anguish, remorse over not finding it sooner, and uncertainty over what to do with it attacked him from all sides. Deep pain followed. He looked at the money day after day until he made a choice, and since then he had hoped it was the right one and that she understood.

He closed his eyes now and pictured Norah the way he'd last seen her. In his mind's eye, he saw her golden hair, her large almond-shaped blue eyes, and her lips, pink and appealing. He'd been bold that last day and held her in his arms. It'd left him wanting more, wishing for a way to stay with her. Their acquaintance had been brief but profound, leaving a mark on his heart that bore her name. If honor had not required him to leave the King farm, he felt certain the affection he felt for Norah would have blossomed into an even deeper emotion.

If he'd found the money even a day sooner, he would have rushed right back to Blackwell and placed it in her hands. He would have told her to put it toward her loan. Financial freedom would have allowed her to call off her engagement to Jake, whom she didn't love anyway. Then he would have begged her for a job on her farm, and he would have worked harder than a man had ever worked while he savored every moment in her presence. And when the time was right, he would have asked to stay with her forever.

A terse chuckle escaped his lips as he berated himself for ever entertaining such an irrational fantasy. By the time he'd found the money, she was married. Running back to her had never been an option. There was no begging for the hand of a married woman. The question became what to do with the money. He'd lost sleep over it, mulling around ideas in his frenzied mind until at last he accepted his good fortune. After all, thanks to Jake, Norah was financially secure. Her farm was safe, and she had been the one to give him the money—albeit inadvertently.

He took the money and headed to the nearest town, deciding to keep his promise to start over and vowing to pay her back when he was able. The bank took his down payment and sold him the deed to the run-down hotel. By the sweat of his brow, he got the place up and running and turning a profit, but still, the guilt riddled him. He worked harder, hoping if he kept his other promises, he'd find peace. But none had come.

He had written a letter to Norah from the small desk in his hotel room. In it he confessed and begged her to forgive him, enclosed double the amount of money he'd found, and promised more if she needed it. He addressed it to Norah Granger of Blackwell, Iowa, and mailed it off. That was a year ago, and he still hoped she would write back one day.

The newly finished rooms of the Mission Hotel filled up with guests just as he'd suspected they would. Sam began work on the store counter, and the café cook was busy pleasing the never-ending line of patrons with her well-seasoned food.

Quincy kissed his plump old head housekeeper, Mrs. Dover, on her rosy cheek when she told him what a fine job he was doing with the place.

"You're a good boy," she said, patting his arm. He was twenty-seven and larger than any man in town, so being called a boy was laughable, but he liked it. He'd been on his own so much of his life, and even when he had been living under the same roof as his mother, he hadn't gotten any affection. His early years had been harsh, leaving him still hungry for more.

"I know you, boy, and that look in your eye tells me you aren't sure if you are a good man or not. Wipe that look off your face and believe me," she said as she shifted the basket of bedding in her arms.

"I suppose I still wonder." He took the basket from her and carried it to the lean-to off the back where the laundry was washed, with the old housekeeper following close behind. It was a dim, muggy room he frequented only when he wanted to make Mrs. Dover's day easier. She had plenty of help working under her, but she still pushed herself too hard, insisting that she liked the work and it kept her young.

"I watch you," she said. Her eyes were caring, soft around the edges, as she looked at him. "You take all those lost souls in because you understand them."

"Is that a question?"

She put a wrinkled hand on his. "No. You're a good man. You don't have to prove it by fixing every problem you come upon. Remember to slow down occasionally and have a little fun."

He set the basket down and straightened his back. The sticky air of the lean-to made his clothes cling to him, and he pulled at his collar. "Mrs. Dover, you can stop looking at me like a lost puppy. I work hard because . . . well, there's lots to do. And I take them in because someone took me in once. That's all."

Mrs. Dover, though she tried, wasn't able to mask her feelings well. Her raised brows and pursed lips told him she didn't believe him. "You're trying to prove something. Maybe just to yourself. But remember, life isn't meant to be all work."

"I suppose you'd rather I frequented the saloon, staying out all night and coming back lost to the bottle. I hear that's a common form of entertainment for men my age. Some even go hours away to the notorious Whetted Whistle. Perhaps I ought to see why the place has such a reputation."

She laughed, unfazed by his wicked humor. "No. I don't think the saloon would suit you, and don't you even think of going to the Whetted Whistle. The tales I hear." She shivered. "You're too worried about being a decent person to be at ease in a place of ill repute. I admire that about you. You're doing good things for this town and for all them folks you keep putting in the basement rooms." She patted his arm then. "But you gotta make peace with whatever it is that weighs on you."

He took a half step backward. "What weighs on me?" He swallowed against the lump in his throat. "I was helped once, and I promised to be better. I'm trying to keep my word."

"Who was it you promised all this to?"

"It makes no difference now. I was lost. And then God put an angel in my path, and I'm doing what I can now to show my gratitude. That's all that matters." Quincy moved to leave but not before saying, "I'd like you to continue keeping my secrets. It's easier for them." He cleared his throat. "It's easier for me too if the past is left in the past."

"You know I will." Mrs. Dover chuckled softly. "I promised you the first time I caught you sneaking downstairs with one of those girls that I'd keep it all a secret. Unless you give me cause, I'll keep my word. But someday I do hope to hear more."

6

ave you tried the apple pie?" Quincy sat across from Sam in the small café. Buying the café had not been his plan, but when the owner died suddenly and the only other soul interested would surely turn it into a house of ill repute, he'd invested his money into it. He'd acquired the store in a similar way. The owner was going farther west and found himself desperate to sell in order to fund his ranching dreams, and Quincy stepped up. He pushed his fork through the flaky crust and ate a bite. "It's good."

Sam's blueberry pie was untouched in front of him. His gaze, and clearly his attention, was focused on the woman who worked in the kitchen, her head only just visible through the glass on the door.

Quincy's fork clanked against his plate, bringing Sam's head back around. "Did you ask me something?"

"Only if you liked the pie."

Sam took a quick bite and nodded. "Sure do."

"You could talk to her." Quincy wiped his face with a napkin and leaned back in his chair. "Tell her you think she has a pretty face."

"Nah." Sam looked down at his pie. "Besides, I bet there are fellas in here every day fighting for a chance to talk to her. It's a waste of my time."

"Suit yourself." Quincy certainly would not force the man's hand. "Half these tables wobble, the chairs have broken spindles, and the kitchen needs more shelving. It's not a fancy job, but if you want it, it's yours."

"Course I want it." Sam licked crumbs of pie crust from his lip. "This pie's real good. Maybe you should pay me in slices."

"I'll pay you cash, and you can spend it on pie whenever you like. The café closes at seven each night. If you work late, on occasion maybe you could offer Alice your arm. She's living with Mrs. Dover in her loft right now. It wouldn't be a far walk, but it'd be a chance to tell her you're taken with her."

"Mrs. Dover's house?" Sam's hand froze above his slice of pie. "Doesn't Alice have family?"

"Not around here."

"I assumed she'd come to town with her family."

"You'll have to ask her about her circumstances." Quincy respected Alice too much to gossip, even to Sam. She worked hard and never complained. How could he not respect a woman with so much grit? He tapped his friend's arm. "She's coming over here now. It's your chance."

Alice was a small woman in frame and height. When Quincy first met her, he'd been surprised to realize she didn't even come up to his shoulder. Her dark hair framed her fair skin, giving her a sophisticated look. She approached now with a swift walk but trembling hands. "Mr. Barnes?"

"Quincy," he corrected. "What can I do for you?"

"Mrs. Dover mentioned some upcoming socials and a baseball game. I know there'll be a lot of spectators."

He nodded. "Are you wanting to go?"

"No . . . well, yes." She flushed red and looked back toward the kitchen like she wanted to abandon her mission. Rather than retreating, she straightened her small shoulders. "I'm not trying to shirk. You know I work hard."

"Put the sign on the door and close up if you wish. I don't see any reason why you can't go." He looked across the table at Sam, who sat motionless, mouth slightly ajar, a bite of pie frozen on his fork. "Have you met Sam Landon?"

"No, nice to meet you." She curtsied slightly in his direction, which seemed to snap him back to reality, then returned her gaze to Quincy. "Might I use the kitchen?"

"You use it every day."

"I was thinking that if folks sit and watch baseball, they might buy cookies and vittles from me. I'd buy my own supplies and cook on my own time," she said, hardly stopping to breathe. "It has nothing to do with this job. I'm grateful for it. I only thought it might be a chance for me to make some extra money."

Quincy tapped the table with his palm and nodded, grateful she'd finally gotten to her point. "Use the kitchen, it's a wonderful idea. Very clever."

"Really?"

"Yes, of course, and Sam will build you a cart to push to the game and sell your food." Quincy turned to Sam. "Do you mind?"

"No, I'd . . . I'd be happy to help." Sam bobbed his head with more enthusiasm than necessary. "It'd be my pleasure."

"You don't have to do that." Alice's blush deepened. "I can't pay you. I'll just carry whatever I make over to the game."

"No need. I'd be happy to make it as a gift," Sam said.

"No. I refuse to be beholden."

Quincy shook his head. Women could be so impossible. Their efforts to be noble often hindered their own path to success. He didn't have time to sit around listening to the two of them go back and forth. "Sam will make the cart for the café. You can keep it in the back and use it when you like, but it'll be my cart and then you don't have to feel the burden of debt."

He brushed his hands together, proud of himself for coming up with a solution.

"If I came by around seven, could I walk you home and then we could discuss what type of cart would work best?" Sam asked Alice. "It wouldn't be putting me out at all, seeing as how Quincy is paying me for repairs on all his businesses."

Alice pushed her dark hair from her face, studying Sam. "Thank you," she said at last. "I wouldn't mind walking home with you."

Quincy fought hard to keep from smirking at his clever matchmaking. He busied himself by scraping the last of the pie from his plate, giving them what privacy he could while still sitting nearby.

He'd been awkward himself when he'd first approached Opal, the infatuation of his youth, and begged her to spend time with him. The memory used to sting, but the throbbing pain had vanished with time and understanding. What they'd shared, it hadn't been love. Opal, Norah—neither had worked out for him, but for very different reasons.

Sam raised his chin high as Alice headed back to the kitchen. "She said yes."

"I heard." Quincy pushed away from the table. "If you

have time, you might want to go home and change your shirt before you walk her home."

Pie filling lay in splotches down Sam's front. "Oh bother," he mumbled as he wiped at the stains with his napkin. "Do you suppose she saw?"

"If she did, she didn't seem to mind. She was as flushed and red as you were."

The two parted ways at the café door, Sam determined to clean up before returning for Alice and Quincy off to wander the streets with no companion other than the twinge of longing in his chest. He'd thought Opal was the girl for him. She was so alluring, so enticing, and she was the first girl who'd been interested in him. For half a year they snuck around together. She watched him fight, cheering him on and celebrating with him or consoling him after each match. He spent what little money he had to shower her with gifts and take her to restaurants he couldn't really afford. And then it ended.

"My parents," she said one fateful afternoon. "They know about us. I thought our fun could go on, but it can't."

His heart sank. His hopes for the future were all based on Opal's continued affection. "We could run away. I'd work hard," he begged, frantically trying to keep her near him. "We could have a life together."

"It was always going to end." She grabbed his hand, and he pulled her close and searched her face. He wanted to see the same sorrow in her features that he felt in his chest, but he saw no remorse, no anguish. He let her go and then lost himself in deep despair. His fights, once won by skill, were then fought with rage. When he saw Opal next, she was married, aloof, and seemingly unaffected by him. What a fool he'd been.

His anger and hurt ran deep. Reckless living became the

norm as he attempted to convince himself that he didn't care. Recalling it now did not bring the old rage or darkness. Just pity for his former self and his naivety.

And then in his darkest moment, there had been Norah. She hadn't loved him, but she had cared about his well-being. No matter her feelings, she had changed him and pointed him on a course far more purposeful than he had ever known before.

He walked faster, hating that even now Norah had a hold over him. That the women in his life had all come and gone, leaving only scars in their wake.

"Any mail?" he asked when he arrived at the post office and greeted old Jim Richardson. "I think there may be a shipment of doorknobs for the hotel coming."

Jim pushed his spectacles farther up on his nose and nodded. "Your name was on half the mail that came through. Wait here and I'll get it." Jim hadn't been lying. He returned from the back of the building with an armload of boxes and letters. "You need help carrying it all?"

"Let me look through it. Some of those might be for the café."

"If they are, I can run them over for you. I have to swing by later for some of that new cook's pie anyway." Jim sat back on his stool and waited while Quincy shuffled through the stack. He found the doorknobs for the hotel, a case of spices for the café, and a book of recipes he'd ordered in hopes they'd inspire the former cook. He set aside a few other packages for the café, then gathered the rest in his arms, thanked Jim, and headed back to his office to read through his correspondence in private.

"Here are the new doorknobs," he said to Mrs. Dover

when he arrived at the hotel. He pried the box open and showed her the gleaming knobs. "I'll see if I can put them on tomorrow or the next day."

She fussed over them, calling them beautiful and complimenting him again for all he'd done to spiff the place up. "This hotel could not have gotten a better owner."

"You flatter me." He smiled, grateful for her unfailing support. "I'll be in my office going through this stack of correspondence. If anyone needs me, let me know."

In his office, he closed the door, sank into his chair, looked at the pile of mail, and groaned. Guests often wrote ahead to let him know when they'd be in town and to request he hold a room for them. Those weren't so hard to deal with, just tedious. There were often letters about business opportunities and invitations to social events that he politely declined. A large smudged and travel-weary letter at the bottom of the heap caught his eye.

He tore into it, stared, then watched the contents fall to the floor. His heart thudded wildly in his chest—like the hoofs of a racehorse it pounded. It couldn't be, could it? The room spun, refusing to slow down. He put his head in his hands— for how long, he was unsure. When at last his senses settled enough that he could force his trembling hand to move, he picked up the two letters from the floor. He devoured the thin sheet of unfamiliar paper first, hungry for an explanation.

Dear Mr. Barnes,

I'm writing to inform you that your letter addressed to Norah Granger was not delivered. It ended up at the dead letter office in Washington, DC, where we had to open it to try and redirect it. We were unsuccessful in locating its intended recipient and have decided the best course of action is to return it to you. All the contents you mailed are enclosed, in addition to the letter. We apologize for the invasion of your privacy and assure you it was done only after all other means of delivering this letter were attempted.

Sincerely,
Penny Ercanbeck,
US Postal Clerk

Daggers could not have caused more pain than these words. For months now he'd assumed his letter was in Norah's hands and that he'd made amends the best he could. He'd lost sleep wondering how his words were received, but he never imagined they remained undelivered. And now . . . now he felt like a thief.

"No!" he bellowed and smacked his hand against the desk. He stood and paced the room. Somehow he had to set it right, but how? He picked up and studied the other paper next. Across the front in legible print, it read "Norah Granger"—there was no mistaking it. What sort of incompetent postal carriers had failed to put it in her hands? How could his neatly addressed letter have been lost for so long? He wadded up the slip of paper from the dead letter office and threw it across the room, then unfolded the letter he'd penned by his own hand. His confession, his plea for forgiveness, and the money. It was all there, staring back at him like a ghost from the past.

"Quincy?" Mrs. Dover's voice came through the thick wooden door.

He took a deep, slow breath before cracking it open and asking, "Yes?"

Mrs. Dover put a hand on her heart, pushed the door farther open, and let herself in. "What's wrong?" She clutched his arm. "Tell me."

Guard down, he thrust the letter into her hands and shared his whole painful story. With unchecked words, he confessed his many indiscretions, then told of his brutal beating and the angel who found him. And then in a hoarse and pained voice, he told of how he walked away from her, only to discover the money.

He collapsed into his chair, weak and bereft from the telling. "I cheated the one soul in the whole world who believed in me. I told myself she would want me to use it to start over. I let myself believe it. She didn't need it, not with Jake's finances there to keep her farm afloat." He rubbed his hands on his thighs. "Mrs. Dover, I wronged her."

"But you tried to make amends." She stepped near him and put a hand on his back. "You sent her a generous sum of money."

"She never got it. Everything I've built is a farce."

"You poor boy," she said under her breath. "Such a burden to carry."

For two years he'd borne this weight, never speaking of it despite shouldering it daily. And now he'd shared it in a burst of words laden with pain. He braced himself, still expecting a blow, not of fists but of words. Surely Mrs. Dover would think on his confession and ridicule his choices and see him for what he really was—a man who had committed a grievous wrong.

Mrs. Dover crossed her arms over her plump chest and

said, "Go make things right. Alice is capable of running the kitchen. I can keep the hotel going, and I'll be sure to check in on the store too. It'll all be here when you get back. Go make amends and then forgive yourself. Surely the Lord has already. Go settle things with Norah so you can get on with your life."

"She's married," he reminded her.

"I didn't say marry the lass. Just go, confess your wrongs, and put the money in her hands. Say what needs saying."

"Go," he whispered. Back to Blackwell, back to the King farm, back to her. He stood, letter in hand, and stepped toward the door. "I'll go." He stopped. "Will you keep this secret too?"

"When I met you, I never suspected you were such a man of mystery." She smiled then, her cheeks round and rosy. "We've all got our secrets. It's an honor you shared yours with me. Now go, and do what you must so you can be on your way."

7

"Blackwell station will be our next stop." The conductor made his way down the aisle. "Gather your belongings if you plan to disembark."

The train journey from Longfield to Blackwell had provided time for Quincy to ponder what lay ahead, but no matter how much time he spent on the matter, he was not entirely certain how he would handle seeing Norah. He'd traveled by train over the last two years, but not once did he stop in Blackwell. He looked away when his train passed through the town, but today there would be no avoiding it.

Out his window, the small farm town of two-story buildings with painted storefronts and a church on the hill came into view. It was a prosperous community in an ideal location on the railroad line. He straightened in his seat. He'd walked away a broken man. What was he now? In many ways he knew the answer was that he was a changed man, but still he wondered.

Ten minutes later, he stood on Blackwell soil with his bag in hand and the money he planned to return tucked in his breast pocket. Today, at last, he would place it in Norah's hand. He hoped her eyes would speak forgiveness so he could walk away and close the door on Blackwell and Norah forever.

"Where might I rent a horse?" he asked the man in the ticket booth. He could walk the eight miles from town to the King property, but a horse would make for a quick escape if those large almond eyes did not contain the clemency he so badly yearned for.

"Livery is down the main street, then turn right after the mercantile and you'll see it."

Quincy thanked the man and then, with a determined tread, followed his directions. In no time at all he had a horse to ride. There was no need to ask for directions. The memory of the day he left Norah's farm was one he would always remember. One turn out of town and then eight long miles of dusty road. Memories rushed at him with fresh candor, filling his mind as he travelled the same road he'd vowed never to pass over again. The time dragged by, and his chest tightened a little more each mile closer to the old King farm, but there was no turning back—not until he put his belated letter in Norah's hand.

The house, with its front porch and wooden rockers, came into view. It was in these fields that she'd rescued him. It was in this house that he'd been revived. And it was from this place that he'd walked to his future, leaving his champion to lead her own life. How surreal it was to be back.

No matter how familiar it felt, he knew it was different. Norah was married. It'd been two years. She might have her long-hoped-for baby in her arms. For all he knew, she may have forgotten she ever rescued a man from not only hungry vultures but also his life of unruliness. His pulse quickened.

He'd rehearsed a clumsy speech, but he feared his words would fail him. If no words came, he'd simply put his letter in her hands and fall down at her feet.

Quincy looked at the garden in hopes she'd be there, but he saw no one. He looked to the barn and rather than Norah's face, he was greeted by the scowling face of a man who Quincy assumed must be Jake. Quincy nodded in greeting. "Afternoon."

"What brings you out this way?" The man's face softened from a scowl to a milder suspicion. "I wasn't expecting anyone."

"Name's Quincy. Sorry to come by unannounced."

"Jake Granger." He put out a hand when Quincy slid from his horse and approached him. Quincy shook the man's hand, reminding himself that Jake was not the enemy.

"I have a delivery." Quincy reached into his pocked but stopped before handing the letter with the money to Jake. "I was hoping I could see your wife. It's a strange request, I know, but I have mail for her. It's a sensitive matter."

"I'm not in favor of honoring such a request." Jake's brow furrowed deeper. "Any correspondence you have for her can be given to me."

Jake was not as big a man as Quincy, but his glare was threatening in its own way. "I'd like to see that it ends up in her hands. It is important she receive it herself."

"You with the post office?"

"No. I wrote the letter, but it was lost." He pulled it from his pocket so Jake could see it but didn't offer it to the man. "Once she has it, I'll leave."

Jake chuckled after eyeing the letter. "That's addressed to Norah Granger. There is no such person."

Quincy shoved the letter back in his pocket. He would not be giving his confession or the money to anyone but Norah. "Why jest about your wife? You want me gone, just tell me where she is."

"There is *no* Norah Granger here. My wife's name is Mary Beth Handley Granger." He said each word slowly as though Quincy were daft. "That letter doesn't belong here. I refused it once already."

Quincy staggered backward a step. He didn't understand. Where was Norah? She and Jake had been days away from marriage when he left. She'd assured him over and over that her future was secure, as was her land, because Jake Granger was to be her husband. Through gritted teeth, he asked, "What do you mean, Norah is not your wife?"

"I told you, my wife's name's Mary Beth."

"What happened to Norah?" he asked, doing all he could to keep the tension from his voice. "Tell me where she is."

He moved a chaw of tobacco around in his mouth. "She wasn't worth my time. I never married her."

Quincy wasn't a dense man, but today, in this moment, he felt the world spinning faster than he could handle. It wasn't making sense, and he *needed* it to. "You were engaged to marry her. Where is she?"

"I don't know. I wanted this land and didn't mind getting a pretty wife out of it, but she turned out to be nothing more than a worthless trollop. Hard to make a name for oneself if you saddle yourself with a woman like that."

Thud.

Quincy's fist connected with Jake's face without reservation. "Norah has more moral character than you'll ever have. You worthless piece of—"

"Get off my land. Now!" Jake shouted as he stumbled about trying to regain his balance.

"This is King land." Quincy took a step toward Jake, who cowered. "Tell me what happened with Norah, or I'll show you again how I feel about you."

"We were going to marry." His once snide voice now quivered. "But word spread around town that she had a man living at her place. She was a tainted woman. I should have known. Her family wasn't well liked, but I'd thought with them dead . . ."

"Go on." Quincy's fists shook at his sides. He wanted to clobber the man so badly.

"She said he was convalescing. Said she found him hurt, but one look at her blushing face and I knew he wasn't some old codger down on his luck." No remorse showed on his aging face. "I called off the wedding, waited a few months for the bank to take the land, and then bought it myself. I think she tried to find work in town. Odd jobs and such, but we all knew what she was by then. No better than her father had been, both weak and worthless. I don't know where she went after that. Someone in town might."

Quincy wanted to defend Norah again. He would have too, but he looked past Jake and saw a young woman with a baby in her arms step outside onto the porch. She deserved better than this man, but Quincy would not hit Jake in front of his wife and child. Instead, he mounted his horse and said, "You're a fool."

He held back the vile words that were on the tip of his tongue and turned away from the farm. Finding Norah was what mattered. He didn't know where to begin looking for her, but he would find her—no matter how long it took.

Was her name even still Norah King, or had she married? Questions rose up like fog around him. With the trains running far and wide across the country, she could be anywhere. How dare Jake turn his back on her. And her town, how could they believe the lies so easily?

His fury turned to despair as he imagined the ache she must have borne as she left the land she loved. Jake had done Norah a terrible injustice when he'd refused to marry her. His fists tightened around the reins—he should have pounded the man a few more times, but no good could come from it.

A gurgling brook ran along the side of the road. Quincy stopped his horse, dismounted, and led the animal to the muddy bank. Norah had loved the water. Her eyes had lit up when she spoke of dipping her feet in it. Did she have a creek where she was now?

A new thought crept its way into his frenzied mind. All this time he'd assumed Norah was a wife, cared for and secure. Quincy had used her misplaced money, thinking she had no dire need of it. And though guilt over his choice had ravaged him, he had never worried about her well-being. Nauseous, he crouched on the bank and splashed his face with water, but there was no washing away the reality of his errors. Jake had been wrong, and there was no denying that his decision had been selfish. But Quincy's hands were dirty too. He'd kept the money she'd needed. If he'd come back . . . *Oh Lord*, he whispered, *this is my fault.*

He rushed from the streambed and mounted his borrowed horse. The guilt may never go away, as the crime was too immense, but he had to try. His need to set the past right multiplied tenfold. And he would. Right there on the outskirts of Blackwell he added a new promise to all the others—*I promise to find her and do whatever I can to make amends. I will find her.* He'd stolen her money, his presence had soured her reputation, and two years of her life were gone. So much couldn't be changed, but he had to do what he could.

Back in Blackwell, he tied the horse to a hitching post, then ran to the church and asked the preacher if he knew where she'd gone, only to see his face droop with remorse. "I've heard of Norah, but she left before I came to town. I wish I could help you."

The storekeeper said he gave her a few menial jobs, but it wasn't enough to sustain her. He believed she'd gone West, and the liveryman said he didn't have time to keep track of loose women. Quincy stopped everyone he saw. Some said, "Good riddance" when Quincy mentioned her name, while others talked of her in hushed tones. But no one knew her whereabouts. When he knocked on the doctor's door, he had no expectation of receiving an answer, not after so many failed attempts.

"Sit down," the doctor said, pointing to a chair in the corner of the small office. "I knew Norah King and all her family. I even treated the man she harbored in her house."

Quincy jerked up his head and looked at the doctor. He'd been so weak and his vision so fuzzy when he last encountered the man, he didn't recognize him. "You did?"

"I'm glad to see you're fully recovered." The doctor smiled, but there was sadness behind his look. "I tried to tell the town that Norah had taken care of a patient, but Jake was set on turning everyone's opinion of her. When a field hand confirmed that you'd been there and you were not an old man, the gossips won. Jake made the circumstances seem much more derisive than they were. I think he may have cared about the farm more than he'd ever cared about Norah."

"Her father gambled. It hardly seems cause to shun her." Quincy ran his hands through his hair. If he'd been alone, he might have screamed. "How could they do this?"

"His gambling cost important people a lot of money, and they made sure no one saw him in a good light again. It wasn't hard to get the gossips talking about the King family."

"So she left?"

"Not right away. She tried to work here for a few months, perhaps longer, I don't recall exactly. She took whatever work she could find, but no one gave her much, and with no home, she was at the mercy of everyone around her. She came to me in tears one night, begging me to help her find a position. Poor thing was thin and her clothes were worn. I feared she'd be forced to resort to unseemly means to feed herself if she didn't find a stable position soon."

The image the doctor created hurt worse than any blows he'd ever taken in the boxing ring, cutting deeper than any gash or wound. He looked up, and without words, he asked the doctor to tell the rest.

"That girl has always had a backbone and a disposition set on seeing the good, but that night she looked lost. I fed her and told her I'd see what I could do to help, but I didn't have the means to hire her on. I offered to post a marriage advertisement."

"What?"

"She refused. She said she couldn't, that after Jake's attack on her honor she was too afraid of the sort of man she'd be saddled with. She wanted to try other means of survival first. In the end, she moved to Warner Crossing, hoping she could find a job in a newer railroad town." The creases around his eyes grew deeper. "I haven't heard from her since."

"I never thought . . ."

"When she came to me, she asked about jobs, but she also asked several times if I thought you were well. She was worried about you, and now I see that same worry in your eyes. I don't know if she's found a safe place in Warner Crossing or not. She may need a friend very badly."

"I never meant her harm."

"She never blamed you." He sighed. "I wish I could give you more direction, but I suggest you go to Warner Crossing to look."

8

Despite his eagerness to rush off to Warner Crossing, Quincy was forced to wait for the next departing train. Two days in Blackwell did nothing to ease his worries. With each passing hour, he grew more agitated and restless, nervous for what was ahead.

The evening before his train's departure, he sat in the lobby of Blackwell's only hotel. He stared out the large glass window, absently watching the town's citizens travel the dusty street. A commotion outside the building caused him to stand. Only slightly interested, he walked out the front entrance of the hotel and followed the ruckus down the main street and then around the back of the saloon. He stood at the edge of the small crowd and waited.

A man shouted above the din, announcing a fight. A chill raced through Quincy. Money was taken and bets were made. It wasn't as organized or as lively as the fights he'd been in, but it still felt too familiar. He turned away, only to have a man put a firm hand on his shoulder. "You the fella who gave Jake a blow across the jaw?"

"I didn't throw any punches that weren't called for." He

stepped out from under the man's hand, eager to get away from this scene before he did something impulsive. In the past, he'd used the fights to try to manage his rage, and since learning of Norah's struggles, he'd been nothing but hot-blooded.

"We got lots of bets being made. You could get in there and make some money. I'd wager on you." The man's speech was garbled enough that Quincy felt certain he'd been drinking. "There's girls too. They came over from the saloon. You win and you could have your choice."

"No." He put more distance between himself and the drunken man. The crowd roared, drawing the man's attention away from Quincy and back to the makeshift ring. Dark alleys, money exchanges, and desperation—he wanted no part in it. They weren't real fixes for what ailed him.

He walked away, but after taking only a few steps, he felt a tug on his sleeve. Irritated by the man's persistence, he grabbed the hand, only to find his fingers wrapped around the thin wrist of a small boy rather than that of the intoxicated man.

"Please," the boy said in a frantic whisper, "help me get away from here."

Quincy looked beyond the boy and back toward the crowd. He saw a thin, wiry man stomping through the throng, eyes peeled, looking for something. Quincy stepped in front of the boy, letting his large frame work as cover. When the wiry man turned away, Quincy grabbed the boy by the shoulder. "Come on."

They wove around the spectators until they were at last free of the crowd. Quincy knelt in front of the child. Surely he was no more than eight or nine. "What troubles you?"

"I just gotta get away." He looked back over his shoulder every few seconds.

"Why? Be straight with me, boy."

"I made a few coins helping with a fight a couple towns back. I was hungry, that's all."

"I don't blame you." Rather the opposite, he felt an instant kinship with this lad. He'd been desperate when he arrived at his first fight. Hunger pains willing him to take any job offered. "What happened?"

"The fellow with the scar on his cheek forced me to go with him. He's the one who's going to all the towns and gettin' everyone excited to have a fight."

"What's he need you for?"

"Makes me and another fella take a few blows to get the crowd excited, and anything else he feels like doing. I take bets, that sort of thing." The boy's face turned hard. "Everyone's mean, and they don't care nothin' 'bout me."

"Have you family?" Quincy asked, but he already knew the boy had no one to care for him.

"I don't got no family. Don't feel I got need for one."

Quincy heard a commotion nearby, so he took the boy's arm and pulled him farther into the shadows. When he felt certain they could leave without being seen, he rushed the boy back toward the hotel but then thought better of taking him inside and instead instructed him to wait behind the livery.

He spent the next hour buying the boy clothes from a local so he'd have something other than rags to wear. He then secured a ticket to Longfield for the lad. Bundle in hand, he found the boy behind the livery where he'd directed him to go.

"I can't go back to Longfield just yet. But I've written you a note to show anyone who questions why you're traveling alone. I have another pressing matter to deal with, but don't be afraid. Go to the Mission Hotel and wait by the lean-to until a plump old woman comes out. She's always doing laundry, so you shouldn't have to wait too long. Tell her Quincy sent you and asked that you be put in one of the lower rooms. You may not believe you need a family, but well, we all need a hand up from time to time."

"And if she won't help?"

"She will." He stared at the boy. "I should have asked your name."

"Nels Anderson." He snatched the clothes and the ticket as though he feared Quincy would change his mind. Quincy knew how Nels felt and why he acted so skittish and untrusting. He could have reached for the boy and forced him on the train, but he chose not to and instead let Nels choose for himself.

Nels disappeared from sight, leaving Quincy alone with only his hope that the boy would find his way to the Mission Hotel or at least away from the men he feared.

Quincy took the first train he could to Warner's Crossing, where he checked in to a hotel room and then began his search for Norah. He knocked on one door after another, asking after Norah. Every shopkeeper shook his head, and every banker, every cook, and every passerby offered him no help. Discouraged but unwilling to accept defeat, he persevered. A drunkard on the street pointed at the infamous Whetted Whistle, grunted, and said there was a Norah there who fit his description. He'd expected to feel relief as he neared the end of his quest, but there was no reprieve to be found. Dread filled him as he walked to the saloon on the edge of the railway boomtown. Nights at the local saloon had once been a regular occurrence for him, but then he'd met Norah. He vowed to be different and not set foot in such an establishment again. Now he was about to enter one more notorious than any he'd ever entered. The irony did not escape him—he'd made the vow because of her, and now he'd break it for her.

Warner Crossing was not his town, but he'd heard of the Whetted Whistle. Men talked in hushed tones about all that transpired within the famed saloon's walls. Evils that even his former self would have shirked away from were common there. The thought of Norah—beautiful, angelic Norah— working within those tainted walls made his stomach clench.

He pulled his hat low on his head and faced the inevitable as he stepped through the swinging front doors and found a seat at a corner table. Heavy smoke filled the air, giving everything a hazy appearance. He fought off a cough, sank low in his seat, and looked around.

A woman wearing a bright dress that hung off her shoulder leaned against the bar. He averted his eyes. It wasn't Norah. Another woman sat beside three men playing cards. She laughed loudly, threw her arm around the man nearest her, and pressed her lips to his. Sickening fear pulsed through him.

"Something to drink, mister?" a young woman stepped up to his table and asked.

"Sarsaparilla," he muttered, knowing he needed to order something if he was going to fill up a seat in the busy place.

"You look like you need something stronger than that." She pulled up a chair and sat too close to him, leaning her body against his. Her presence made him uneasy. "Want a whiskey?"

"No. A sarsaparilla will do." He scooted to the far side of his chair, ignoring her. Relief flooded him when he heard her chair scratch the floor as she went for his weak drink.

His discomfort grew as he waited for her to return. The laughing, the coarse language, the lack of morals. There'd been a time when he'd felt at ease in saloons with drunken men and enterprising women, but he no longer belonged here. He saw the dancers, the women leading men away from the crowd, and the empty look in the women's eyes. If not for Norah, he would have run away by now.

"You're not from around here, are you?" the girl said when she returned with his drink. "You passing through?"

"I'm looking for someone," he said. "I think there's a woman here I used to know."

She sat beside him again, her thigh touching his. "I've been here two years. I know everyone. I'll take good care of you."

"Do you know Norah King?"

"Yeah." She straightened in her chair. "I don't know why everyone always wants Norah."

"What do you mean?"

"One fellow said it was because she wasn't hardened like the rest of us. Don't make no sense to me. The rest of us got experience she don't. The men can't keep their eyes off her. But Percy won't let them have her. Not yet."

"Where is she?" he asked, disgusted by the scene she painted. "I need to see her right away."

"Percy doesn't let the girls make social calls while they're working. It's part of our contracts." She pointed at a large man on the far side of the room. "You'll have to wait."

"I don't care what Percy says or about any contract." He pushed away from the table with enough force that his chair fell to the ground behind him. Eyes that had ignored him before were on him now. Rather than remain civil, he growled like a bear. "I'm not leaving this place until I find her. Tell me where she is."

Percy stepped from the shadows. "I own this place. You got a problem, come talk to me. You pick a fight, and I'll throw you out."

"I don't want a fight." Quincy uncurled his hands, but his insides remained clenched. "I'm looking for an old friend. I was told she works here."

The crowd watched the exchange in eager silence, the tension palpable in the air. Were they all waiting for a fight, eager for some sort of action? He'd fought in front of crowds before. He knew the appetite of mobs. They were rarely satisfied, always wanting more.

"You want to talk to one of *my* girls," he sneered, "you'll have to wait until they aren't working. I share them with my paying guests, but there won't be any social calls." Vile laughter ripped through the room. "But they're mine. Ask anyone. They all know that these are Percy's girls."

Percy challenged him with his stance and his eyes. Quincy might have stepped away from his former life, but something deep inside him remembered and anticipated what was to come. This wasn't going to be a peaceful exchange. His body was ready to fight. This time not for survival or money but for Norah. If a confrontation was the only way to end this, then he'd accept it. What he wouldn't accept was to walk away from this saloon without Norah at his side.

"I'll pay for her time." He reached into his pocket and waved money he hoped Percy wouldn't resist. One last attempt at a simple resolution, despicable as it was. "Where is Norah?"

A low murmur filled the room when he said her name. The sudden excitement alarmed him. What piece of this puzzle was he missing?

"You can have some other girl's time." Percy reached for the money, but Quincy pulled it back. Percy scowled and barked at everyone in the room, "Drink, play your cards." He glared at Quincy. "And you—come talk to me out back."

Quincy narrowed his eyes. This situation screamed of impending danger. Come what may, Norah was worth the risk. He owed her that much, and so much more. They walked through the maze of tables. Neither man spoke as they stepped through the back door. The night air was cooler than that of the smoke-filled saloon, but it was still warm and sticky.

"Look," Quincy said, breaking the silence, "I need to see Norah, not some other girl, and then I'll go. I don't want to cause trouble."

"She's in one of the rooms upstairs—"

"No!" He could not keep the horror from his voice. "She would never."

"She would and she did. She came to me begging for work." He spat a long string of tobacco from his mouth. The brown spittle landed near Quincy's boots. "I offered her a spot working upstairs. She refused and was going to leave, but business is better if I have pretty faces working for me.

Besides, it's only a matter of time before I convince them to do more than serve drinks."

"Then why is she up there now?"

"I'm working on convincing her. I got men lined up, ready to pay a high price. Relax, she's a grown woman, and this is where she wants to be. She signed her name on the contract, so she's one of Percy's girls now. We got other girls—"

"No." Quincy stepped away from Percy. He didn't have time to play games. He came for Norah, and he was going to leave with her. He'd get her himself—no permission needed, at least not from Percy.

Percy's hand landed on Quincy's shoulder. "Where you going?"

"I'm going inside, and I'm getting what I came for." Quincy pushed his hand away. "Let me pass, and you won't have trouble."

"You go up there now and that whole roomful of men will be at your throat. They been waiting for me to let them have her. You can't walk off with her."

He shoved the man with both hands and went through the back door. He didn't make eye contact with anyone as he stormed past the bar to the stairs. Taking them two at a time still didn't feel fast enough.

A hallway full of closed doors met his gaze, and he banged on the first. "Norah!"

"Go away, there ain't no Norah here," a man's voice said from within, followed by a woman's giggles.

"Norah!" he said, banging on the next door and the next. After pounding his fist on the fourth door and shouting her name, he heard a weak reply. He grabbed the handle, only to find it locked. Men were coming up the stairs. His time was running out. With all the force he could muster, he kicked the door. It cracked with his first kick and swung open with his second.

There she was. The angel who'd rescued him sat curled in the corner, shaking with fear. A protectiveness like nothing he'd ever felt before raced through his veins. Here before him was the girl who'd visited him in his dreams. Only now, she was in the flesh. His rage returned, magnified by the sight of her sunken eyes and thin frame. Whatever had happened in the last two years had altered her appearance, but it was the fear he sensed in her that he found most alarming.

"Norah," he said as he crossed the floor.

Her eyes, which had been so full of fear, sprang to life. "You should go." She pushed at his arm. "Go, before he kills you."

"No." He put his hand out, ready to pull her to her feet and rush her from this wretched place. "I'm not leaving without you."

"Get out of this room." Percy's voice boomed from behind him. "She works for me. She's mine."

Quincy turned, fist up, and swung. This was not a warning blow. It was full of force, meant to put its recipient on the ground—and it did. Percy didn't sway or stagger; he collapsed. The two men who stood behind Percy looked from their sprawled-out employer to the raging bear Quincy had become. "I *am* taking this woman out of here." His voice was hoarse but full of power. "He doesn't own her."

"D-d-does she want to go?" the larger of the two men asked. "What about her contract?"

Quincy bent down, sliding one arm behind Norah's back and the other under her knees. "Ready, Norah?"

She nodded, and that was all he needed. With her in his arms, he stepped over Percy and past the two men. She was light as a feather, and he hardly felt her in his arms. Halfway down the stairs, someone pulled back on his shoulder. He struggled to keep his balance. Pain shot through his back as a foot kicked him hard. With all his power, he tried to stay upright, but he failed, and they went down, skidding and toppling to the bottom of the stairs.

He sprang back onto his feet quick as he could, only to have a fist connect with his jaw. In a ring with an opponent, he always kept his bearings about him. But here in this moment, he struggled to make sense of what was happening. Norah was on the floor. Noise was all around him, and Percy was approaching from the stairway.

He swung at one of Percy's men, sending him tumbling across a table. He swung at another man, earning him a cheer from the crowd.

"Quincy!" Norah's voice cut through the commotion. He jerked his head to the side just as Percy swung and missed. Quincy went for the man's chest, hitting him with an upward force, stealing the man's breath.

Percy bent over, grabbed his sides, and gasped for air. Quincy went for Norah. In a single motion, he picked her up, glared like an angry bull at the drunken crowd, and walked out. No one followed.

They made the walk from the Whetted Whistle to the hotel in silence. Gone were his worries over retribution or confessions. Caring for Norah's immediate needs was his only aim, and the rest could wait.

He shoved open the hotel doors. "Someone! Fetch a doctor!"

9

The doctor, a squatty man with thinning hair, arrived ten minutes later. Despite his girth, he moved quickly and had a commanding presence. "Give me room to work," he instructed, shooing the extra bodies from the room. "Who are you?" he asked Quincy when he didn't leave. "I said I needed room to work."

"I'm her friend." At least he hoped he had a right to call her a friend. With a heavy heart, he told the doctor about the condition he found her in and the fall down the stairs. "She's been crying but unable to tell us what ails her."

"She's been through a lot. She'll calm." He pulled his stethoscope from his bag and held one end to Norah's thin chest. "You go on out. I'll speak with you after I examine her."

Reluctantly, he left.

Lord, help her, he prayed as he waited. In the quiet of the hall, his emotions overwhelmed him. The anguish over her condition, the guilt for his role in it, and his desperate need to ease her suffering. How bad had her life been? He wasn't sure he could stomach the answer.

The minutes passed by at an agonizingly slow pace. At last, the doctor stepped into the hall, closing the door behind him.

"How is she?" Quincy asked in a hushed tone.

"Norah is a brave woman." The doctor led him farther down the hall to a bench. "Sit if it'll help. You look rather tightly wound."

"I knew her before she had her turn of misfortune." He grimaced. What a careless choice of words. This was not some trite misfortune. "I don't like seeing her in such a disturbing condition."

"Let me put your mind at ease. The fall down the stairs has left her with a broken arm. I set the bone and it will be well again in four, perhaps six, weeks at the most. Her ribs are injured, but I don't believe they're broken. She appears to have a lot of bruising but didn't want to talk about their origins. I do not believe they were all from the fall."

Quincy understood his meaning. Knowing the wounds were not the result of his actions should have eased his mind, but it did not. Instead, he felt anger. Someone, Percy, had hurt her. Unsure how to respond to such bitter news, he simply waited to hear more.

"Other than that, she seems to have suffered from malnourishment and unsettled nerves. I don't know . . . well, I don't know if Percy had . . . you know what I'm saying. She is distraught, so I did not ask." Quincy met his eyes then and saw a sadness in them. "Percy is a beast."

"What can I do?"

"Reassure her. Listen when she wants to talk and do what you can to not add to her anguish. Try not to distress her. With time she'll make a full recovery." He patted Quincy on the shoulder. "Food and friendship will no doubt be good medicine, but you ought to know that hardship like she's seen changes people. Scars do not come only from physical wounds. Some of the deepest wounds are unseen."

Quincy nodded. There would be time later to sort it all out. "I intend to take a train to Longfield with her tomorrow if you think she's well enough to travel."

"Is she willing to go?"

"I'm going to ask, but what else can she do? She can't go back to that place, and I know for a fact she has no family. I can keep her safe."

The doctor looked him over. Quincy didn't shy from his gaze—he let him look. The doctor would find him sincere and free of malicious intent.

"Very well. I'll talk to Susannah. She's an old friend of my daughter's and works at this hotel. I'll see if she can help Norah bathe. If she's cleaned up, she'll draw less attention. With you beside her, I do believe she'll be capable of travel." His features lost their professional seriousness and grew softer. "Remember to be patient, son. Some wounds are slow to heal."

"I will." Patience was not a natural trait of his, but he would learn it.

Quincy paid the doctor for his time, then together they found Susannah and made arrangements for Norah's care. A bath was ordered and would be ready in half an hour. Susannah even offered to give Norah an old dress of hers. Over the course of a day, Quincy had witnessed the best and worst in humankind.

"Go sit with her," Susannah said to Quincy. "I'll let you know when I'm ready to help her bathe."

He had been bold at the saloon, kicking through doors and using his fists. He'd been too on guard to be frightened, but stepping into the silence of the sickroom now with no looming threats, he felt afraid. *Don't distress her*, he reminded himself. Now was not the time to do anything but offer comfort.

"Norah," he whispered. How right it felt on his tongue. "It's Quincy."

The room was dim but light enough that he could still make out her features. Her large eyes stared up at the ceiling. A damp trail ran across her sunken right cheek where a recent tear had traveled. Her right arm was casted and resting on the bed beside her. Much about her was changed, but he still felt he knew her. The same pull he'd felt two years ago existed even now, urging him closer.

"Norah," he said again as he settled into the chair beside the bed. His words croaked from him, the lump in his throat so large. "I don't know what to say. I thought I would, but I don't."

She didn't turn toward him. Her eyes stayed on the ceiling. When she spoke, her voice had a far-off quality. "I thought he was going to kill me."

He rubbed his forehead. How was he supposed to keep her from being distressed when she had such a vile man in her life?

"He said he would. Said if I wouldn't start entertaining the men like the other girls, he'd kill me. He kept talking about taking bids and my time running out." Her voice was stoic and cold, laced with pain that cut at his heart. "I was sure I'd die. Part of me wanted to. I was so tired . . . I was tired of it all."

"No." He reached for her uninjured hand. She flinched but let him hold it. What a strange turn of events. She'd held his hand, nursed him back to health, and now here he sat with their roles reversed. Her hand had once touched his own, the touch offering him hope and compassion. He brought her fingers to his lips and kissed them. "Did he . . . did—"

She turned her head away. In a voice laced with pain, she whispered, "I had nowhere to go. I tried for so long. I shouldn't have gone there, but I didn't know what to do."

Each word pierced his heart. How desperately he wished he could undo all that had been done. With her head still turned away, she continued. "He let me believe it would be nothing but serving drinks." A sob crept from her lips. "At first he was kind, but then he got angry. He wanted me upstairs. He locked me in the room. He hurt me and told me he'd break me."

"Percy won't hurt you again." He would protect her. "You're safe, do you hear me? If you'll let me, I'll take you to Longfield. You will be far away from this place."

"Longfield?"

"I started over in that town. I have a hotel, and you can stay there as long as you want. It's a respectable place, nothing like Percy's."

"You started over." She whispered the words. "I knew you would. I was so sure . . . When you walked away, I prayed you'd begin again."

"You cared for me when I had no one. I will give you the same in return."

"You owe me nothing." She let her gaze meet his, and for the first time since he'd reentered her life, he saw fire in her eyes. "I'd almost given up, and then you came."

He shifted his weight, uncomfortable with her words. He hadn't rescued her, or been the answer to her prayers. All her pain never should have happened. He could have prevented it all if he'd not been selfish and kept the money. In a voice as controlled as he could muster, he said, "I'm glad I was there. No more talk of who owes who. Say that you'll come with me. Once you're better, you can have any life you wish." In a softer voice he said, "I wish I had come soon—"

"Hush," she whispered, tears running freely down her face. "You didn't know."

"I went to Blackwell. I was . . . I was going to tell you about my businesses and all that happened. You weren't there, and I had to find you."

She bit her lip, her eyes never leaving his. "I wondered so often about you."

If she'd not been so battered and weary, he would have gathered her in his arms and held her and promised her the world. But instead, he ran his finger along the bridge of her knuckles. "A bath has been ordered for you—"

Her eyes went dark again, and she turned to the wall. "I look frightful. I saw my face in a mirror. I don't look like me. I was never a beauty. I don't claim that, but now—"

He put a hand on her ashen cheek and gently urged her to look at him. "Do you recall our first meeting?"

She nodded, her battered body curling away from him as though she wished she could disappear.

"I was half-dead, bruised, and soiled. I must have smelled awful." He leaned very near her. With his face so close to hers, he made it impossible for her to look away. He said, "You are a raving beauty in comparison."

Despite her condition, she smiled. "I've never smelled

something so foul as you on that day. It was so bad, I almost let the birds have you."

Hope filled his heart at her jesting. The woman he'd dreamed of, she was still in there—inside this broken frame. "See, there's proof. I was in far worse shape. But I have no desire to leave you to the birds."

He wanted to make her smile again, but there was a knock on the door and when he opened it, Susannah said she had the bath ready. Quincy left the women and went to his own room, where he packed his few belongings and readied to leave on the first train out in the morning.

Susannah flushed brightly when she found him later in the parlor and told him about Norah's terrible bruises. "I've never seen someone so badly hurt. I put her in one of my nightdresses and gave her a dress for tomorrow, but she's so thin, it'll hang on her."

"I'm grateful for the care you've shown her."

Quincy asked Susannah if she would stay the night with Norah in case she had needs that arose. To his great relief, she agreed, and even refused the money he offered as compensation. One night was all that stood between him and getting away from Warner Crossing. It still didn't seem soon enough.

Mrs. Dover would help him care for Norah, he was sure of that, but how would he explain Norah's presence to the rest of the town? He wanted them to accept her and give her the loving welcome she'd been deprived of in Warner Crossing. He fretted through the night, but with the rising sun came no answers. He would simply meet her needs and tackle the rest as he went.

At dawn he ordered food for Norah and Susannah and had it delivered to her room. Susannah had Norah ready to travel long before the train was set to arrive. Norah had on a pale blue dress that was a vast improvement over the rags she'd worn the day before, but it did not fit properly. Her thin body looked lost in the large garment, but it was clean and modest. The two women shared an embrace before Norah took his arm and they headed for the station.

"Do you have anything back where . . . where you stayed that you need to get? I'd face Percy again if you wish," he said as they walked toward the tracks, the town fading behind them. Their pace was slow and tedious, but at least they were moving away from this wretched place. He checked behind them every few steps, making sure Percy wasn't following.

"No. Jake didn't let me take anything from my old place. Everything went with the farm when it was sold." Her chin trembled. "Jake didn't marry me. I thought he would protect me and that I'd be able to keep my land. I thought I'd grow old and be buried there."

"I know." He guided her around the muddy tire ruts. "I told you yesterday that I went there first."

She stopped walking and put a hand on her stomach. "I still don't understand."

"I wanted to know how you fared and to prove to you I was the changed man I said I would be. I never imagined . . . I promise you, I believed you to be married." Sweat beaded his forehead. "When you weren't on your land, I asked around. The doctor told me he thought you were in Warner Crossing, so I came here." He nearly said more, but the doctor who'd tended to her had told him not to distress her. "I had to ask around awhile until a drunkard told me one of Percy's girls was named Norah."

She flinched. "I wish you'd found me under better circumstances. Will you tell me how my land looked?"

"Jake is a snake, but he knows about farming, and he has the place looking fine." Was that the answer she wanted? He wasn't sure. When one had been deprived of their heart's desire, did they wish their beloved land well or ill? "But not as good as when you were there."

"I wasn't doing so well at farming, not without my father. But I did love the land. I still do." Longing crept into her voice. "I wanted to save it, but I lost everything. And I fear I'll always be known as one of Percy's girls now."

"Norah."

"Yes?"

"The doctor said you should take it easy. I aim to do all he said and to care for you. I'll help you get well." He patted her hand, feigning confidence when, in fact, he had no experience nursing. Mrs. Dover's mother-hen ways were the best example he had. "What if we get you feeling better, and then we talk about the reasons for my trip and about all you've suffered? In fact, what if when we get to Longfield, we put you in one of the hotel's finest rooms and for an entire week you do nothing but read books? I have a rather extensive collection now."

"A full week to read books." She pulled her lips into a thin line, but still she blubbered. "That dream was from a lifetime ago. I'd forgotten until now."

"But it was a good dream." If he could turn back the clock, he'd have fulfilled it sooner. Was it too late? His stubborn, headstrong nature refused to accept that. "Some dreams take time."

"Yes," she agreed. "Some do."

He urged her toward the train, eager to be on it and moving toward something good and welcoming and away from the evil and heartache of Warner Crossing. Twice he thought he saw someone staring at them. Perhaps he was merely paranoid, but the eerie foreboding was hard to shake.

The strain of the walk to the train station was evident in her movements, but there would be time for rest later. She paused near the tracks and ran her hand over her dress. "I feel vain for caring," she whispered. "But I don't like being a spectacle."

"Don't worry about it." He put his arm around her, offering his strength to her. "I'm certain you are not the first woman to board this train in an ill-fitting dress."

She stifled a laugh. "You are as brash as I remember."

"For that I apologize."

"Don't. Your honesty appealed to me before, and I find it refreshing now. Shocking but refreshing." She tightened her grip on his arm.

He bowed his head ever so slightly. "Come along, Miss Norah King. This brash and shocking man is getting you out of here."

10

The train ride to Longfield began uneventfully. Several times Norah nearly asked the questions that were marching through her mind, but the train was full, and without some level of privacy, her queries would have to wait. Instead, she watched out the window as Warner Crossing grew smaller and smaller until she could no longer see it. She breathed easier knowing Percy and the Whetted Whistle were out of sight. If only she could kick the memories and fears away so easily. But she would cling to the hope that with time and distance, she could find peace.

Quincy said very little as they rambled down the tracks. His back was straight and his eyes alert like an animal watching for danger. When he engaged in conversation with a man near him, she allowed herself to steal a lingering glance. He was much as she remembered him, large and strong. He was injured when she saw him two years ago. Now he was well, though his nose still had the slightest crook to it. She'd believed him to be a man with a good heart when she found him in her field, and now he'd rescued her and offered her safety, solidifying her belief.

When she'd prayed for liberation, not once had she imagined Quincy would be her answer. His return had come at the perfect time. She didn't understand why he'd come or what he'd been doing all this time, but he had come, and she would forever be grateful. A faint smile pulled at the corners of her mouth. Quincy had kept his word. He'd changed his ways and made a new life for himself—he'd done what he set out to do.

As the train jostled, the aches in her body screamed louder, stealing her breath. The train ride was tiresome and long, and she attempted sleep but it was elusive.

"Norah." Quincy's voice startled her. "I'm sorry. You're awfully skittish. I only wanted to tell you that's Longfield up ahead."

Out her window she saw a town on the horizon surrounded by farmland that looked so much like home she nearly cried. "How did you end up in Longfield?"

"I was passing through, and an opportunity presented itself." He scooted closer and in a whisper that made her long for more answers said, "I'll tell you all of that when you're feeling better. Right now, we have to decide what to tell people in town about you."

"What do you mean?"

"You walk into town telling folks you were one of Percy's girls and that might be all they can ever see, and"—he looked up a moment—"I don't think that's what you want. It's certainly not all you are. I got a fresh start once. Seems now it's your turn."

"I don't want to embarrass you." She looked past Longfield. The tracks kept going. Perhaps she should too. "I also don't like lying."

"It's you I'm worried about, and I don't think it's lying to not bring up the unpleasant past. I was a boxer, and I fought for money in despicable places. You know that, but this town doesn't." He scratched his head. "I don't know the right way to go about moving on from the past. But I don't think the peace we gotta make with all that has happened is between us and all the other people out there."

A sickening feeling built inside of her. "Quincy," she said, leaning in, "I'm afraid to go into a new town." She pressed a hand to her stomach, willing it to settle. "I confess I want to hide for a while in a room that's safe. And then some-day I want to start over and live a life of my own choosing. But what if Longfield rejects me like Warner Crossing and Blackwell did?"

His firm jaw flexed. "When we get to the station, we'll go the long way to the hotel and go in the back door. I think if we're careful, we won't be seen. Once you're feeling better, you can have a job at any of my businesses. You can have whatever life you choose."

"And if someone asks—"

"I could tell them I'm your brother." He laughed, and she couldn't help but smile at the sound of it. How like him to jest when life was so serious. "But I think it might be better to simply say we are old acquaintances. There's no lie in that."

"I recall you doing a fine job of listening like a brother would."

"On that we will have to disagree," he said with a change in his tone. "I'm not much of a family man."

"Are you not the one who just spoke to me of reform and futures untarnished by the past? You could become a family man." She turned back toward the window, baffled by the sound of her own silly chatter. At the Whetted Whistle she'd been quiet, cautious. "There's no need for you to claim me as kin."

"Norah." She turned back and looked into his hazel eyes. "I am not embarrassed in any way to be associated with you. I simply think we need to both know what our story is. We will have to live with whatever we tell people."

"Very well. If someone asks, tell them I'm an acquaintance—an old friend who has had a nasty turn of fortune that's left me destitute." The indignation she felt every time she thought of Jake stealing her farm made it impossible to look away dismissively. "Jake said he'd marry me," she whispered through gritted teeth, "and so I didn't look for other help. I might have been able to find a way, but I was so sure he wanted to marry me. I thought if I was a good wife, we'd be able to build a life together."

Quincy's arm came around her, and he pulled her to his shoulder. "He is a fool."

"He's living in my house, on my land, and he's married now. I heard talk of it before leaving town."

"I saw his wife when I went there." Quincy pulled her a little tighter. "I felt sorry for her."

"Jake proved himself a selfish man, but at least his wife has a roof over her head. It's a dreadful prospect we women face. So many sacrifices are made so one can be dry in the rain."

"Look." Quincy pointed toward an enormous hotel. Three stories, made of brick, with a sign reading MISSION HOTEL. "That'll be your roof, and there is no one like Jake or Percy in the entire building. It's a roof for your taking, and no man will require anything of you. Let it rain. You'll be dry."

She blinked back tears, grateful and at the same time aware that he would never understand how the Jakes and the Percys of the world were always with her no matter where she went. They filled her mind when she slept and taunted her during the day by sauntering through her memories, declaring her one of Percy's girls, no matter how far away she was. She would do her best to push the memories aside and hope someday they would no longer haunt her as she built a new life so strong the pain could not get through.

"If you can wipe your tears and muster your courage, I'll get us to that roof you're yearning for." Quincy stood when the train stopped. "There's a lot I can't fix"—he held out his hand—"but I can put you up in a room and send Mrs. Dover to fuss over you." When she looked at him confused, he said, "She's the head housekeeper and a rather motherly sort."

"Ah." She took his hand. "You've found yourself a mama. You are more of a family man than you claim to be."

"Perhaps."

She rose on shaky legs, lightheaded from the unhealed wounds and many hours of sitting.

"Let's hurry and get you settled with your pile of books."

As stealthily as possible, they crept off the train and through the backstreets of town.

"Your roof!" He threw his arm before him like a manservant when they reached the back door of the hotel.

She grabbed both sides of her overlarge dress and dipped a curtsy to thank him. She stepped inside and followed him up the stairs to room eight on the second floor at the end of the hall, where he left her to get settled.

"You look lost." Mrs. Dover waddled down the hall toward him after he left Norah in her room. "This is home, boy, you ought to be smiling."

He did smile then. How could he not? Having someone care if he was here or there was a balm to his weary soul. He embraced the older woman and asked, "How did you fare here while I was away?"

"I managed without you, but you were sorely missed." She chuckled, her extra chin shaking. "Your baseball team complained about you not being here. There was an awful lot of talk about you being back in time for the big game. I'd say half the town was missing you. The other half was thrilled you were gone and hoping you'd stay away until after the game."

"I see why I'm wanted."

"They say you have more talent on the field than anyone else on the team. That's a fine compliment."

"It's good to be needed, but I had hoped someone would miss more than my athleticism."

She grinned. "Very well. If it makes you feel better, I'll tell you the truth. I missed you, and I don't care one hoot about baseball."

He put a hand to his heart. "And I missed you terribly. I had no one around to keep me out of trouble."

"Oh dear, did you break your promise to yourself?"

"My promise?"

"To be an upstanding, honest citizen." She clucked her tongue good-naturedly. "Tell me, did you find the woman?"

In an effort to deflect, he said, "I do believe I've reformed. I used my fist only when necessary."

"You laugh, but I can tell it didn't go like you wanted it

to. What happened?" Her hand went to his arm. "You know you're going to end up telling me. No stalling, out with it."

He looked back toward Norah's door. "I ruined her life."

"It was only money, and you said she married into plenty. I can't imagine she'd hate you for it."

"It's so much more than money." A guest walked past them, unlocked room six, and stepped inside. He waited until they were out of sight to say more. "I own this grand hotel. I own a store and a café." He choked on his words. "I have clothes made to fit me and food to eat whenever I want it—"

"Stop rambling," she said with force. "I know all this. Tell me how it's ruined her life and what has you so distraught."

"She never married." He leaned heavily against the wall, suddenly aware of how truly tired he was. "I always believed she had. But her betrothed called off the wedding days after I walked out of her life. If she'd had the money, she may have been able to save the farm and herself from so much harm and heartache. My very presence tarnished her name. She even ended up at the Whetted Whistle."

Mrs. Dover gasped and said under her breath, "One of Percy's girls?"

"It's a wretched place." With the gates of remorse open, he poured the whole story out to his dear, motherly house-keeper. "I'm going to make it right."

"You've brought her back," she said at last when his words ran dry. "She's here."

"Yes. She's resting in room eight now. I expect she'll keep to her room for a few days, but what then? She claims to want an independent life, and I'll do what I can to give it to her, but the scars and the hurts are so deep. No one saw us arrive, so for now she can recover in peace, and we can decide how to introduce her later. I don't know how to fix it all, and I don't know enough about Percy. What if he's the type to come after her?"

She pursed her lips. "Quincy, slow down. You hear me? Slow down and take care of her. Help her get to feeling better. That's all you can do. You did the right thing, bringing her here."

"I told her about you and that you'd be looking in on her. And you should know, I . . . I haven't told her my secret." His fancy hotel with its shiny new doorknobs jeered at him. None of this should be his. "She doesn't know about the money or why I really went to see her."

"Ah." Mrs. Dover furrowed her brows. "You're afraid."

"Yes," he said, knowing if he were talking to anyone else, he'd have trouble confessing the truth. "I don't want to distress her, that's true—"

"But it's more than that. You care about this girl. Best remember, you can't build a life on lies. You will have to tell her—and the sooner, the better."

"I'll tell her when the time is right, and it's not right yet." He started down the hall. "I'm going to send for the doctor. Will you show him to Norah's room when he comes? Ask him to be discreet." He stopped walking and turned back. "Has a young boy come here?"

"A boy? I haven't seen a boy around here."

Another disappointment. He'd hoped that young Nels had used the train ticket he'd bought. "I met a boy in Warner Crossing, and I told him to come here. I thought I could help, but he must not have trusted me."

"You can't take everyone in."

"No, I suppose not."

"If he ends up here, I'll give him a plateful of cookies and convince him to stay." She waved him off. "See to your other businesses so you can come back and catch up on sleep. You look more than a little tired."

"I haven't slept much."

"Don't worry about Norah. I'll make sure she's settled and the doctor gives her a thorough exam. And I'll tell her all about you."

"Ah, only the good things though."

Mrs. Dover shuffled down the hall. "I'll tell her the good things and maybe a few things to make her laugh."

———————

Norah stroked the soft fabric of the thick drapes that hung near the window while she peered at the city below. There were more brick buildings here than in Warner Crossing, and the streets were wider. She leaned closer to the window and looked to her right and then to her left. Her eyes stopped on the saloon. She took a quick step back from the window and yanked the drapes closed.

Percy's not here, she reminded herself, hating the fear that gripped her so tightly. She forced herself away from the window and busied herself by exploring the room. If she'd not been so travel weary, she'd have asked Quincy more about his hotel and how he'd come to own it. When she met him two years ago, they shared an openness unlike any she'd known before, but now with time between them and a switch of life stations, she wasn't sure what to say or how to say it.

The room was furnished with well-crafted wooden furniture. She pulled open a dresser drawer despite having nothing to put in it, then closed it again. It slid in easily, so she pulled out another one and let herself imagine for one brief moment that she was an important person with fine clothes and a box of jewels to put away. Such a ridiculous fancy, but pleasant nonetheless. A knock forced it to end.

"Yes?" she said before opening the door.

"It's Mrs. Dover," a woman with a commanding but sympathetic voice said. "Quincy asked me to check in on you."

"Come in."

A plump woman with a face full of creases stepped inside, holding a stack of books. She walked past Norah and put them on the stand beside the bed, then turned and appraised Norah. Her scrutinizing eyes, though unnerving, were caring. "You and I are going to be good friends."

"We are?"

"Yes, of course." She walked to the desk, pulled out the chair, and sat on it. "Go ahead, sit on the bed and rest while we talk."

Norah did as she was asked and sat on the edge of the large bed. The mattress was soft, reminding her once again that she was not in Warner Crossing but set free.

"That's better. You look pale."

Norah reached a hand to her face. "I, well . . . I—"

"No need to explain. Quincy already told me about you."

"He did? I thought . . . well, he told me he wasn't sure what he'd tell people."

"He'll be careful about your past, but I'm not just anybody. Quincy doesn't have family, so I suppose you could say I've adopted the man. He's a big fellow, but he still needs people looking out for him, and I've never been shy about offering my motherly guidance. It's worked out well for both of us.

He's a son worth being proud of." She beamed like a mother ought to when talking about her child. "Had I raised him, I would have ironed out some of the wrinkles in his manners, but I suppose we can forgive him for his rough ways."

"He can be a bit coarse."

"That's what I'm talking about. He speaks rather bluntly. Once he told a man to leave with no words at all. He simply picked him up and threw him out. Don't tell him, but sometimes his ways have me laughing for days. Now"—she clasped her hands together—"he says you've been through an ordeal, and I'm to see to your needs."

"I don't—"

"No need to object. I'm going to take your measurements so we can have dresses made for you. The doctor is going to make sure you're healing up well, and then I was told to bring you as many books as you like. That pile there will be a start, but don't be shy about asking for more. It's about time those books Quincy keeps buying are put to use." She motioned for Norah to stand. "Up with you. Let's get these measurements fast so you can get to sleep. Both you and Quincy look weary as can be."

While writing down Norah's size, Mrs. Dover spoke pleasantly about the hotel and all its recent improvements. "Quincy's been working nonstop since he bought the place."

"When did he buy it?" she asked, amazed that he'd been able to do so much in so short a time. Surely it'd taken him time to save up the money.

Mrs. Dover's eyes found hers, and she paused before saying, "It's been about two years."

Norah reached for the corner of the four-poster bed, steadying herself. "How?"

"Don't you worry about any of that. Not now. Quincy is a good man. He'll answer all your questions when you're feeling better. It's quite the tale."

Once her measurements were taken, Norah sat again on the edge of the bed and tried to piece together the little she knew of Quincy's path to Longfield. Perhaps he'd been awarded a loan with ease because he was a man. How unfair the world could be. She did not begrudge him his success, even if she wished she'd experienced some of it herself.

Mrs. Dover sat beside her and took her hand. "Quincy says you lost your family."

And everything else, she nearly said but instead simply nodded.

"My husband died, and my children are grown and settled. They went West, claiming the land was better, and left me here. Quincy's my boy now and"—she squeezed Norah's hand—"and if you're looking for family, you can be my girl."

"It's been so long . . ." Norah couldn't fight the tears any longer. They came in full force, running down her cheeks until Mrs. Dover put her arm around her and let her find comfort in her embrace.

"Go on and cry," Mrs. Dover consoled her. "You've much to grieve. When you're ready, in your own time, we're going to give you plenty to smile about."

11

Quincy had found the store well stocked and busier than ever, which was a relief since his store manager, George, was relatively new and hadn't handled inventory on his own before. Thankfully, the man had been competent and eager to learn. The café had suffered more in his absence than his other businesses, with one waitress marrying and another leaving the area with no explanation. Poor Alice had been left to not only cook but also serve as best she could with only the help of one other woman. He had reassured Alice that he'd find her more help, but he could tell from the tired look on her face that she was doubtful.

After stopping by the store and café, Quincy met up with Sam to chat.

"I'm about ready to start on the café repairs," Sam said as he walked beside Quincy on the streets of Longfield.

"Did you finish Alice's cart?" Quincy slowed his pace. He'd only run into Sam by chance, but now, being back with his friend, he was in no rush to be on with his day.

Sam nodded. "I did. I think it's what she was after."

Quincy raised a brow and studied his friend. "She said she was eager to have you work on the café."

"She did?"

"I think she might have even blushed when she said it." Quincy laughed, and it felt like they were boys, not men. "I think she's sweet on you."

"Nah."

"Is she easy to talk to when you stop in?"

Sam ran a hand through his hair. "Sometimes I trip over my words when she's around. I keep thinking about all the failed attempts at courtship I've had, and then I blabber even more. I doubt she thinks I'm very smart. And . . . I asked her about her family, and she didn't seem to want to tell me. She started talking about other things."

"Give it time," he said. "If she isn't proud of her past, she might not want to talk about it until she trusts you. You can't blame her for that."

"I suppose you're right. The whole time we were talking, I kept hoping she wouldn't ask me about the girls I've courted." He pulled his hand from his pocket and rubbed his scruffy jaw. "I wouldn't mind telling her once I know she won't laugh at my misfortune."

"She doesn't seem like the sort of woman who would laugh, but I think it's alright to start with easy conversations and work toward the more difficult topics." How strange to hear himself giving someone advice about women when he understood so little of the opposite sex. "You ought to ask the preacher or Mrs. Dover for advice. She was married a good long time, and she's always telling me what I should do. I'm sure she'd be happy to give you advice, and you'd probably listen. She'd love that."

"For now, I'm merely friends with Alice, and I expect it'll stay that way." Sam stopped talking and waved at one of his married sisters as she rode into town with her husband beside her. "Will you excuse me? I haven't seen Rhoda in weeks."

"Of course. Go see your sister. Perhaps she'll have advice for you."

Sam's eyes grew wide. "Don't tell my sisters or my mother about Alice. They'll scare her off for sure. They're always badgering me to settle down. It's taken me years to convince them I'm content as I am."

Quincy held his hands up in innocence. "I wouldn't dare tell them that you still think of giving up your bachelor ways."

"I never said that." Sam laughed as he crossed the street and helped his sister out of the wagon. Quincy had heard him complain from time to time about his large family of sisters, but seeing him now with one of them reaffirmed his long-held belief that Sam adored his family.

Quincy headed back to the hotel, nervous and eager to see Norah.

He leaned against the side of the building before entering. When he'd met Norah two years before, they'd been at ease in each other's presence. Could they have that again? There were secrets between them now. The blatant honesty of the past was now buried beneath a thin layer of deceit. Since walking away from her, he'd prided himself on his integrity. He wasn't perfect. He lost his patience and even cursed from time to time, a habit he found difficult to break, but he tried his best to be honest. And now she was back in his life, but he hadn't told her why. He looked up at the fine brick walls of his hotel, knowing she was there, in his building. Once she was recovered, he would have no choice but to confess the words that suffocated him. The doctor said it would take four weeks, perhaps longer, for her arm to heal. He'd wait until then to tell her. For her sake.

A boy running across the street drew his attention. Nels? Quincy took off after him. He turned the corner, only to see the boy disappear behind the bank. Quincy increased his speed, overtaking the youngster. Recognition dawned on him. "Nels!"

The boy slowed to a stop. He scowled when Quincy's hand went to his shoulder. "Get away from me," he shouted. "I didn't take it."

"Didn't take what?"

Nels wiped the back of a dirty hand across his forehead. The new clothes Quincy had given him were now torn and covered in filth. "Sit down." He kept a firm hand on the boy as they slid down the back wall of the bank and sat side by side. "I won't hurt you. Just tell me what you're about."

"I was just walking on the street, that's all. That ain't no crime."

"And . . ."

Nels crossed his arms and looked away, his thin body full of defiant tension. "I was hungry."

Quincy leaned his head back against the wall. "So you took something."

"I don't see what all the fuss is about. It was just a bit of bread." He looked up then with dark eyes full of pleading, begging him to have mercy. "I asked for work. Honest, I did, but I ain't been able to find none. No one wants to hire a rat, that's what they say."

"I told you to go to the Mission Hotel."

Nels shrugged. "I couldn't 'member where you told me to go. I used your ticket. I came, but then I had no luck. And now that big man says he'll catch me and throw me to his dogs."

Quincy chuckled. "No one's throwing you to the dogs. Big men talk and act fiercer than they are."

"I know all about what they do," Nels said. "I'm getting out of here. I'm going somewhere better."

"Stay here in Longfield."

"No." Nels scuffed his shoes back and forth in the dry dirt. "I ain't gonna live here where they already hate me."

"Where to next, then? Azure Springs isn't too far, but you don't have a horse. I guess you could sneak on the train and hope you don't get caught." Quincy tapped his jaw. "If you got on at night, that might work. But what then? You'd be begging for work again, and then you'd get hungry, and soon you'd have a big man chasing you down again."

A groan from Nels was enough for Quincy to know he'd gotten to the boy. "I'll give you a job, and if it goes well and you prove trustworthy, I'll see about sending you to school so you can learn. I'll give you a chance to make something of yourself."

Nels's head twisted around quick as a boxer's in the ring. "What kinda job?"

Thinking fast, Quincy said, "I have a friend who is sick. She's hurt and needs someone to sit by her. And when she's feeling better, she'll need someone to walk with her so she can get outside and breathe the fresh air. I think she'd rather walk with a friend than by herself. I intend to sit by her whenever I can, but I have business that will require my attention much of the day."

"I just got to sit by her?"

"Not all the time, as I'm sure she'd like some time to herself. I might have you help Mrs. Dover too. She's the housekeeper for my hotel. You could carry the guests' luggage to their rooms. And my café is shorthanded. You learn a few manners, and I'll have you serve food there. I'll keep you busy, and I'll pay you fair wages and feed you." Quincy held out his hand. "I expect you to work hard and represent my establishment. Do we have a deal?"

Nels threw his hand into Quincy's. "I'll work for you. But you gotta promise you won't let that big man catch me."

"I think I know who you're talking about." Quincy rose, brushed the dust off his pants, and motioned for Nels to follow him. "Come along. Let's go settle it now so it's not looming over you." Nels pivoted, about to flee, but he wasn't quick enough. Quincy grabbed the top of the boy's shirt, stopping him. "I'll go with you. He won't hurt you. You have my word."

"Aw, fine." Nels trudged after him toward the bakery. Warm, fragrant air met them at the threshold, making Quincy's stomach rumble and the boy's shoulders stiffen.

"Willard."

"Quincy." A large man with a white apron stepped toward them. He stopped short when he saw Nels. "You know this boy?"

"We're recently acquainted. He's a thief and a runner." Nels squirmed beneath Quincy's hand. "But he's promised to change, and he's starting with you. What does he owe you?"

"Two cents, and we'll be settled." Willard scowled down at Nels, sending a warning with his look. "What do you want with this little street urchin?"

Quincy cleared his throat. "I think I'll start by putting food in his stomach and cleaning him up. I'll make him useful." He squeezed Nels's shoulder. "I could use a hand around the hotel. You never know, he might turn out alright."

"Seems to me there are more able-bodied men around, but suit yourself." Willard took the two pennies Quincy offered, smiled at him, and then grunted at Nels as they left the shop.

Nels pried himself free. "You don't want to help me. You just want to make me work."

"Work for pay, boy. That's an honorable way to get by in this world. And trust me when I tell you I know about the less honorable ways. Take what I'm offering." He let Nels move away from him, showing him they could trust each other. "I helped you once before. I plan to do it again if you'll let me. Besides, you owe me two cents' worth of labor. Then you can go free if you want, but then you'll be running from one set of troubles to the next. A lot of running wears a fella out. Here's your chance to face your troubles and be done with them" He softened his expression. "Come on, let's get you something to eat."

Nels looked over his shoulder a couple more times before following Quincy back to the hotel. The boy's eyes shifted to the ceiling with its gold-painted trim. They grew wider when he looked to his left and saw the small restaurant that served breakfast to the hotel guests.

"Think you could wait to eat until you've been cleaned up?" Quincy asked. "I could have a whole meal from the café waiting for you when you're done."

Nels nodded. "I been needing a scrub. I always know it's time when I can't see me own freckles."

Quincy tousled the boy's hair. "I've been in your spot

before. That grime will wash off, and then we'll get a good look at you."

Mrs. Dover arrived then and immediately gushed over the lad. She shooed Quincy away, telling him to check on Norah and leave her to tend to Nels. As he walked away, he heard her laughing. "We do run the strangest hotel, don't we?"

He turned back and, with a grin on his face, said, "Yes, Mrs. Dover, we do."

Mrs. Dover had been correct. Rest had been exactly what Norah needed. She smiled, picturing the kind, matronly woman who'd received her tears with such compassion. Liberating those captive tears had left Norah exhausted but also more composed than she had been when they were trapped inside.

With her good hand, she pushed herself to sitting, cradled her injured arm in her lap, and yawned. If she were well, she would have to question her quick acceptance of Quincy's charity—but with her wounds fresh, she'd been at his mercy. She couldn't help but feel an odd gratitude for the pain and the way it had led her here. What luxury to live in this room while she recovered. Since leaving her childhood home, she'd not had such fine accommodations. She swung her legs off the side of the bed so she could sit and look at the stack of books.

She picked up the book on the top and admired its gold lettering. *Persuasion* by Jane Austen. She pulled the book to her face and breathed in the scent of it—heavenly. She'd owned this heart-wrenching but ultimately satisfying tale of love when she was still a girl, free of worries. She'd left her copy, inscribed by her mother, with all her other belongings when her property was seized. She hadn't held a book since.

"Norah." Quincy's voice from behind the closed door interrupted her thoughts of home.

She put down the book and wiped her eyes. "Yes?"

"It's Quincy. Do you mind if I step inside?"

Norah nearly laughed. It'd been so long since she'd spent time with anyone who worried about who went in whose room. "Come in."

He opened the door and stepped just over the threshold. "If you were fully recovered, I'd suggest we talk in the lobby. As it is, do you mind . . ."

"There's a chair by the desk. Come in and sit. We've never been formal with one another, so why start now? I believe our entire history is rather unconventional." She picked up the book again. "Thank you."

"Mrs. Dover picked that one out. She told me if I was building my library, I ought to have a few romantic reads."

"Have you read it?"

He shook his head. "No. I can read, thanks to a few years of schooling, but I didn't ever do it for pleasure."

"Then why do you have so many books?"

"I plan to read more. I just haven't yet." He shifted on the small wooden chair. "I did something . . ."

"What do you mean?"

"I . . . uh, well." He tugged at his sleeve before saying, "It's hot in here. Are you too warm?"

"No, I'm comfortable. More so than I've been in a long time." He sat awkwardly beside her, wiggling like a child in church. She waited, eager to know if her mind had played tricks on her these last two years or if they truly had shared a singular closeness. On particularly lonely nights, Norah had often let her mind wander to Quincy, imagining him as the one her heart could have loved had circumstances been different. Logic told her such fancies were foolish, but even so, they'd been a comfort. "You can tell me whatever it is. I assure you I can handle it, no matter what the doctor advised. I have been distressed many times since we first met, and I have persevered."

"I have no wish to be the cause of your distress," he mumbled. His expression changed, and he seemed to relax a bit. "I only . . . I only wanted to tell you that I took in a stray boy."

"A boy?"

He recounted meeting Nels on the streets and telling him to come to the Mission Hotel. "It was a rash invitation. He was dirty and desperate to be away from the boxing. I saw so much in his face . . ."

"You saw yourself," she whispered, reassured that she, at least to some degree, did know this man. "You told me you lived on the streets. And I know about your boxing history."

"Yes, I saw myself," he whispered back. "And I wanted to help him, to show him there was another way. I told him I'd give him work and maybe schooling."

"I was thinking only moments ago that I'd like a way to be useful." She smiled then, truly eager to help. "I could teach him, even with my arm healing and my ribs so sore. It would be no strain at all to teach him the basics."

He slapped his leg and grinned. "I was worried I'd be asking too much. He wouldn't have to be in here with you all the time, but maybe an hour or two a day. I could get you whatever you needed. Anything at all you might want for schooling him." He grew more serious and somber. "You will tell me if it's too much?"

"It won't be too much. It will be my pleasure. All boys, all children, they deserve care and proper teaching."

"I'm afraid his language is rather coarse." He winced. "Guess that's like me too. Though I try awful hard to control it now."

"Very admirable." Excitement grew inside her at the thought of helping Nels. "I can hardly wait. If it is helping you, then I will feel like less of a burden myself."

He rose, walked quickly to the door, then softly said, "You could never be a burden."

A simple proclamation said so quietly she could almost believe it was not meant for her, but she had heard it and it proved powerful. She stared at the doorway where he had stood, hand pressed against her wildly beating heart, amazed at how it soared. Percy had not turned it to stone like she had once believed. No, she was not dead. Injured, yes, but she was alive and ready to see what tomorrow held.

12

Five days of teaching Nels had flown by, and already Norah adored the little rascal. He had absolutely no reservations about bodily noises or wiping at his nose with his hand. He laughed far too loudly, and when he grew frustrated, he used foul language. His ways should have appalled her, but instead she found herself drawn to the boy, eager to show him the gentleness he'd never known. She found his determination admirable, his resilience inspiring, and his tender heart endearing. After a little guidance, this boy, with all his spunk and zest for life, would surely grow to be a man who led others and made a difference in the world. Not so unlike his benefactor, Quincy Barnes, who each day proved himself a truly good man.

Quincy had moved a second desk to her room, bought her every schoolbook the store carried, and promised to get her anything else she wanted. Having never taught before, she wasn't certain what she would need but was grateful for the offer. For her first lesson with Nels, she'd begun with letters and numbers. He'd proved clever and a generally willing pupil.

"I wish my pa could see me now," Nels said after tracing his name on the small slate in his hands. "He never thought I'd amount to nothin'. I ain't even ten yet, and I'm writin' my own name and doin' proper work."

Nels pulled his mouth to one side as he traced the letters again. Norah smiled as she observed. Had Quincy been like this boy? Belittled by the very people who should have adored him? Had his grit and tenacity been stifled when it should have been channeled and nurtured? "Nels."

"Yes?"

"Did your mother believe you could learn?"

His small shoulders sagged. "She left. I don't 'member her. I don't know where she went, but my pa always said 'good riddance.'" He kept his focus on the slate, pressing the chalk hard against it. "I don't know if she were as bad as pa said, but she ain't never come back."

"And so, you left too?" Norah kept her voice calm despite the queasy feeling growing within her. "Did you run away?"

He held up his slate for her to see. "I did it. There's my name."

"It's very nice." She grinned. "You learned quickly. At this rate you'll be a regular scholar soon."

"That'd sure be something." He wiped his slate clean. Norah wanted to know more about his past, but she didn't press further. If he wanted to speak about it, he would. If the memories were too painful or laced with regret, then he was free to keep them to himself.

To her surprise, he spoke up on his own. "My pa left me at home. He said he was going to work, but he didn't come back. I waited a long time, but then I took off. My pa didn't want me anyway. He told me most every day." He spoke in an unaffected voice, but she saw the hint of loss in his posture and unsteady breathing. "I been doin' alright, and Quincy says he'll pay me wages."

"Wages?"

"For looking after you and helping 'round the hotel. Said if I can find my manners, he'll let me work at the café and maybe someday go to school." He leaned in closer and flashed her an adorable smile. "Mrs. Dover makes me wash behind my ears and even checks my fingernails. I ain't never had nobody care 'bout that before."

Norah laughed. "My mother always checked to see if I was good and clean too."

"Do ya think Mrs. Dover likes me? 'Cause when she tugged at my ear and told me to wash again, I wasn't sure." He folded his arms then and scowled, a veil of forced indignation hiding the smile of moments before. "But I don't care none if she likes me."

"She likes you." A lump grew in her throat. She hadn't trusted anyone herself for such a long time, yet she wanted to believe, for this boy's sake, that the world was still full of good-hearted souls. "I think Mrs. Dover is a good woman. She just likes clean ears."

"She said she likes you." Nels scratched his head, making his long hair fall from side to side. "She said I had to be nice to you 'cause you been through a hard time. She said I couldn't use curse words, and I been trying not to but—"

"I don't fault you. With time you'll find better alternatives."

"I suppose, but sometimes I think a curse works best."

She laughed at how much he sounded like Quincy—blunt and brash, a little world-weary. "I will have to disagree with you on that. And if I have my way, one day you'll change your mind."

"I suppose." He scratched his nose. "What happened to ya anyway?"

Norah scooted closer to him and held out her arm for him to see. He'd seen it before, of course he had, but she'd never spoken of her injuries. "I hurt my arm and my side, and it felt like every part of me was bruised, but I'm healing up. I suppose you could say I was trapped with a bad man, but I'm free of him now. Inside, I still hurt, but it's getting better every day."

Nels put his small hand on her hurt arm. "No one shoulda hurt you. I'm never gonna be like that."

"I believe you," she whispered. "I felt very alone before, but now I believe things will get better. I have you for a friend and Mrs. Dover to watch over me—"

"And Quincy."

"Yes, Quincy has been good to me. He brought me here to be safe and to get better."

"Then you gonna go away?" He tilted his head to one side and looked up at her. "I plan on moving on when I got money in my pockets. Don't seem right stayin' here living off charity, 'course Quincy says this is honest work and better'n thieving."

"I believe he's right. And now that we're all friends, you'd be missed if you were gone."

"How long will you stay?"

"I don't know. I used to have a place that felt like home. The farmland went on forever, and it smelled like happiness. I'd like to have that again, but I'm not sure how. So for now, I plan to enjoy my time at this hotel."

"The eatin' is good." Nels rubbed his thin belly and grunted. "I might stay for that."

Norah glanced at the clock. They'd spent much longer gabbing than she had intended. She took his slate and stacked it by the books Quincy had brought. "Mrs. Dover asked you to help her with the bedding. I didn't mean to keep you so long."

He held up his hands and looked at his nails, then turned them toward Norah. "Think I better scrub up again before I see her?"

"It wouldn't hurt." Norah stood on stiff legs and walked with him to the door. "Tomorrow we'll work harder on your letters."

He groaned, but she saw the gleam in his eyes as he left. His step was already lighter and more carefree than it'd been when she first met him. Norah eased herself onto the bed and laid on her side. Life had left her weary. The soft heaviness of sleep was descending on her when she heard a knock at her door.

She wiped the tiredness from her eyes the best she could before opening it.

"I woke you," Quincy said upon seeing her.

"I wasn't sleeping." She motioned for him to come in. "I was merely thinking of sleeping."

"I can come back." He shifted uneasily. "I don't even have an important reason for coming. I only wanted to see how your lesson went with Nels."

"Oh, Quincy! I adore him. He's clever and funny and sometimes bad-mannered just like you, but his little heart is so good. I can feel it."

"Are you saying I'm clever or bad-mannered? Or are you making an observation about my heart?"

"I would not be so bold as to make comments about your heart." Norah studied the man in front of her. Large and powerful yet gentle—a strange combination of traits. "As for your manners, they are much improved. Mrs. Dover has done well with you. I do think you're clever, and so is Nels. Your business is proof of that." She inched closer, drawn to this man who'd rescued her in her moment of greatest need. She longed to know all there was to know about Quincy Barnes.

Her large friend squirmed under her scrutinizing eye. "Is Nels learning quickly?"

"Very. He's so proud of his learning, and you're the one who made it happen. You gave him that." Aware that she'd crept too close to him, she took a step back and sat on the edge of the bed. "I think our Nels will grow up just fine, if he follows your lead."

Quincy rubbed the back of his neck. "You flatter me. Now, tell me what I can do to make your stay here more pleasant. Do you need anything? More books?"

"I have read three already. You really ought to read them all."

"Which was your favorite?"

"*Persuasion*." She picked up the book and handed it to him. "It's so hopeful."

"How so?"

"Read it and you'll see."

He bounced the novel between his hands several times before nodding and putting it on the bedside table next to the pile of other books. "For you, I'll read it. You say you like the books and the room, but is there something more you want?"

"Nels has come five times now, and we sit and talk while

I teach him. Then I feel a little sad when he goes." She smoothed the lap of her skirt. It was the first of the new dresses to arrive off the measurements Mrs. Dover had taken, and it fit her perfectly, unlike the one from Susannah. With her new clothes that made her feel almost pretty and this safe town to live in, she *ought* to be content. "I don't think I need anything else."

"But you'd like something. What is it?"

"I thought I wanted solitude, but I find I enjoy company."

He pulled the chair from the desk to the side of the bed and sat by her. "You're lonely. I've neglected you."

"You've been nothing but good to me. But I think I might like going out and seeing the town. Here under this fine roof, I feel more like my old self than I ever thought possible." She looked toward her window and at the town beyond. "I can almost believe that in Longfield I can lead a full life. Perhaps I could even find friends." Heat raced to her cheeks. She was embarrassed that at her age she still had to solicit friends. What was it about Quincy that loosened her tongue? "I seem to always throw my dreams at you. Pay them no mind."

"It used to be all that was thrown at me was punches." He raised his hands up as though he were blocking a blow and jerked left, then right. "I know what to do with those, but I'll try my best to handle whatever dreams you throw my way."

She fisted her hand and swung it playfully. "I'll have to work on my punches. They'd be easier to take than a list of silly ambitions."

"You're small, but if your aim was good, you could defend yourself. Not that you'll need to around here."

"When I'm feeling up to it, I would like to learn. Add that to my list—learn to throw a punch but never have reason to."

Quincy's laugh came deep and rich, and she grinned back at him. Soon their laughter mixed, and for a moment she could not remember what it was they were laughing about, only that it felt good. Just like the tears she'd shed with Mrs. Dover had washed away a great many of her fears, this laughter took away some of her tension and made it easier to smile.

"How do you feel about baseball?" Quincy asked when they'd settled down.

"I don't think I feel any particular way about baseball. I know of it, but I've never watched. I suppose it could be entertaining."

"I think seeing a baseball game should be one of your dreams."

"You do?"

"Yes. You should desperately want to see a game." His features took on the mischievous quality she'd been so intrigued by when she first met him. "It should be a goal you want to see come to fruition very badly. You should beg me to take you to a game."

"Very well. I find that I do have a keen interest in seeing a game of baseball. In fact, I don't know how I'll even think of other things until I witness for myself a man running from base to base."

"Done." He stood and reached for her good hand and pulled her from the bed. She winced slightly. "I'm sorry."

"Don't be. It's nothing. The pain is better every day."

He looked her over, gauging her condition for himself. "A month or so ago, the town divided into two teams, the North and the South. We've been practicing once or twice a week since, and today is the big game. You say you want to meet

149

the town, come to the game. Let me make that dream come true. Come and watch and cheer us on." He cocked a brow. "You will cheer for my team, won't you? I'd hate to take you and have you cheer traitorously for the South."

"I don't know," she said with mock innocence. "I do know that I owe you a great deal, but what if the other side has a dashing man on it and I'm so smitten that I simply must cheer for him?"

"There it is." He practically shouted.

"There is what?" She looked behind her.

"Your wit! You're as clever as I remember."

She fought a giggle and forced a straight face. "What makes you think I'm jesting?"

He stepped closer and tapped the side of her cheek. "Right there is your tell. The corners of your mouth can't stay down."

His finger barely touched her, but heat raced through her from the corners of her lips clear to the tips of her toes. It was an innocent, insignificant gesture, and yet her cheeks burned. Thrown off guard, she simply smiled back at him and said, "Very well, I'll cheer for you."

"Good. Now, there are a lot of people who will want to meet you."

I want this to feel like home, she reminded herself when a wave of nerves washed over her. "I'm ready to meet them. I know I look somewhat frail, but the bruising on my face is nearly gone and no one will know about the ribs." She tucked her hand against herself. "My arm is not such an easy hide, but—"

"No need to worry. I'll tell them you were injured elsewhere and came here to recover and would prefer to not talk about it. You will walk in on my arm and tell the town that we are old friends. They'll have questions, no doubt, but we'll get through it. We've nothing to hide. Let them gossip and their tongues wag, and we'll smile through it all." He pulled his pocket watch from his vest. "Let me change, and I'll come back for you in a few minutes."

"Don't forget your book."

"*Persuasion*," he said, picking it up and pressing it to his heart. "I nearly forgot."

When he left, she hurried to the mirror and stared at her reflection. The blush he'd brought about gave her sallow cheeks a fresh glow. Her hair was pinned nicely, thanks to Mrs. Dover, who had insisted she help Norah with it. And her new clothes, though far from fancy, fit her well. She looked more closely and smiled. Before her in the glass was a woman about to start over. *Be brave*, she instructed herself, *be brave*.

13

Quincy had a bounce in his step as he walked from Norah's room to his own with the novel in his hand. How was it she had such sway over his very reasoning? A novel, a romance novel, and he'd said yes. He laughed, drawing curious looks from an elderly couple who were leaving their room.

He waved a hand in their direction, then ducked into his room, where he changed into his uniform. A white jersey with green lettering made by one of his teammates' wives so they would easily be distinguished from the South, who would wear brown and red. To his great relief, his broad shoulders fit inside the uniform top with room to spare.

Boxing had kept him fed, his blood had thumped rapidly through him when he entered the ring, but it'd been an off-colored excitement motivated by survival and rage. What he felt now, heading out to play baseball for fun, was wholesome and good. Knowing Norah would be watching only added to that pleasure.

He grabbed his ball and bat and headed down the hall to her room, whistling like a champ as he went. When he knocked, she joined him in the hallway, taking his offered arm as they began to walk.

"I hardly recognized you in your jersey," she said, looking him over. "I didn't realize you loved baseball so much. You're grinning from ear to ear."

"Maybe I'm smiling because there's a beautiful woman on my arm."

She blushed. "You shouldn't say such things."

He stopped walking and looked at her, taking in the curve of her cheek, the color of her hair, every detail. "I told you when I left your farm that I'd be an honest man. Having you here, it makes me smile. That's the truth."

She said nothing at first, making his palms sweat. But then she tilted her head in his direction and smiled. "Thank you."

"You're welcome."

They resumed their slow pace, only now his heart felt two sizes bigger. Something about stepping out with Norah so close made the world feel brighter. The grass greener and the sky bluer. "I do like baseball, but it's more than that. It's slowing down, spending time with my town and being a part of a team. I like all that comes with the baseball game. Plus, I think it's high time the people of Longfield meet you. You've been here for close to a week. It's time I showed my dear old acquaintance to the world. I'll make them all green with envy."

She rolled her eyes. "I don't imagine they'll be green."

"We'll have to watch and see. Green or not, we'll get the flap jaws going." His first days in Longfield had been nothing but meeting new people, dissolving rumors about where he'd come from, and assuring everyone he would do right by the town. They'd scrutinized him, but ultimately the money in his hands quieted their worries. With time, his hard work earned him their respect. Norah had no wealth to calm whatever rumors might spring up about her, but he'd lead the way, showing them she was someone they wanted in their midst. "I think the town will love you before long."

"I'd be content with them finding me tolerable." She looked over her shoulder toward the hotel. "Does Mrs. Dover care for baseball? I thought I might sit by her."

"I asked her if she was coming, but she said she planned to stay behind with Nels and wash windows. She's a strange woman."

"I think she's wonderful. A clean window has a way of making everything look better. But if you play again, we will have to convince her and Nels to come. I think he would like the game."

"A quiet afternoon with Mrs. Dover's full attention will do him well."

"Do you think I ought to stay back and help somehow?"

"I'd much rather have you at the game. I'm determined to hit a ball so far, you lose sight of it. I wouldn't want you missing that." Several women on the other side of the street waved in their direction. Quincy nodded in return. He was glad the citizens of Longfield had accepted him, but he could do without the constant attention from the women. When he turned back toward Norah, she was looking at him with a bit of skepticism. He cleared his throat before saying, "You won't be alone. I thought sitting by Alice might suit you. She's friendly and will help you get to know others."

"Alice . . . is she . . . your friend?"

"She cooks at the café and plans to sell cookies and such at the game. Before that she worked at the hotel under Mrs.

Dover." When she looked unsure, he added, "She's welcoming, so no need to worry. You'll be friends in no time."

"I do hope so," she said with a nervous but buoyant smile. "I haven't had many true friends. I'm afraid I won't know what to say to her."

"You've always had a loose enough tongue around me."

"You're different. I don't know why, but I've always been strangely at ease around you."

"Be at ease now. I think you'll be better received than you expect." He urged her to go a little faster, and soon they were on the field that only a month ago had been for cattle. When the town caught baseball fever, they converted it to a playing field and built seating for the onlookers. The once tall grass was now splotchy and worn from the many eager feet that had trampled through it. Quincy pointed when he saw Alice and her cart. "There's Alice. Let's go meet her."

She gripped his arm tighter but walked tall.

"Look at all this," he said to Alice as they approached. "You've brought a feast."

"I used the kitchen, but not during café hours," Alice said, pink with pride.

"It all looks delicious to me," he said before glancing over his shoulder and waving at Sam. "I see the boys from my club have arrived. I better go. First, though, this is Norah. She's a friend of mine and new to town. Do you think she could watch the game by you?"

"Of course."

"Thank you." He put a palm on the small of Norah's back and leaned in. "I'll walk you home. Wait for me after the game?"

"I will."

Then in a soft voice, he said, "Remember, you're worth befriending."

Quincy's hand left her back. Norah floundered only a moment before saying, "I can help you sell your goods if you like."

"I'd like that." Alice smiled as though they were already well acquainted. Could friendship begin so easily? "I'm glad you're here so I don't have to stand around looking sheepish all by myself."

"It all looks wonderful. I expect you'll be surrounded by customers before long." Norah's eyes roamed over the cookies, candies, and popped corn. "Quincy said this would be a good chance for me to get out and meet people, but meeting so many new people all at once . . . it's got me shaking in my skin."

"No need to worry. Let me tell you about everyone I know." Alice paused when a woman came over and inquired about her prices. She bought fifteen cents' worth of baked goods before walking away, leaving a grinning Alice. "Oh my, it's working." She put the coins in a small box, then turned back to Norah. "Do you see the woman with the oversized hat?"

Norah glanced toward the seats. "With the feathers?"

"Yes. That's the preacher's wife, Lea Townsend. She's sweet and calls everyone a 'dear child.' I once even heard her call a woman older than her that." She looked harder at the stands. "And beside her is Jessica Bosse. She's married to the head of the bank. He plays on the team from the south of town. She comes in the café with her friend May Simpson and talks forever. She's very loud, so I can hear everything she says."

Alice discretely pointed and whispered about nearly every spectator, sharing what details she could. Norah followed her finger and tried to memorize the faces and names of each person, hoping someday they'd be her friends as well.

"Who are the women in the front row? They look related."

"On the North team is a man named Sam Landon." Alice's voice grew hushed. "He has nine sisters. I haven't met them, but I know who they are. Everyone does."

"They're all so tall and lean."

"So is Sam. I don't know why he's not married. He's not a bad-looking man, and he works hard. Men are strange creatures though. You think you know them, but they all seem to have a secret," Alice said more to herself than to Norah. "Sam usually finds a reason to talk to me. Once you meet him, you can decide for yourself what sort of man he is."

Norah followed Alice's eyes to the field, where Quincy was throwing a ball back and forth with a tall stranger who had to be Sam. His features were more masculine than the women in the front row, but the resemblance was striking. "How curious that he finds reasons to come and talk to you. Perhaps his secret is that he's sweet on you."

"If he is, he's made no indication of his feelings. He usually just mumbles and gets red in the face."

"A red face and trouble speaking could mean he's nervous. It's kind of endearing, don't you think?"

"I haven't decided yet."

They watched the baseball players in comfortable silence. Norah's eyes continually went back to Quincy.

"It's fun, isn't it?" Alice asked. "Everyone together like this."

She kept her eyes on the men in matching uniforms. Quincy tossed the ball, then his gaze found hers and he threw her a roguish smile. "I can see the appeal."

"And the game hasn't even begun." Alice made another sale, then squealed. "It's working!"

Feeling unexpectedly giddy for her new friend's success, she asked, "Do you have plans for your money?"

"I do. I plan to buy a tiny house someday and plant lilac bushes on the sides of the door. Lilacs make me think of Mama."

"It sounds lovely." Norah knew about sights and smells trapping memories. The sloshing sounds of a creek or the smell of wheat being harvested were enough to send her heart racing back in time. "I think we ought to sell more of your cookies so you can have your lilacs. Maybe we should ask your Sam fellow how he feels about little houses with flowers by the door."

"We will not." She laughed loud enough that the men on the field nearest them looked their way. Alice waved and pretended nothing was amiss. "I think you and I will be good friends." She handed Norah a cream-colored cookie. "Tell me what you think."

Norah took a bite of the soft cookie and nodded her approval while wiping crumbs from the corner of her lips. "It's excellent and will no doubt be the means of earning you enough money to buy many lilac bushes. I didn't have time to ask Quincy, so if you're willing, I'd love to know how this game works."

Alice stepped closer. "The main thing to remember is to

cheer when the team you want to win makes it all the way around the field and goes back to that base." She pointed at a dusty spot in the ground. "I'm assuming since you walked in on Quincy's arm that you are cheering for the North too. That means you want to cheer for the men in green and white."

"I can do that."

Alice rearranged the food on her cart while talking. "Are you staying at the hotel?"

"I am." Movement caught Norah's eye. She elbowed Alice and whispered, "That Sam fellow is coming our way."

Alice straightened, brushed at her hair with her hands, and smiled. Norah took a step back and watched her new friend interact with the lanky man. "Can I get you something, Sam?"

He nodded, looked back over his shoulder at his eager team, and waved them off. "I got to hurry, but, well, I worried it'd all be gone if I didn't come soon."

"Tell me what you want and I'll hold it for you."

Sam reached into his pocket and pulled out a handful of coins. "Will this cover popped corn for my sisters? They're on the front row. They all came to watch the game. I thought . . . I thought they'd like it."

"It'll more than cover the cost." Alice started counting the coins, but he put his hand on hers. Alice's gaze darted from her hand to Sam. Their eyes met, and Alice eased her hand away from his.

"Keep the extra." Sam looked over his shoulder, then back at Alice. "Will you take it to my sisters? They're in the front row. I think the team needs me now."

"I will," Alice said. "And, Sam, the cart is very fine."

"It was nothing." He paused, staring at her until she patted his arm and told him to go play.

Norah waited, unsure if she should acknowledge the exchange. Alice watched Sam's departing back for a moment before smoothing her skirts.

"Will you help me carry popped corn to Sam's sisters?" she asked matter-of-factly. "I'm nervous to meet them. It'd be easier going over there with someone else."

"They look nice," Norah said, already grabbing one of the bags.

Alice turned away from the stands and pushed her loose hairs into place. Her chest rose and fell as she breathed deeply. "How do I look? My face gets red when I'm nervous. Do I look nervous?"

"It's not too red. More of a pink, and with the sun so bright, they'll think it's from the heat."

"Oh, good. Sam has been so kind to me, and I want his sisters to like me." Alice's cheeks went from pink to red. "I know it's silly to care when I have plans for a house all of my own. I'm not after a husband or any such nonsense." She shook her head, flustered. "Let's just take these bags over there and be done with it."

Together they approached the line of matching women, walking carefully so they didn't spill their goods. The sisters were sweet, complimenting their brother's kindness and thanking Norah and Alice for bringing the popcorn.

"I haven't met you yet," one of the women said to Norah.

"Didn't you walk in on Quincy's arm?" an older sister asked. "I was sure it was you I saw him with."

"We're old acquaintances. He's insisted I stay at his hotel while my arm heals." She exhaled deeply, then added, "I don't know how long I'll be here. I'm at a bit of a cross-roads."

Two of the sisters looked at each other, and she felt certain they were questioning her story. But when they returned their gazes to her, she saw no malice in their expressions. "We're glad to have you as long as you're here. Sam always speaks highly of Quincy." Her eyes went to Alice. "He also has lots to say about your cooking."

Alice stiffened beside Norah. "He does?"

"Yes. He's much quieter than the rest of us, but lately he's been rather talkative about the café, the cart he made and how it had to be perfect, and of course, about your pie." The sister leaned closer and said, "I've never seen him act so starry-eyed."

"He did a fine job on the cart." Alice tugged on Norah's sleeve. "We best get back in case anyone else wants vittles. Enjoy the game!"

"We will. And we will have to get together again soon."

Alice nodded and retreated like a racehorse who'd only just had the reins loosened. Norah thanked them and scurried after her friend, taking long strides to catch her. Once out of earshot, Norah whispered, "They seem very nice."

"But there are so many of them. I'm not normally a coward, but I felt like one with all their eyes on me."

"Sam having sisters may not be a bad thing. I would guess that he knows a great deal about women and is probably kinder than most men because of it."

Alice chewed on her bottom lip. "I suppose. I do think if I were to end up married, I would need a man who realized women were capable and strong. But this is all ridiculous.

Sam and I . . . it could never happen. I expect it will end before it has ever begun."

"I have little experience with romance. I wish I had wisdom to share." Norah looked toward the field. "Oh, look, the game has started."

———— | ————

Throughout the first half of the game, people bought Alice's treats. Several women walked by and bought nothing but inquired after Norah, wanting to know who she was and where she'd come from. Norah's heart raced every time, but to her great relief, everyone spoke kindly and seemed genuine in their interest. Every welcoming smile added to the happiness blooming inside her, and soon she was smiling even when no one was talking to her.

Once Alice's cart was emptied, they stood together on the edge of the field and watched the game. The score remained close, with the North trailing the South by one most of the game. Quincy often looked in her direction and smiled or even waved, sending an unfamiliar thrill racing through her.

"Do you find him a handsome man?" Alice asked when she caught Norah staring.

"He's not so bad."

"I don't know if I've ever seen a man so large and strong. He's like a giant ox with a crooked grin."

"I'm surprised that I do not find his size intimidating."

"I saw him angry once," Alice said. "Someone at the hotel was drunk. He was being unruly and"—she cleared her throat—"the man made untoward comments to me. The moment the man touched my arm, Quincy became a bear. He picked up the guest and threw him out."

"I've seen that side too. But still, he doesn't scare me." Norah pried her eyes away from Quincy, embarrassed she'd been caught ogling the man. Instead, she studied her cuff, a far less intriguing topic of study. "Do you know him well?"

"I worked at the hotel, but I spoke more to Mrs. Dover than to Quincy. I can't say I know much of his past, but I know he's liked here. The women in town would love to be on his arm, but he's shown little interest in any of them. He spends his time on his businesses. He's very savvy. I've no complaints about how he runs the café, though he does need to hire more help."

"If you are still in need when my arm is recovered, I would like to work at the café." Perhaps independence could be found in Longfield.

"Quincy does all the hiring, but I don't see why he'd turn you down. He might make you promise not to marry though."

"Not marry?" She looked up from the cuff she'd been so consumed with. "I don't understand."

"He keeps hiring servers and they stay a few weeks or a month, and then they run off and marry the farmers or the railroad men they meet in the café. Don't look so worried. I can't imagine he'd actually put it in a contract." Alice cocked her head. "You in a hurry to marry? Is that what worries you?"

"No, it's not that." It was the thought of contracts and consequences that had her squirming. Percy had demanded she sign her name. She'd been starving, and in an act of self-preservation, she'd succumbed. The act had haunted her ever since. But they were talking of marriage, not houses of ill repute. "I have moments when I want someone to be in my life, but those moments are brief and all hinge on the idea that there's a good man out there who would want me for a wife. I believe independence is a more realistic goal. Perhaps my house can be near yours, and we will start Spinster Row."

"Clever! It can be the lane that women move to when they've given up on men. We will run the café and drink tea and plant flowers when we're not working." Alice spoke with conviction, yet her eyes lingered on the men in uniform. "It's easier to only have oneself to care for."

"Do you believe that?"

"When you have a story like mine, you fight off all romantic notions the best you can. It's better to aim for a reasonable target."

Norah felt her jaw fall open. What did Alice mean?

"Watch Quincy. It's better than worrying over the past." Alice directed her attention back to the field, and Norah forced her eyes to follow despite the plethora of questions that filled her mind.

Quincy stood on a square in the center of the field. He threw the ball to a man at the front who swung and missed. Half the crowd cheered and the other half yelled at the man, telling him to watch the ball. Quincy threw again. This time the man hit the ball, but it didn't go far. Quincy raced forward, picked it up, and threw it to a man at the first plate. More cheering, more yelling.

Alice clapped with the rest of the crowd at the right moments. Her dancing eyes led Norah to believe that perhaps her secret was not as drastic as she feared. A broken heart could leave a woman wanting solitude. Had the man she loved jilted her? Or was it possible that Alice knew the pain of betrayal, rejection, and fear that she herself knew?

Consumed by her thoughts, Norah leaned back against the cart, only to topple to the ground, landing hard on her backside. The cart that had just been there had rolled a few feet away, leaving her with no support. She pushed herself to sitting with her good arm and fought the sting of tears that sprang to her eyes.

Alice jumped to her side and bent to help her up. Embarrassed by the spectacle she'd likely become, she hurried to her feet and turned away from the crowd.

"Are you hurt?"

It took Norah several seconds to catch her breath before she was able to fully straighten. When she did, she saw Quincy running across the field toward her. Afraid he'd make a scene, she waved him away and stepped farther from the field.

"Let me help you," Alice begged.

"I'm alright now." She worked a smile onto her lips and brushed the dirt from her backside. "I think I'll head back to the hotel. The game is enjoyable, but I . . . I've pushed myself hard enough for one day. Will you tell Quincy? Tell him not to worry."

Alice stayed by her side. "You're hurt. I could get Quincy or Sam to help you back. I know they wouldn't mind. Or we could find you a seat and you could rest."

"My pride is more hurt than my body." She put a hand on Alice's arm. "Go back and get your cart. I'll be better in no time. Let's visit again soon. I want to hear how you came to Longfield."

"And I confess I'm rather curious to know how you came here yourself." She looked back toward her cart and the field. "You promise you'll be safe going back?"

"I'll be fine. The hotel is not far."

Once out of sight of the field, Norah hurried down the street, wrestling with her embarrassment and gratitude. She cringed as she relived her fall over and over, but then she smiled at the memory of Alice offering help and Quincy being ready to leave the game to console her. In a soft voice, she whispered aloud the names of all the kind women she'd met, doing her best to remember them. Longfield was not her beloved family land, but perhaps this town could someday feel like home.

She stepped near the stores and allowed herself to pretend she was shopping in her hometown. In the mercantile, she admired the displays of books, bonnets, and baskets—all begging to be bought. Through the post office window, she saw the rows and rows of little boxes stacked on top of each other. Would her name be on one someday?

And then her feet froze. The wistfulness vanished. Ahead of her was a saloon, and she had to walk past it to get to the hotel. Ominous and threatening, it taunted her, bringing memories of darker days to the forefront of her mind. Her heart beat rapidly, and her neck grew warm. Quincy had been beside her when she went to the game. She wasn't afraid then, but now . . .

Percy is not here, she repeated in her mind, but her feet would not move. Like the stumps of the tall oaks she'd climbed as a child, her legs were rooted to the ground. Her breath came shallow and fast, her mind filled with fear and the memories of threats and the sting of Percy's hand on her cheek.

"*I'll break you*," he'd said before slapping her hard enough to knock her to the floor. She'd shielded her face with her hands as she lay curled on the floor. His booted foot connected with her side, not once but many times, before he left and locked the door behind him.

Norah pressed her back against the post office wall and tried to steady her breathing. Forging bravery when she had no real confidence was never easy, but she'd managed before. Gathering all her reserve, she stepped into the street. She was halfway past the saloon when a man staggered out and waved. "Ain't you a pretty thing."

No longer caring how she appeared, she grabbed her skirts and sprinted for the hotel. She ran into the lobby like a mouse scurrying from a cat. She didn't stop to talk but simply waved a hand at Mrs. Dover and went straight up the stairs, tripping once, but sprang back up and darted into the safety of her room.

14

The smooth wood of the bat in Quincy's hand and the cheering of the crowd should have been enough excitement to hold his attention, but it wasn't. *Where did she go?* Swinging the bat felt trivial in the very moment it should have felt important. The score was tied up for the first time in the game, and with the swing of his bat, he could bring his team into the lead.

"Bring 'em home!" Sam slapped him on the back. "Listen to them. Our half of the town is sure glad it's you up next."

Quincy nodded, tightened his grip on the bat, and stepped up to the dusty home plate. Again, his eyes swept across the many faces, wanting her to be there.

"Quin-cy! Quin-cy!" A chant rippled through the audience. He raised his bat, watched the ball, and then swung. The other half of the town cheered as he missed the ball. The next pitch was slow and low, and he missed again.

Out of the corner of his eye, he saw a man slap his leg and another mutter under his breath. He needed to focus, but where was she? He fixed his attention on the man pitching the ball and closed out the rest of the commotion from his mind. This time when the ball came toward him, his bat connected with it. The ball soared high and far, past the edge of the field. He took off running from one base to the next until he'd circled the diamond and returned home again.

The crowd exploded—some cheering, some groaning, but everyone reacting. The North had taken the lead, and with only one inning left, he'd likely won the game. Victory was close, almost within their reach, and everyone knew it. But why wasn't she here sharing the moment?

He smiled at the crowd and accepted their cheers. As quick as he could, he went to Alice while his teammates batted. "Where did Norah go?"

"She said she wanted to go back to rest, but I think she was embarrassed after her fall." Alice shook her head, clearly disturbed by her new friend's departure. "I'm so sorry. I should have gone with her."

"You're sure she was well enough to go by herself?"

"I think so. She seemed eager to go, but not because of pain." Alice looked back toward the field where the game was carrying on without Quincy. "Looks like they're switching who is up to bat now. Better go and be with your team."

Blast this baseball. He wanted to check on Norah and relieve his worries. "I hope it ends soon."

"It will." She startled him by putting her hand on his arm. "You don't have to fix everyone else's problems. She'll manage."

He shrugged her arm off and turned back toward the game. "This is different. It's not like when you or the others came. I want to help where I can, but this . . . this is . . . I don't know what this is, but it's different."

"Hmm," she said.

The ponderous noise sent him walking back to the game. He wasn't ready to answer any questions about him and Norah. Somehow he endured the last inning, even tagging two men from the opposite team out. Celebrating broke out as the North's victory was called. He joined in only long enough to be polite, and then he grabbed his bat, glove, and ball and left the field. When he'd suggested the outing, he'd envisioned Norah cheering for him, his eye catching hers and finding the familiar twinkle in her gaze as she celebrated with him from the stands. He'd hoped she'd begin finding her place in the town and that this outing into the fresh air would be a step toward her recovery. But she'd left. And now he walked as swiftly as he could back to the hotel, anxious to know how she fared.

Upon entering, he ran for Mrs. Dover. "Have you seen Norah?"

"She's in her room. She hurried in here a half hour ago or so, waving at me to leave her be. I've walked by her door a few times, and it's quiet inside." Mrs. Dover set down the rag she held before asking, "Did you tell her? Is that what this is about?"

"No. I didn't tell her." He groaned before slamming his bat, ball, and glove onto the counter. His ball rolled to the floor, but he didn't bother to pick it up. He walked past Mrs. Dover. "We may need a doctor."

"Check on her. If she needs a doctor, I'll go for him myself."

"I shouldn't have suggested the baseball game," he muttered as he walked to her room at the end of the second-story hall. He knocked and waited, his worry increasing with each moment that passed. "Norah."

"Quincy, is that you?"

"Yes, open up. I know you're hurt." He gritted his teeth. He'd not meant to speak so harshly. "Will you let me in?"

Metal sliding against metal told him she was unlocking her door. "Come in."

He looked behind him, and no one was in the hall. He slid through the door and into her bedchamber, making sure to leave the door open. Only then did he get a good look at her tear-streaked face. "What's wrong? Tell me where you're hurt."

"Stop." Norah's face puckered, and new tears came. "It's not that."

She leaned against the nearest wall and then slid down and sat in a heap on the floor. He was at a loss for what to do, so he just sat next to her and waited, hoping she'd tell him what was wrong if he was patient enough. But thunderation! This waiting was torture.

"I want to help, but I can't if you aren't willing to tell me what's wrong."

With her face still down, she whispered, "I'm afraid."

Silence followed. Give him an angry opponent or a business problem and he would come out swinging, but a woman in tears and he froze. Norah was afraid, and he didn't know how to fix it.

She looked up and their eyes met. The twinkle in her eyes was gone. All he saw was fear. His arms went around her, and he pulled her close. She melted into him, resting her head against his chest. She shook as she sobbed, but she didn't pull away. His arms tightened around her, offering her whatever strength she wanted to take from him. Her tears were plentiful, falling like great gushing waters from her eyes, running down her cheeks, and landing on him. He put a hand to her cheek and let his thumb wipe at the trail of tears.

"Don't be afraid," he said in a hoarse voice. "Fight off the vultures, yell at them. Tell them they can't have you."

Since bringing Norah to Longfield, he'd seen glimpses of the woman he'd met two years ago, enough to give him hope she was still in there. The outspoken, stubbornly optimistic woman who'd nudged him toward a fresh start and stolen his heart quicker than a pitcher throws a ball. She was in his arms, only now she was battered and plagued by a foe he could not see. His heart skipped a beat as he realized how close she was to him, sprawled nearly on top of him, shedding tears onto his shoulder. Trusting him, vulnerable. Every protective instinct he'd ever known was alive and wildly begging him to keep her from pain.

"Norah." He inched his face closer to hers. Unruly pieces of her hair brushed his nose as he brought his cheek close enough that it rested on the top of her head. Her scent, the feel of her against him—all of it was intoxicating. How could he care so much for a woman he still hardly knew? Did the *how* matter, or did it only matter that what he felt was real? With his head against hers, he said, "Will you tell me what you're afraid of?"

His question roused her, and she wriggled away from him. An emptiness existed where she'd been only seconds before. He ached to hold her again, to console her and give her enough love that she'd be able to fight the demons that tormented her.

"You'll think I'm weak," she said, wiping her face. "I was clumsy and fell at the game. I left, but I wasn't running, not then. I was only embarrassed." With each word, his desire to hold her grew. "While I walked back, I was looking at the town and thinking that maybe it could feel like home someday. But I was wrong. I think only King land can make me feel that way." She sniffled. "Maybe I'll never feel safe again. I wish I could go back to my house and my creek. What if I never have a home again?"

"You have a home, here at the hotel—"

"I have a roof, not a home. I can hide in here, in this little room, but outside I am too afraid to even walk by the saloon. Just looking at the saloon, I crumbled. I lost all my bravery." She swallowed. "I don't know how to explain it, but I froze. I couldn't get my legs to carry me past it. I kept thinking of Percy and how he hurt me."

Quincy put a hand on her shoulder, slowly and tentatively. "He won't come here."

"He could. He's chased a woman down before. She ran away, and he got the law to bring her back because she'd signed a contract. I tried telling myself I was safe here, but all my fears, they just crashed around me. I finally got my legs working, and I ran and tried to hide from it all, but it won't go away. I'm still afraid." She tipped her head back against the wall and closed her eyes. "I want to tell the vultures they can't have me, but they've already taken so much. Percy may not be here, but he circles inside my head. He's never really gone."

"No. Norah, look at me." She tilted her head toward him, but still she looked afraid. "You told me once that I may have gotten my fresh start in an uncanny way, but that I'd gotten it and I should take it. I haven't been perfect. Lord knows I still have a great deal to tell you about all that, but right now I want you to hear your own words and act on them." He reached for her hand, brought it to his lips, and said, "You're here in Longfield now. You may have come in an unusual way, but you're here now and you *can* have a new life. Alice wants to be your friend, so do Nels and Mrs. Dover, and so many others will too when they get to know you. And I am here to help you. I'll keep you safe, you have my word." He scooted nearer to her, their legs now close enough that they touched, but it still didn't feel close enough. "I'll fumble my way along, but I'll be here. I'm even going to read that book you wanted me to read. I'll sit beside you, and I'll tell you all my favorite parts." Her small hand trembled in his large one. "You're not alone. In fact, I'll let you cry in my lap anytime you wish. I rather like that part of helping you recover. We could make a daily thing of it."

"You're a regular rogue," she whispered, but beneath her tears he saw her smile. "I should be appalled."

"But you're not, and you don't have to be afraid. Longfield is not Warner Crossing, and I am not Percy."

She leaned closer, resting her head on his shoulder. "I don't think you're a rogue, not really."

"If a big fellow like me doesn't scare you, then I'd say you're mighty brave." He rubbed her arm.

"It's not just Percy that scares me," she said. "I'm afraid of coming close to happiness, only to lose it again. I'm afraid of wicked men who might hurt me and of always being seen as one of Percy's girls. I'm afraid of so much, and now I'm afraid you'll think I'm nothing more than a weeping woman too broken to fix."

"I say, if a good cry helps, then cry. I don't know much about women, but I don't think tears mean you're broken, just that you're human." He stood and offered her a hand. When they were both standing, he said, "There's a lock on your door and window. What else can I do to help you feel safe?"

"I wasn't afraid when I was at the baseball game. I enjoyed talking to Alice, and everyone I met was kind. It was only the saloon that reminded me of Percy and his threats." She pursed her lips before saying, "I suppose if you want to help, you could tear down the saloon and turn it into a church." Her small smile turned serious. "I don't know if I'll feel afraid again or not. It attacked me unexpectedly."

"I'll work on tearing the saloon down, but for now I'll go with you if you go out so you're not alone."

"I couldn't expect—"

"I want to. I'll show you all the reasons this town *is* a good place for you to call home." He touched her cheek. Her skin was smooth, tear-stained, and altogether perfect. "Besides, you've already got family here."

"Yes," she said, her voice breathless. "I've a brother."

"I've never cared for that role. I'll forfeit it to Nels. He can play the part of rowdy little brother, and Mrs. Dover is rather motherly. And I will . . . Well, I'm not sure which family role I should play, but I am here to help you."

"Thank you. And thank you for listening to me." She smiled then, and with it the tension in his chest relaxed. "I may seem fickle, but I feel better now than I did before you came. You are a good remedy for my troubles, as was the game. Who won?"

"The North. And I have to say that the ball I hit near the end of the game helped get us that victory."

"Look at you boasting. I'm sorry I missed it." She wiped the remaining wetness from her face and stood straighter. "I want to watch another game, and I want to go out and walk the streets again. Percy said he'd break me, but I don't want him to." She poked one finger at his chest. "I'll cheer for you."

"You sure? No dashing man from the South caught your eye?"

"You were so big out there, it was hard to see anyone else."

"I've never been so grateful for my size." He wanted to stay and watch over her like she had watched over him in his time of need. He wanted more than to care for her . . . He wanted so much more. But he also wanted to treat her like a gentleman would, so he moved for the door. "Rest up, and tomorrow we'll find more ways to scare off the vultures." He lowered his voice and said, "Because they can't have you."

"No need for a doctor," Quincy said to Mrs. Dover in the hall after leaving Norah's room. Repairing a painful rib would have been easier than mending damaged spirits and chasing away ghosts of the past, but he'd never shied from a challenge. And judging by the gleam in Norah's eye when he left, she wasn't giving up either. "She's resting."

"Poor dear has been through so much."

"The doctor in Warner Crossing said it would take time. That she had pain inside as well as out." He ran his hands through his hair. "I think he was right."

"We will all give her the medicine she needs."

"But there's no medicine for this," he muttered. "I wish there was."

"Patience is excellent medicine. Time, peace, and gentleness." She looked toward Norah's room. "And maybe a little love. I'll let you take care of that part."

15

Alice worked at the café later in the day, so she made a habit of stopping by in the mornings to visit with Norah. And Norah savored their daily visits. During her second week in town, they'd become so close that Mrs. Dover had declared them practically sisters.

"You two women act like silly girls when you're together," she said with a smile full of motherly warmth.

"You're welcome to come giggle with us anytime you like," Alice said. "We were just talking about the men in town."

Mrs. Dover swatted at the air. "I'm well past those days. I'm happier scrubbing floors and seeing them glisten than I would be fussing over a man again."

"But you did care for your husband?" Norah asked.

"My goodness, yes. I never tired of that man. He could make me swoon by tipping his hat in my direction." She moved toward the door of Norah's room. "But it's your turn now, and I'll just stand back and smile while I watch the two of you in love with such fine men."

"We aren't actually in love." Norah put a hand to her heart. She certainly didn't need that rumor spreading. Not now while she was just dipping her toes in the waters of Longfield and trying to find her bearings. "We were merely discussing possibilities. But we aren't sure we even want men in our life. All this talk is a diversion, that's all."

"Hmm . . . some diversions become husbands. But there's no rush." Mrs. Dover paused at the door. "You're strong women, some of the strongest I know. But don't forget that loving a respectable man doesn't make you weak."

Norah nodded, knowing that she'd never felt stronger than she did when Quincy was beside her. Mrs. Dover left, chuckling under her breath as she went.

"My mother was not nearly as outspoken as Mrs. Dover," Norah said.

"Mine was bossy but in the best sort of way." Alice ran her hand over Norah's quilt. "I was bullheaded and stubborn. I think that's why I want lilacs and ways to feel closer to her." She sighed. "She died before I'd grown up and realized how good she was."

"It hurts, doesn't it? Wishing they were still here. I was always dreaming of growing up and falling in love and leaving home, but now I'd give anything to have my land back and my family." They'd still not broached the most painful memories, but each day they became bolder as they grew more trusting of each other. "Now it's hard to know what to want and what to risk going after."

"At least we've found a place where we can breathe and dream a little."

"Is Sam part of your dreams?" Norah asked in a cautious tone, ready to back off if Alice seemed hesitant to answer. "Has he asked to court you?"

"No. But he walks me home if we finish work at the

same time, and I don't mind his company." She stood and brushed the wrinkles from her simple dress. "For now, he's a diversion, like we told Mrs. Dover. He's . . . pleasant." She shrugged as she walked toward the door. "I need to get bread rising at the café. I'll see you soon."

Alice left, and Norah found herself with time to spare before Nels was due to come for his daily lesson. Most days she read when she was alone, but today she wanted to do something different. Perhaps her conversation with Alice was to blame for her sudden desire to give Quincy a gift.

With one arm in a cast, her options were limited. She had use of her fingers on both hands though. She wiggled them for several minutes while she thought of ideas—until at last she landed on one.

"Mrs. Dover," Norah said as soon as she found her. "I was wondering if you might help me."

"Is your hair falling out of its pins?" Mrs. Dover inspected her appearance.

"No, it's holding fast." She touched her hair, which remained exactly how Mrs. Dover had fixed it earlier that morning. "I have time to spare and thought I could use it for good. I'd like to help you more, and I thought I might make something for Quincy." She blushed, since gift giving could be misconstrued as a romantic gesture. "I wanted to give him something as a thank-you for all he's done for me."

"What did you have in mind?"

"I thought I might make a new shirt for him. I thought if we had the dressmaker make one less dress for me, I could use that fabric to make him a shirt. It would take me a long time with my hand how it is, but I think I could manage." She sucked in her bottom lip, embarrassed by how forward she sounded. "I could keep thinking. I only thought of that because once a long time ago, I cut his shirt off him."

"Oh dear."

She covered her mouth, mortified by her own words. "He was hurt . . . I was helping him with his wounds." She groaned. "I should let you work. I'm sorry—"

Mrs. Dover's chortle came then. Her belly and chin jiggled along with it. "Don't be sorry. If you cut the man's shirt off him, then a new shirt is an excellent gift."

"It seemed like a good idea until I said it out loud." But even Norah laughed then.

"Come along, and I'll fetch you one of his shirts from the laundry that you can use for a pattern." Norah followed Mrs. Dover through the hotel and out to the humid lean-to, where she handed her a freshly washed shirt. "I'll get your fabric and thread soon as I can, and if you have trouble cutting it out with your bad arm, just holler and I'll gladly come."

"Thank you."

Norah hid Quincy's shirt in the back of her dresser. She wasn't alone for long, as Nels soon came for his daily lesson. After only two weeks of being her pupil, he was already reading simple words, adding sums, and writing his name with no prompts. They stayed on topic most of the time, but he often begged her to read him stories, and sometimes he'd sit beside her and lean his head on her shoulder. A strange motherly pull grew inside her, and she couldn't help but care about more than his academic well-being. Hopes long forgotten, like dormant bulbs hidden beneath the snows of winter, pushed upward, trying with all their might to bloom. Someday, Lord willing, she would like to have a child of her own. One who called her Mama.

For three weeks she walked outside with Quincy nearly every day. Often on their walks they'd visit with the townsfolk or stop and eat at the café or simply meander through the streets, peering in shop windows. Her list of names and faces grew with each outing. Today was like so many others. They waved and smiled but also savored their time walking alone.

"Quincy"—Norah lifted her skirts a little higher and stepped around a pile of droppings—"do you think Nels needs something more than we're giving him?"

"What do you mean?" he asked as they rounded the side of the hotel and headed for the open fields that bordered the edge of town. "He's fed, working, and you're teaching him."

"That's true, and I think you've done a good thing taking him in—"

"But . . ."

"He's still so young. Everyone at the hotel is a makeshift family and it works, but it's all temporary. It could all be gone in an instant, and then what would he do? I wonder if he might like having a more permanent family. He looks at me sometimes the way I remember looking at my mother, and I can't help but think . . . It's hard to explain, but I think he wants family that he doesn't have to worry about losing."

Quincy scratched his cheek. "You want me to find him a home?"

"I would miss him if he were gone. He's worked his way into my heart, but I do wonder what would be best for him." Even mentioning finding Nels a permanent family made her queasy, but she cared deeply for him and wanted what was best, no matter the cost to herself. "If we did find him a home, it would have to be a very good one. I can't bear the thought of him living with someone unkind. He'd need a family that would overlook some of his rougher ways and see the gem that's beneath it all."

Quincy waved at someone across the street before speaking again to her. "Together we'll figure out something good for the lad. For now, we'll just keep teaching him and helping him settle down. He doesn't talk about running away anymore."

"He likes it here. I can tell." She moved easier these days, their pace no longer the slow crawl it had been when her body was so stiff and sore. Her cast would soon be removed and inwardly, she'd relaxed. It was rare for her to feel the panic that had once been so powerful. Even when she walked by the saloon, she felt her courage rising. Granted, she rarely went out alone. Even so, her soul felt more at ease with each passing day.

She read, helped Mrs. Dover, and worked in secret on the shirt for Quincy. Twice he'd mentioned his best shirt and how it'd gone missing. She planned to return it soon, once she was sure the one she was sewing was the correct size. It was tedious work, but every stitch brought a lightness to her heart.

Quincy visited her most afternoons, often staying until the late evening, sometimes alone and sometimes with Nels joining them. Their conversations were easy and natural as they discussed Quincy's businesses, the weather, food, the changing seasons, the weekly sermon, and occasionally their dreams. And like the good friend he was proving to be, he'd even begun trudging through *Persuasion* one page at a time.

"She never should have rejected Wentworth to begin with," Quincy said when he was partway through *Persuasion*. "It's nothing but boring drivel about a woman with a fickle mind. She should have married when she had the chance. She's miserable, but it's her own fault."

"She was young." Norah defended not only Anne from the story but also every woman who'd made a decision and then regretted it. "She didn't know her own mind or what lay ahead. She was persuaded to believe it'd be a match she'd one day regret."

"She was afraid she would be poor." Quincy's voice rose in agitation. "I think she was foolish and shortsighted."

"I agree."

"You agree?"

"Yes, she should have married him, but we have the luxury of saying that knowing what her life looked like after her decision. She didn't know how dismal her lot would be when she rejected him. I think it's rather harsh to think that one error in judgment should keep her from all future happiness. She's already had enough miserable years taking care of her ungrateful family."

He paused his tirade against the fictional Miss Elliot and studied Norah. His eyes were on her as they walked through the town and turned toward the garden behind the hotel. Did he see in her the regret she bore? Had she known him capable of so quick a transformation, perhaps their past could have been different. And they could merge their dreams into a common one.

"I concede," he said, his eyes still searching her. "She should get a happy ending, but I still think she worried too much about keeping her wealth and pleasing her family."

"I suppose. But a woman is often at the mercy of the man she marries. She does not have the opportunity to simply work her way out of poverty. I would have married Jake to save my land. Anne Elliot rejected her suitor on similar grounds."

"Hmm . . . and you were unwise as well. Jake was always a snake and being married to him to save a piece of land was never a good idea."

She swatted his arm and groaned. "You weren't telling me to jilt him then. You know I had no alternatives." She laughed. Nothing about the past was funny, but she laughed anyway. How ridiculous it was to compare her life to the fictional Anne Elliot, who had a writer creating her life and making the impossible happen. "I must be feeling better. You've been so careful not to disturb me, but now you're back to your frank ways—telling me how foolish I was. As much as I hate to admit it, you are right. Marrying Jake would have been a horrible sentence to bear." She made a face just thinking of it, earning her a laugh from Quincy. "Had I known he'd reject me, I could have solicited other land-hungry men with deep pockets. I'm sure some man would have taken me on in order to put their name on the deed to my little piece of heaven."

"You sound rather mercenary. I thought with all your struggles, you would look back and wish you'd found a man you could have loved, or at least liked." He led them to a bench in the garden and they sat together, surrounded by trimmed bushes, stone paths, and weeping willow trees.

"As I said, we women are rather limited in our choices." She leaned back and sighed as the warm sun beat against her face. "I would have liked marrying for love *and* keeping my land." She shaded her eyes as she watched the white clouds drift across the blue sky. "Do you see why I care for this book? I feel a kinship with Anne. I regret the past, but only now can I think of ways I could have handled it differently."

"And yet you believe Anne Elliot deserves a happy ending despite her foolish decision. Does that mean you believe the same for yourself?"

She opened her mouth, ready to speak of happy endings, but before she could get the words out, he stood, leaving her on the bench. "I think I had better read the end to see if the fickle woman can make the right choice—and if she gets another chance."

Two hours later, he pounded on her door. They'd become more careful about appearances—meeting in the lobby, the gardens, and the café, and avoiding each other's rooms—but he'd clearly now forgotten all thoughts of propriety and appearances. He entered with boldness, and a satisfied smile played across his lips as he neared her side. "I've read it, and Anne has gotten her second chance."

"Did you love his letter?" Norah brightened at the thought of Captain Wentworth's romantic confession of love. "I had tears in my eyes when I read it."

"'Course I didn't cry. He's not even real, but I was glad she got her second chance. I would have thrown the wretched book in the fire had she said no again."

"She was *not* going to say no." Norah laughed, enjoying the exchange. "She loves Wentworth, she always did, and . . . and I believe she always will. It's what every woman wants—a man who knows his heart and commits it to her, and she gives hers in return."

Quincy took a step closer to her. Her heart stirred, unsure what he was about. He took her hand, sending a thrill racing through her. They'd held hands many times during their separate bouts of convalescing, but this felt different. It was not his touch so much as the intensity in his eyes that had her holding her breath in anticipation. "Is that another dream?"

She swallowed. "To be loved?"

"Yes."

"I don't know." She pulled away, retreating several steps. "Who wouldn't want what Anne and Captain Wentworth found? But I don't have an author weaving words together, ensuring a happy ending. Real life is much more complicated." Unsteady on her legs, she leaned against the wall. "Shall we read another book? We could pick an adventure this time."

"You do have an author," he whispered. "He's there, working for your good. You helped me to see that and to know it's true."

It was true, she knew it was. The greatest of all authors was there, and she'd seen his hand. He'd answered her prayer of desperation by sending Quincy to rescue her. Surely, if it was his will, love could come too. "You're right. I will try to trust that good things are ahead for me."

"And I will read another book."

Over the course of the next week, they met daily, walking and discussing fictional adventures and bickering good-naturedly about outcomes for imaginary characters. It was safe, entertaining, and pleasant. One day he even confessed that his missing shirt had miraculously returned, and he declared it cause to celebrate. That night he wore his shirt and they ate two slices of Alice's pie. She'd never smiled so much or felt so at ease. Never before had a man cared so deeply about her opinion or begged to spend time with her. Often at night, when she was alone, she lay awake wishing these days could go on forever.

"You're a rather opinionated woman," Quincy said one lazy late-summer afternoon. They'd ventured outside with Nels to discuss their latest read. Nels had scurried off to catch grasshoppers, leaving the two of them alone to sit back on the picnic blanket in the garden and enjoy the sun.

"I wasn't always." She smoothed her green skirts out around her. "With Jake I was always so quiet. I suppose I did have opinions, but I rarely voiced them. But with you it's different. It's easier and even fun. Your eyebrows wrinkle up when you think I'm wrong and you get that edge in your voice. It's all rather amusing."

"I'm glad you find my riled spirits entertaining. I find you amusing as well."

"Do you?" She pursed her lips. "And what is it I do when I'm feeling passionate about our book debates?"

"You talk so fast that I can hardly keep up, and then when I disagree with you, your lips go in a hard line. It's rather adorable." He lay back on the blanket and looked up at the cloudless blue sky. She stared at him, amused but not shocked by his statement. "I'm glad you can tell me what you really feel. Even if it's only about a book we're discussing."

She lay beside him with one arm behind her head. "I knew when I first met you that you were a man I could trust, and though I still have nightmares that haunt me, I can forget them when you're nearby. My land was always my sanctuary. I find that you are a satisfying alternative."

He rolled to his side. "Do you miss it a great deal?"

"My land and home?" She closed her eyes. "I do. I think if I could go back, I would be happy and carefree again. It's naive thinking, I know, but I can't help but picture my creek and the wheat fields and the house when I close my eyes."

He closed his eyes and allowed himself to picture her land. "Ah, dreaming again. I wish I could make it come true somehow. But I'll be your alternative as long as you like." Flashes of memory—Norah tending his wounds, her fiery eyes when she saved him from the rooster, and the sincerity of her words when she told him to go be a better man. If it was her land she wanted, there must be a way to get it for her. Would that not, in some way, set things right? Would Jake sell?

Quincy pushed himself to sitting. Norah had been in Longfield for over four weeks now, and not a single day had passed without him wondering how to right his wrong. He'd stalled and not offered his confession. At first he was leaning on the doctor's command to avoid distressing her. But now, he could divulge the truth about the money, yet he still kept the secret to himself, burying it deeper and deeper every day. He'd piled his own hopes on top of it, and he feared he'd lose it all if he uncovered it.

He rubbed his tight chest. There was no peace in keeping secrets, but so much was at stake. A new thought swiftly consumed him. He stood and paced the garden. If he could buy back the land she'd lost, he could set things right. Although that was not entirely right—time could not be returned. But surely when he gave her the soil she longed for, she would know how deeply he wished to correct all that was wrong.

She propped herself up on one elbow. He swallowed the urge to tell her every thought as it entered his mind. How easily they conversed. This was different. He would settle with Jake before giving her hope. He cleared his throat, buying himself a few seconds more to form the words to explain his newly hatched plan.

"I may have to go away for a few days," he said when he finally spoke. "Would you be alright here while I'm gone? We've had no sign of Percy since you got here. I think you're safe."

She rose and came to him. The closer she got, the more he wrestled with his decision. This plan was made in such haste, but for her . . . he would go.

"You needn't worry about me. I have Nels and Mrs. Dover, and I've only read half your collection of books. What is it that calls you away?"

"It's a . . . a matter of business."

She remained silent a moment, giving him time to tell her more. When he did not, she nodded, apparently accepting his mysterious departure. "I will miss knowing you are under the same roof as me. Oh dear, that sounded improper."

"That does sound improper." He laughed. "But don't apologize. I find I rather like hearing that you think of me at night."

"Quincy, you are impossible." She laughed loud enough that Nels looked up from his playing. She lowered her voice and said, "I think of you because you are big and strong, and I know if there were some villains about, you'd scare them off."

"I'd clobber any man who tried to hurt you. But you're safe here, and I won't be gone long."

"I'll keep myself busy by spending time with Nels. We've been making wonderful progress. He's so bright—and he's stubborn."

Quincy looked at the boy and smiled. "If he's stubborn about the right things, then it may not be his downfall."

"If I have my way, he will be immovable about all the right things."

"He may always be a little unruly, but you wouldn't want a perfect gentleman, would you?" He smiled playfully, enjoying the banter. "A little callousness is fun, right?"

"Well . . ." She bit her lip, the moment stretching on in a delightful way. "Every girl wants a gentleman, don't they?"

Nels ran back toward them before Quincy could answer, his hands cupped around something. "I found a grasshopper!" he shouted as he got closer. "I wanted to show you both."

"Do show us!" Norah leaned close, encouraging him.

Nels opened his hands and out jumped the insect, doing its best to flee its entrapment, but it didn't get far. It landed in Norah's hair. She batted at it with frantic hands. Pins fell from her hair. "Get it out!" she squawked. "Quincy!"

Nels and Quincy laughed as they tried to work the creature from the snarls of hair that surrounded it.

"Stop flailing, and I'll get it," Quincy said. His fingers sank deeper into her hair, savoring her nearness. "I've got it," he said, freeing the grasshopper. He cleared his throat. "And now we are even."

"Even?"

"You once saved me from a vicious rooster, and now I've saved you from a terribly vicious grasshopper."

"You're a perfect knight in shining armor, aren't you?" Her hands were on her hair, attempting to smooth it. Nels giggled beside her. "Are you laughing because Quincy was once attacked by a little old rooster? Or because of my hair?"

"I ain't sure I should answer that. You told me I was supposed to think about my words before I say them. And I'm thinking that you don't want me telling you what you look like."

"Excellent choice. You're practically a gentleman already. And next time, be more careful with your grasshopper."

"I will." Quincy watched the boy pull his mouth to one side. "What's the right way for me to tell you that your hair looks like a bird's nest?"

Quincy tried covering his laugh with a cough, but the look Norah shot him said she wasn't fooled. Norah put a hand on Nels' shoulder. "No need to say anything."

"We better let Norah go on inside and fix the hair that we aren't mentioning." Quincy took a step toward the hotel, only to stop and lock eyes with Nels. "But first I have a question for you."

"I'm listenin'," Nels said.

"I'm going to head out of town for a few days. You think I could trust you to take care of a few things here while I'm gone? You've proven to me that you're a hard, responsible worker."

"I could manage whatever you need."

Quincy smiled, proud of Nels in a fatherly way. "I imagine you could."

"Don't give him too much to do," she said. "I don't want him shirking his lessons. He's a regular scholar."

"I won't shirk. I can run this place and do my studies."

Nels puffed his small chest out when he spoke. "I can work hard. You don't got to worry about nothing."

"I feel better leaving knowing you'll be here to man the place." Quincy gave the boy instructions, including checking in with the store manager and Alice every morning to see if there were any unusual needs and to help if he could. In an emergency of any sort, he was to tell Mrs. Dover and have her send a telegram to him. Nels nodded after each of his requests. And to think that just over a month ago, this lad had been accused of being a *street rat*.

"Most important above all your other duties"—Quincy looked him right in the eye—"is for you to make sure Norah smiles and laughs every day. And if you catch a grasshopper, show it to her from far away."

When Quincy found Mrs. Dover later in the humid lean-to working on the laundry, he told her his plan to go to Blackwell and try to buy Norah's land. She agreed to help but was less enthusiastic than he'd expected. "Are you sure this is what you want to do?"

"She lost it because of me." He owed Norah so much more than land, but time could not be given back as easily as acreage. After listening to her talk about her beloved land and all the memories and hope it held, he knew he had to try. If he were being honest, he also hoped that somehow it would ease his guilt. "I stole it, and now I'm going to give it back."

"You didn't steal it. That's useless talk. You made a mistake. Who's to say that if she'd had the money, she would have been able to keep the farm anyway? Farming is hard work. She's a small woman, stubborn and hardworking to be sure, but she couldn't have kept up a place that big for long."

"I'll get it back for her, and she can choose what she wants to do with it." He wasn't asking for her permission, only for her help. "She will be at the hotel with Nels, and I'd like you to check in on her. If she did need something, I'm afraid she wouldn't ask."

"Checking in on that dear girl is a privilege. Don't you worry about her." Mrs. Dover shook her head in dismay. "She's been smiling more lately, especially if you're around. You sure this isn't going to stir the pot and bring back all her dark memories?"

"I won't tell her where I'm going. And when I get back, I won't tell her where I've been unless I've made a deal for the land. I don't want her hopes up." He raked his hands through his hair. This decision to return to Blackwell had been so sudden, but he was stubborn himself and he was going. "I'll handle all of that when I return."

If he could get her land, what would she do when he gave it to her? Would she turn her back on Longfield and on him? If she chose a life away from him, there would forever be a hole in his heart. He would bear it. Giving her back what was lost was the right thing to do.

He pressed a hand against his forehead, wishing for an easier way. He'd been selfish once before and it'd hurt her. Everything was different now. He was different, and he was going to show her that by making amends, no matter the cost to himself. "I think this is for the best. She deserves to choose what she wants out of this life."

"But you care about Norah." Mrs. Dover looked near

tears. "You've finally found someone who helps you slow down and enjoy life."

"I do care." He filled his chest with air as he fought his worries. "I've cared about her since the moment I met her. I can't explain it, but every day those feelings grow."

"Why not tell her that—and tell her the truth about what happened with the money you found?"

"When she looks at me, I can see the trust in her eyes. I'm going to give her land back to her and show her I'm an honest man."

"Do what you must." Mrs. Dover frowned. "But it doesn't seem right. You're trying to fix it without really fixing it."

"I can't undo what's done." His voice was rough and strained. He wanted Mrs. Dover to confirm his course, not question it. "If I can get her land and she goes back there . . ." He winced, knowing how bad it would hurt if she left him, refusing to let him be a part of her life. But he'd wronged her and could not expect her forgiveness, only hope for it. "I'd ache for her. But Jake and Percy did not let her pick her course. I won't be like them. If she wants me to go back with her, then I will. If she doesn't, then I will have to let her go."

"She can't choose if she doesn't know what her choices are. You haven't told her how you feel, and you haven't told her how sorry you are."

"I'm going to get her land. I'll give her the means to take care of herself for years to come. Until I can offer her that . . . I have to go, and then I'll decide what needs telling."

Tenderness crept over her features, erasing the thick lines of judgment. "You make my mama heart proud. I can see in your eyes that you want to do what's right. It's good of you, but—" She cut herself off and, with her lips pressed firmly together, nodded. "You'll do what is right. I'm sure of it."

Nels rushed up to Quincy, ending their conversation. His face was flushed from his hurrying. "There's a girl here— she's all dirty. Said she needs to speak to you."

"Did she say her name?" he asked, already moving to follow Nels.

"I didn't ask. Come with me."

Quincy slowed down and turned to Mrs. Dover. "I'll send her around back. I trust you can get her settled." She nodded, and he quickened his pace and caught up with Nels before they reached the front of the hotel, where he grimaced at the sight of the woman.

"See if Alice needs help at the café. I'll handle this," he barked at Nels, sending him scurrying off. Someday, if Nels was still around, he'd explain it all, but not now. He sat next to the woman, who'd seated herself in the empty dining room. This was a fine mess, being seen in daylight with such a woman. Her tattered clothes hung from her shoulder. Her dirty and sunken skin practically screamed her past profession. "Who sent you?"

The stringy-haired woman looked up at him, her chin quivering before she even spoke. "I was working in Beckford, but it got real bad and I ran off. Came here. I didn't know what to do, but the preacher told me to find you at the hotel. Said you might be able to put me up and get me on my feet. You'll take me in, won't you?"

"What's your name?"

"They called me Flower there, but that ain't my name. I'm Irene. I don't got nobody else."

"Go around back. Try to go unseen if you can. There's a woman waiting in the lean-to who will help you."

Quincy watched her go, then put his head in his hands and took several deep breaths. But, still, his head spun. Would life ever settle down or was he destined to always be jumping about, trying to make amends in one way or another?

———————|———————

Quincy was leaving tomorrow, and the very idea of him being gone left Norah's stomach in knots. Their endless days of comfortable chatter would be interrupted. Would they ever resume? When Quincy was near her, she felt important and cared for. His very presence brought a smile to her face. He would be missed.

"It's only a few days," she whispered to her reflection as she repinned her hair the best she could with one free hand and one still mostly immobile. She froze. When he walked away two years ago, she regretted not telling him how she felt. Though it would have changed nothing then, could it make a difference now?

If he was going to go, what could it hurt to say the things she'd been wanting to say to him? In *Persuasion*, Captain Wentworth asked in a letter if he was too late and if Anne cared for him still. Could she be so daring? No. She shook her head. She was not as bold as the romantic captain, but she could thank Quincy for what he'd done and attempt to write a piece of her heart onto the page.

With new resolve, she sat at her desk and wrote quickly, refusing to permit herself to overthink her words.

Dear Quincy,

When you left my farm in Blackwell, there were things I wish I had said. I should have told you how grateful I was to have someone listen to me and how I enjoyed the sound of your laugh. You are going away again. You will be back, but still I feel the urge to write and tell you that my time in Longfield has been some of the happiest days I have known. I will forever be thankful for the generosity you have shown me.

I will be anxiously awaiting your return so we might resume our afternoon walks and book debates. Please accept this shirt as a token of my gratitude for your kindness. Sorry I had to borrow your other shirt for so long.

> *Be safe in your travels,*
> *Norah*

She scowled at the letter. It was hardly the romantic gesture Captain Wentworth handed Anne. She added,

I told you once I dreamed of dancing. I still dream of that, but now I think I'd like that dance to be with you.

16

Nels entered Quincy's office and thrust a crumpled letter and a parcel wrapped in brown paper into Quincy's hands and stood back, waiting to see what it was. "Norah said to give this to you. She was all red and splotchy when she handed it to me. I think it might be somethin' bad. My reading ain't that good or I woulda read it before I gave it to you."

With an anxious hand, Quincy unfolded the letter and read her brief note. He smiled at the beginning and laughed when he got to the part about her taking his shirt. Her final line gave him pause. It was not like the rest. It was vulnerable, a step they'd both skirted around but never taken. His heart leapt within his chest as the reality of her words sank in. She wanted to dance with him.

"What'd she say?" Nels asked, giving no heed to rules of privacy or etiquette. "You ain't going to keep a secret from me, are you?"

"She hopes I travel safely."

Nels grunted. "That don't seem important enough for her to be acting so strange. I don't think I'll ever understand women."

"You're kind of young to be worried about that."

"Nah, way I figure it, if a fella don't start worrying young, then when he's a man he won't know nothin' about women and they'll all turn their noses up at him." He folded his arms across his chest, confident and sure of himself. "So, tell me why she's flustered if all she wanted to say was travel safe. It's not like you're going away for good, are you?"

Quincy had to admit that the boy made a solid point. He'd given little thought to the fairer sex until he suddenly found himself intrigued by them, but he had no foundation. He knew nothing about the workings of a woman's heart when he set out to win Opal's affections so many years before. Even after that he struggled to learn about courtship and romance. "I fear I am not the man to teach you about women."

"Why not? All the women in town stare at you when we go out, and Norah cares about you."

"Do you think so?" He chided himself for asking a child's opinion, but the boy *was* observant. And in this moment, he very much wanted someone else's thoughts on the matter.

"Maybe she don't, but she asks about you an awful lot, and she's always telling me that I ought to grow up and be like you. And she sent whatever is in that bundle." He picked at a scab on the side of his arm. When it bled, he pressed his thumb against it. "I told ya, I don't know 'bout women. You gonna open that?"

Quincy nodded, and though he kept his face free of emotion, it did not escape him that this was the first gift he'd ever unwrapped. He shook out the shirt she'd sewn and held it against his chest. Tiny stitches, perfectly straight. Four buttons that went halfway down and a collar on top. His heart swelled at the sight of such a fine gift.

"Aw, it's just a shirt." Nels frowned.

"It's not," he said. "It's much more than that."

"Just looks like a shirt to me." Nels shrugged and wiped again at his scab. "Want me to tell her anything for you?"

"Yes, wait a moment." Quincy moved to his large desk and laid out a sheet of paper to write on.

Nels wiped his thumb on his pants, then sank into the chair across from him with a plop. "I can tell her what you want to say. You don't gotta write it down. Besides, I want to know what you're telling her."

"Maybe I don't want you knowing. These words are for Norah alone." Quincy didn't look up, but he knew his little friend wouldn't like such a response. He softened it by adding, "Sometimes words on paper have a different effect than words spoken."

"Maybe I ain't old enough to learn about women, 'cause that don't make sense to me."

"Just remember it. One day you might have important words to say, and you'll decide to write them down rather than spew them out and make a mess of them." He turned his attention back to his sheet of paper and hoped he'd be able to express himself with more grace than he ever had speaking. When he finished writing, he folded the paper and sent it with the impatient Nels to give to Norah, instructing him to place it in her hands alone. Nels rolled his eyes before tucking the note into his pocket and leaving to make his delivery.

Quincy immediately questioned the words he'd written, but it was too late. They would be handed off in a moment's time. He would simply have to reap the consequences of what he'd sown.

"This is for you." Nels put the letter into Norah's hand. "I don't know why you two can't just talk to each other. You're in the same building. You're both acting awful strange."

"It's not strange to write letters." She turned away from him to open her mail, but he skirted around her and looked at her face.

"There you go, gettin' all red again."

"I'm not red." She touched her face, only to find it warm to her touch. "Nels, doesn't Mrs. Dover need you for something? Or Alice at the café?"

"Mrs. Dover told me to come find her as soon as I was done helping you. I'm waiting."

"For what?"

"I thought maybe you was going to write Quincy back again. Besides, I want you to tell me what he says on that paper."

She tucked the letter into her pocket. "I prefer to read my correspondence in private, and you, being the little gentleman you are, will respect that. If I need you, I'll come get you, but I think you ought to go see what Mrs. Dover needs."

"Aw, fine," he muttered under his breath before leaving her to read her letter in peace.

She adored the boy, but she was nervous to read Quincy's words and didn't want to do so with an audience. Besides, no one had written her a letter in years, and she wanted to savor each word. Before opening it, she held it in her hands and admired the crooked way her name was scrawled across the front. At last, she unfolded the paper and slowly read the gifted words.

Dear Norah,

I have little practice with letter writing, so I imagine this will not read as smoothly as Captain Wentworth's in Persuasion, *though I share some of his same sentiments. I find myself experiencing the same agony and hope he wrote of. You write of wanting to dance with me, and I find that your dream is also my dream. I see no reason to wait when we are both united in our desire. I have a fine new shirt and would love nothing better than a special occasion to wear it for. And so, I ask, will you dance with me tonight before I leave? I don't want to wait for your cast to come off. Meet me, dear friend, in the lean-to behind the hotel at seven o'clock and we'll share a dance.*

And promise me that no matter the condition of your arm, you'll be here when I return from my business. I find that I have a great many dreams that involve you, and if you're gone, I'll be left wondering if those dreams will ever come true.

Nels is muttering about how long this is taking and how foolish it is for me to write when you are in the same building. He may be right, but I am a coward, not in the boxing ring and not when I am up to bat, but I am with you. I worry I'll scare you off. I fear you will see me for the imperfect man I am and you will go. For tonight, I beg you to come and dance with me. Say yes. Agree to live that dream with me.

> *With hope,*
> *Quincy*

The breath she'd been holding while reading left her in one giant exhale. He *wanted* to dance with her not at some distant time but now—tonight. Her knees went weak. She put a hand on the wall to steady herself before walking to her armoire and looking at the row of dresses she'd had so little reason to wear until today. She'd worn only the plainest ones, hardly giving the others notice.

But dancing in Quincy's arms seemed like reason enough to wear a dress that flattered the curves that had slowly returned since leaving Percy's establishment. Tonight she'd wear a dress that complemented her coloring and swayed when she danced—a dress suited for romance.

Ducking into the hall, she checked for Quincy and was relieved when she didn't see him. She wasn't ready, not yet. She went for Mrs. Dover, who was a couple of rooms down with Nels, taking bedding off an empty bed.

"Mrs. Dover."

"What did I tell you, boy? Here she is." She shot him a conspiratorial look that did nothing to settle Norah's racing nerves. Mrs. Dover brushed her hands on her apron, patted Nels on the shoulder, and said, "You finish up this room. I'm going to help Norah change her dress and get ready for an evening free of worries."

"You know?" she said when Mrs. Dover was beside her and they were walking down the hall.

"Quincy was here a minute before you—"

"Oh no." She looked around, afraid she'd see him before she was ready. "I can't see him yet."

"He's not here. He said he had to make plans before leaving town, but he told me the two of you were going courting tonight."

"No, it's not like that— Did he say that?" She stopped walking, too consumed with thought to move. "I told him once, long ago, that I wanted to dance. He's always trying to make my silly dreams come true. That's all this is."

"A man is trying to make your dreams come true—that's courting, my dear. That big boy of yours isn't looking around at all the other girls. His eyes are on you." She looked her over. "Have you chosen a dress to wear?"

"No, not yet. I looked, but didn't decide on one . . . It's courting? Do you really think Quincy wants to court me?"

"Mm-hmm, I do. Quincy never sits still, and then you came along. Now he's always sitting beside you, reading with you, and doing whatever he can to help you heal. He's being patient, waiting for you to tackle what haunts you— like a good man ought to. I daresay he has his own worries plaguing him. But he's antsy to sidle up beside you and show you what he's got bottled up inside him. I can tell. You being his angel and him your rescuer, I don't know if there's ever been a match more fitting."

Norah couldn't help but sigh. Mrs. Dover painted a compelling scene. But she'd read perfect scenes before, all the figment of an author's imagination. One could dream up perfectly romantic stories, but that was not the same as living one.

"I'm not sure it's all so simple."

"He's a good man and nothing like those men from your past. Let him dance with you and see what happens."

Her pulse quickened, and her toes wanted to tap to the music already. She'd been happy these last few weeks and less afraid. Tonight she would risk her heart, gamble it on what was likely a fantasy. "He said to meet him in the lean-to. It's not where I pictured dancing, but I don't even care where it is, only that we dance."

"Don't you worry. I told him that was a horrible plan. I'm having dinner prepared for you both in the main dining room. We'll close it off, and it'll be just the two of you." She pulled on Norah's hand and led her down the hall. "Quincy has not stopped working long enough to even look at a girl since buying this hotel. I told him to over and over, but he never listened. I think it's always been you he's wanted."

"Had circumstances been different . . . I wonder if . . . Well, it makes no difference now. Nothing could have happened then. But now, I can almost believe we've been given a second chance."

Mrs. Dover patted her hand before entering Norah's room and rummaging through her dresses.

"I think . . ." Mrs. Dover held up a blue and a pink dress next to Norah. "You should wear the pink. It's pale enough that I think it'll shimmer in the candlelight. You'll look beautiful."

Mrs. Dover helped her get ready for the night. In no time at all, she was wearing the pink dress and inspecting her reflection. "My father loved it when I wore this color."

"If he could see you, he'd tell you that you look exquisite." Mrs. Dover stood behind her, both of them looking at her reflection in the mirror. "I'll tell Quincy you're ready for him to fetch you when he's back from whatever errands he was running."

"You make it sound so formal."

"Courting was not designed to be casual. A man who is interested in a woman ought to go to great lengths to show her that he cares." She patted Norah's cheek in a tender, protective way. For a moment she could almost believe her own mother would have touched her the same way. "Courting doesn't last long. You've got to learn what you can about a man while you court. A man who doesn't know how to greet you at your door, offer his arm, and write you a letter isn't going to suddenly know how to when you're hitched."

"Marriage still seems like a distant dream."

"It starts with a first step." Mrs. Dover's eyes twinkled. "And with honesty. Tell him when you see him that you want to know everything about him."

"I do want that, and he does talk to me. I know about his boxing and his years on the streets. I even know he thought himself in love once, only to realize it wasn't so. Unlike other men I've known, Quincy does talk to me."

"Keep him talking."

Unsure what she meant, Norah simply nodded. Mrs. Dover smiled. "Have a wonderful evening."

Alone again, Norah faced her mirror and inspected herself. She'd never been a raving beauty, but tonight she felt pretty. Her skin had lost its ashen color and was once again bright and clear, and her blue eyes seemed to be dancing already.

While waiting for Quincy, she thought back, remembering every interaction she'd shared with him. She scrutinized each word they'd ever spoken to each other. Memories settled over her like mist, reminding her of every kind deed, every laugh, every look. She now felt certain that what they shared was more than mere friendship—it was special.

His knock brought her from the past to the present. She pulled open the door, and there he stood, dressed in a fine dark suit with the shirt she'd made beneath it. He held a bundle of flowers. "I . . . I remember seeing flowers at your farm. I thought . . . I hoped you'd like them." He thrust them toward her. She didn't take them right away, as her eyes were still busy wandering over his freshly shaved face and parted and combed hair. "You . . . you look real nice."

"Thank you, and thank you for these black-eyed Susans." She took the flowers from him and buried her face in them, inhaling their pleasant scent. Then she set them on the small table beside her bed. "My mother would pick them every year and put them in a vase on our kitchen table."

"We will have to get you a vase to put them in." He bowed and held his hand out to her. "Might I escort you to dinner?"

"Aww, you've become a gentleman." She curtsied before taking his arm. After so many hours spent together, it felt strange and exciting being so proper. "I'm sorry I had your favorite shirt for so long. Mrs. Dover gave it to me so I would have a pattern."

He tugged at the collar of his new shirt. "That old shirt? I doubt I'll have much need of it. This is my favorite one now. I've never seen anything so fine."

"That's very generous of you. It's rather ordinary. In fact, it looks a lot like the shirt you were wearing when I found you in my field."

He smirked.

"What?" she asked.

"You still feeling bad you cut that old shirt off me?"

"You were hurt! No more talk of such things. Mrs. Dover told me that we ought to be proper tonight."

"I've always told you I'm not much of a gentleman, but I'll try."

With grins on their faces, they made their way to the

restaurant, drawing looks from the other guests and whispers from the staff. Norah wasn't fond of the attention, but Quincy smiled back, pulled her close, and whispered, "We're going dancing and there's nothing wrong with that, so no shrinking away. Besides, if everyone thinks you're my girl, I won't have to worry about all the men in town coming to call while I'm gone."

"I would not worry on that account."

"Any man who doesn't look twice at you must be a simpleton." Quincy pushed open the door to the restaurant and held it for her.

"Look how lovely Mrs. Dover has made it—and so quickly." She gasped when she saw the one table dressed in a white tablecloth and set with the hotel's finest dishes among the many ordinary, undecorated tables.

"She insisted and put Nels to work on it too. It'll do the lad good. I had no examples of proper romance growing up, and it's left me at a disadvantage." He pulled out her chair for her and she sat. "Mrs. Dover seems eager to instruct me, so with any luck, I'll learn quickly. I can only hope you'll be patient with me."

"So this is to be a romance?" She tilted her head and waited for his reply. "A proper one?"

Quincy took his seat. "If you're willing, I would like this to be the most romantic romance there ever was. You had me read *Persuasion* and told me you believe Anne deserved a chance with her captain, and I agree. Choice separated them, but you and I never chose to be apart. You were engaged to a cad and bound by a duty to your land." He shook his napkin out and laid it across his lap. "What I'm saying is that you and I haven't even had our first chance at courting, and yet, if you are like me, you want it."

"She wants it." Mrs. Dover entered with a tray in her hands. "I wasn't eavesdropping! Well, maybe I was, but only to bring you dinner." She served them both, then smiled with her hand on her heart. "Your speech, my boy, nearly brought me to tears. I wonder if your business trip ought to wait and you just stay here and woo this woman with your attention and *honesty*."

Quincy's jaw clenched. "I have to go. You know that."

"So you said. Enjoy your meal. And stop your scowling. You know I want happiness for you both."

When she left, they sat quietly and ate the first of their meal. Norah took a bite of the roast and chewed it slowly, all the while loving the warm feeling of being wanted. Jake had never said so fine of words as Quincy. He had never made her feel anything. It was her land that caught his eye, not her. Their relationship had been practical and nothing more. But Quincy made her feel like she might soar right out of her chair and into his arms if she didn't control herself.

"You usually talk a lot." His fork clanked against his plate, bringing her eyes to him. "Did I botch it? I wanted to let you heal and settle in before asking if you wanted to court me. But your note gave me hope. And you've been so happy lately, I believed you were doing well and I got to thinking that you cared for me—at least a little."

"Quincy Barnes, I would very much like to court you." She set her fork down, met his gaze, and with an unwavering voice said, "You've not botched anything. I'm only quiet because I'm sitting here wondering if this can be real. I want it to be, very badly."

He let out one giant, ungentlemanly whoop before digging into his dinner. Every time their eyes found each other's across the table, they held their gaze longer than normal, as though they both wished they could cling to what they were feeling and never let it go. Already they'd shared tears, healing, and conversation, but they'd done so as friends, companions through grief, not as two people openly seeking love and affection. Like flowers bursting from the ground, their suppressed longing for more filled the air like a tangible cloud of happiness.

"What business has you leaving town?" she asked, wishing he did not have to go.

"I'm going to the larger towns to view their inventory and see if there are things I should stock here. While I'm traveling, I have a few other stops to make as well. I hear they have the finest broom and duster factory in Monticello, so I may go there." He shoveled a bite of potatoes into his mouth, chewing slowly before saying, "When I come back, I'll take you for buggy rides and strolls down Main Street and to a social." He scratched his head. "I'll ask Mrs. Dover for more ideas."

"Buggy rides and socials—I can hardly wait for you to return, and you're not even gone."

"I'll hurry back."

Their conversation, like so many others before, found an easy rhythm, bouncing melodically from trivial things like his store being out of nails to much more serious issues, like whether a family could enjoy living in a hotel rather than a house. On this they never decided, and then the conversation went to the café.

"Alice told me that everyone at the café is always running

off and getting married," Norah said between bites. "She says you're good about finding new workers though."

"I worry she'll do the same before long, but I can hardly begrudge her happiness."

"You think Alice will marry? You must mean Sam, but she says he's still so quiet. He must care for her though. He stops in often."

"He's timid, and for good reason. He's been jilted before, but I think he might one day tell Alice that he has a soft spot for her. Likely he's worried that his sisters will find out and make a muddle of it all, so he's keeping it to himself for now. Or perhaps he's intimidated by Alice's outspoken nature."

"A woman ought to know her own mind."

"I agree. I've known from the start you were far wiser than I am. Alice no doubt is too."

Norah pursed her lips playfully. "I like a man who recognizes that the fairer sex is not a weaker sex. I do believe Alice suspects his feelings. There's something she isn't telling me though, and I don't know if that will keep her from ever settling down. I haven't pressed her for details, so I can't say what it is. She talks of independence and having her own home surrounded by lilacs and not of marriage or children. We joke about living side by side on Spinster Row. I wonder, though, if she says that's what she wants because she fears it's what she'll get. I've spent many nights convincing myself that what I want is to live a solitary life."

"But that's not what you want. You don't truly want to live on Spinster Row, do you?"

She wiped the corners of her mouth, giving herself time to find her words. "Percy, and even Jake, taught me that not all men are the dashing suitors I'd believed your sex to be when I was a girl. I know now that men can be evil and vile. If I were to choose between a lifetime married to a man I had no respect for or a life alone, I would choose a life alone."

"But if you were to find a man—"

"One I loved, who loved me, and whom I trusted completely—then I would let my dream of marrying and having children resurface. Altered, of course, because I can no longer dream of life on my family land, but I think it's possible I could find happiness in other dreams, or at least I want to believe so." Warmth filled her heart, bringing happy tears to her eyes. Dreams of family she had suppressed for so long tickled her insides as they found their wings anew. "If family is God's will for me, then I will be forever grateful."

"Another dream." He stood and held out his hand. "Will you dance with me?"

She took it, leaving their table and dinner behind. He led her a few feet away, where the floor was open. "There's no music," she said.

"I have a confession." His hand came around her waist, and with his other hand he ever so gingerly took her casted arm. "I don't know how to dance. No one ever taught me."

"You've never danced?"

"No, I've never danced before, and until this moment I've never minded." He moved his hand, bringing her closer to him. "I don't even know if this is right. I hope it is. I find I enjoy having you in my arms and close to me. If this is all I have to do, I say let's dance every day, all day."

"It's right for a waltz." She moved her hand up farther on his shoulder. His muscular build was hard to ignore with him so close. "My parents made sure I knew how to dance. It would be easier to teach you without my cast, but I can try."

"When I come back, you'll have to teach me. Until then, let me pretend I know what I'm doing." He swayed with her in his arms, and then he surprised her again by pressing his lips to her forehead, sending delight through her entire body. "I'll never tire of holding you."

He kissed her again in the same gentle way. She smiled at the warmth of his touch—how right it felt. She looked up when he pulled back, only to see a matching smile on his face. When she spoke, her voice came out in a far more alluring whisper than she'd intended. "I've another dream."

"You do?"

She nodded, swallowed, and tried to put the desire of her heart into words. "I've dreamed you'd . . . that you'd . . ."

"Tell me," he begged.

She let her hand wander from his shoulder to his neck and then to his cheek. His freshly shaved face was smooth to the touch. She stilled her hand but let her thumb graze his skin. "You'll think me brazen."

"No, I could never." He tilted his head down, and she lifted her chin and looked up at him. They were close enough that she could feel his breath on her skin. He moved closer still. She closed her eyes, afraid this wasn't real. And then she felt his lips find hers, and every nerve in her body reacted. Heat filled her from the tips of her toes to the crown of her head. She melted into him, loving the feel of his lips on hers. Quincy's touch was gentle, full of hope and the promise of deeper passion to come.

When he inched away from her, she could do nothing but smile. "Another dream," she whispered. "You are finding ways to make them all come true."

17

Quincy grinned as he walked the halls of the hotel. He couldn't stop . . . He didn't want to. Holding Norah, kissing Norah, loving Norah was the rightest thing he'd ever felt in his life. Reluctantly, he had walked her to her room and kissed her again at the door, lingering only a moment before stepping away with the promise to return from his travels as quickly as he could.

He needed to pack, write instructions for his employees, and look over his accounts so he knew exactly what he could offer Jake for his land. Mrs. Dover, with her eagle eyes, saw him before he reached his room and swooped in like a mighty bird of prey.

"I worked late," she said, justifying her presence before he had time to ask. "Besides, I wanted to hear about your night with Norah."

"Tell me, is it normal for a mother to attack her children with questions after they've escorted a woman to dinner?"

"Depends on the mother. But for this one, yes. All my children knew they were to tell me their good news and their bad news, and they knew they better not wait to tell me."

She leaned against the wall and folded her hands across her chest. "Does she love you back?"

He rubbed his jaw and nodded. Like a fool, he opened his mouth then shut it again, unable to form the words to describe the depth of his feelings and his hopes for the future. What he felt for Norah was more real than anything he had ever felt for anyone before, yet a war still raged within him. One side was begging him to go on living this fantasy—courting, kissing, and savoring Norah's love. The other side was reminding him again and again that he was in her debt and had to repay and repair what he'd done.

"Spit it out, boy." She chuckled under her breath. "Has she stolen your voice along with your heart?"

"I believe she has." He pushed both sides away and spoke. "I had hoped she could someday care for me. When I first met her, she was an angel beyond my reach, and now she is willing to love me back. If I were a more selfish man, I would take all her love and never look back. Perhaps I am selfish. We talked of romance and she spoke of her trust in me, and still I could not voice the truth."

"You may not have spoken your secret, but I think you found ways to tell her how you feel."

He laughed, convinced this woman knew him far too well. "I assure you that we did nothing improper, but you are right, she let me hold her. Everything about her feels right and begs me to crumble at her feet and love her always."

"But you won't, because you are a man of honor."

"Blast it all, I wish I weren't."

"Put yourself out of your misery and knock on her door and tell her the truth."

Tell her? He couldn't. He'd lose everything. Anger spiked

within, causing his voice to rise and come out terse. "The truth is, I love this woman. I want to care for her and make every dream she's ever had come true. Why can't that be enough?" He fisted his hands, frustrated with himself and the wretched secret he bore that he didn't know how to free himself of. "I'll buy her land. It'll be my retribution. Won't that set it right?"

"Only you know that." Mrs. Dover's voice was steady and soft. "I'll say nothing more about it, but before I do, I'll say this. It's better for you to tell your secret than have it told for you."

"No one knows." He tensed his jaw and through gritted teeth said, "And no one needs to. I'll tell her I worked hard for this hotel. That's not a lie. The rest can be left unsaid." He saw Mrs. Dover's disapproving look. "You don't like my plan to buy her land. You say it'll only stir the pot, yet you want me to tell her about a mistake I made two years ago. Think what that would do to her."

Her silence pricked his conscience, riddling him with guilt. He didn't want these chains or this endlessly heavy weight that followed him wherever he went. But freeing himself could mean losing her. He looked out the window and muttered, "I'm going to Blackwell. You don't have to like it, but I'm going."

"Quincy," she said, "I didn't mean to upset you. I wish, for your sake and for hers, that the past was different. She's good for you, and I don't want you to lose her."

"It's not just about my losing her. I want to be good for her too. But how can I be if she runs off all because I made a mistake?" He didn't know how to explain to her what was at stake—that both his and her happiness could be lost. The hotel, the café, the store—none of it mattered if she left. Here in Longfield, he could protect her and give her a good life filled with love. He cringed, recognizing the faults in his plan. When he gave Norah her beloved land, she might leave. No matter what he did, he could lose her.

Unwilling to rehash his rationale with Mrs. Dover, he changed the subject. "How is Irene?"

"She's downstairs. The doctor has seen to her. He's been paid and has agreed like always to keep things quiet."

"Have you told her our terms?"

"I have. She is ready to reform and make a new life, and she's agreed to keep your role in her recovery quiet. Poor thing, she's half-starved and more skittish than a deer." She patted his arm. "Be safe while you travel, and don't worry about anything here."

"I'll be safe."

She shooed him toward the door. "Go to bed, dream of Norah and the evening you shared. No use heading out with a load of worries. They'll be here for you when you get back. With time and wisdom, this will be sorted out."

"I hope you're right."

Each bump along the train tracks brought him closer to Blackwell, closer to Jake, and closer to Norah's land. He'd stayed up late the night before poring over his account books, not going to bed until well after midnight, and even then he'd been restless. If Jake resisted, Quincy could dangle more and more money in front of him, but even then, the man may not agree to his proposition. Quincy's businesses were doing well, but getting the land back might cost him the deed to one or all three of his properties in Longfield. A sore loss, but he was willing to risk it.

How would he tell Mrs. Dover, Alice, and everyone else that worked for him that their jobs were in jeopardy, left to the mercy of whoever bought his businesses? Livelihoods depended on him, but so did Norah's dreams and his restitution. A sickening tug this way and that battled inside of him. He finally settled the storm by telling himself that if he had to sell his businesses, he would go to great lengths to make sure they were sold to someone who would not deprive his employees of wages or proper working conditions. It was all he could do. He had to make things right with Norah.

When at last the train jerked to a stop, he disembarked and walked to the livery, where he rented a horse. The eight-mile ride to the farm was peaceful. The flat land, with its rich soil, stretched as far as the eye could see. He breathed deeply, savoring the smells, trying to connect with what it was Norah loved about this place. He wanted to understand so he knew what it was he was fighting for. Having never had a childhood home full of good memories, he did not understand her deep yearning for a place.

The farmhouse came into view, growing larger with each step his horse took, and soon the fields he traveled on were those tilled by Jake. He kicked his heels into his horse, anxious now to confront Jake and be done with his quest.

"Get off my land!" Jake came around from behind the house the moment Quincy slid off his horse.

"I will as soon as you hear me out."

"No." He turned toward his house and yelled, "You'll leave now!"

Quincy had never shied away from a fight, and he wasn't

about to mount his horse and take off before he'd even made his offer. "I got an offer to make."

"I said leave." Jake rubbed his jaw in the very spot Quincy had punched him the last time he was there. "Mary Beth, fetch my gun."

Quincy's defenses went up. "It doesn't have to be like this."

Jake didn't acknowledge him. His eyes were on the house. A woman emerged with a gun in her hands.

"I just want to talk." Quincy tried again to ease the tension in the air. "I want to make you an offer."

"I said no." Jake moved closer to Mary Beth, going for the gun. He didn't know Jake well enough to know if he was all talk and no action or if he'd fire the gun when he got to it. This was no time to find out.

Like an ox, he plowed into Jake, pushing him to the ground before he could get to Mary Beth and the gun. Jake landed on his stomach. He tried to roll over, but Quincy was quick, and in a single motion, he had Jake's hands pinned behind his back. When he was sure Jake couldn't free himself, he looked up at Mary Beth. She held the gun in her hands, shaking and looking between her husband and the house.

"Let him go," she said. "We don't want a fight. I have a baby, and that's his father."

"I won't hurt him. But I can't let him up until you put that gun somewhere far away."

Mary Beth stood still a moment, until Jake barked at her to put the gun away.

"I need to talk to you both, and then I'll go. It's a business matter." He tightened his grip on Jake and leaned close so Mary Beth couldn't hear. "I'm going to let you up, but if you start something, it'll be you who'll need a doctor." The part of Quincy that had thrived in the ring and loved the feel of wild rage racing through him was long gone. He wanted this over and handled peaceably.

"Let me up," Jake said, lifting his head from the ground enough that he could look at his young wife. Dirt covered the side of his face that had been pressed to the ground. Quincy waited. "Let me up. I won't fight you."

Quincy let him go. "I want to buy this place,"

Jake shook his head. "If we sell, we've got to start over somewhere. I'm not willing. I bought this land without breaking any laws, and I've been farming it since. Everyone in town will tell you that this is Granger land, and that's how it'll stay."

"Name your price." Quincy folded his arms across his chest and waited, unwilling to be the first to throw out numbers. "Don't tell me there isn't an amount big enough to get you to clear out."

"I'm not selling," he said again, his nose twitching like the weasel he was.

"Every man has a price."

"Fine." He smirked. "Four thousand dollars and not a cent less."

The price was much higher than the land and home were worth, but Quincy could do it. He'd have to sell one business for sure, maybe two, and drain his savings, but he could manage. He'd have to find a buyer and speak with the bank . . . the wheels of possibility spun in his head.

His wife took a step closer. "But Jake—"

"Let me handle this," he growled.

"It'll take time for me to get the money," Quincy said,

trying not to look at Mary Beth. "I'll write to you when I'm ready."

Jake wiped a hand across his forehead. Speechless, he stared at Quincy. "I thought I was getting a bargain buying this land from the bank when I did. It's turning out better than I ever hoped. Mary Beth, stop your whimpering. We'll be making a hefty profit."

His words sickened Quincy, but he said nothing. Driving the man off the land by other means would have been more satisfying, but Mary Beth, with her scared eyes, didn't deserve that and certainly the baby didn't. Still, he hated knowing Jake would profit from his heartless choices, pocketing money he hadn't earned and smirking as he walked away. It made Quincy's skin crawl thinking of it, but he'd learned that some battles weren't his to fight.

"When Norah moves back here, you leave her alone." Quincy glared, and Jake cowered under the threat, shrinking away from Quincy's clenched fists.

"I don't want anything to do with her," he said.

"Keep it that way." Quincy mounted his horse, knowing if he stayed longer, he would not be able to hold back the angst he felt. He expected to feel relief knowing he could give Norah what she'd lost, but he didn't. He kept seeing Mary Beth's scared eyes and thinking of his life in Longfield that would never be the same. It was a small price, though, to give Norah what he'd taken.

The ride back to Blackwell felt tedious and long, but the miles passed and soon enough he was back in Blackwell. He wired Mrs. Dover to let her know he would return in a few days. He kept the outcome of his visit with Jake to himself. He needed time to plan his next move and space to think through his options and make peace with what lay ahead. Rather than rush back, he stalled and decided to spend some time doing what he'd told Norah the trip was for—inspecting the inventory of other stores.

After all, his businesses weren't sold yet, and until they were, he'd treat them as he always had—with the finest care. And perhaps by the time he returned to Longfield, he would know how to give Norah the gift of her land and the freedom to truly choose her path.

18

"Do you always smile at nothing?" Alice asked as she walked beside Norah through the streets of Long-field. "It's Quincy, isn't it? Has he finally confessed his feelings?"

"What makes you think he cares for me?" Norah tried to force the corners of her mouth down so she could say she wasn't smiling, but they disobeyed by creeping up again. How could they not? She'd felt nothing but blissfully happy since the night before. "I only just learned for myself of his feelings."

"I think everyone who's seen the two of you together suspects it. I hear talk of it in the café, but mostly from jealous women." She swung the basket in her hand back and forth as they walked the quiet streets. "Quincy is the bachelor all the women have been pining over. You know that. You've seen him after church and at the hotel—everyone makes up an excuse to talk to him."

"What do these women say about me?"

"Only that they don't understand where you came from

or how you ensnared him." She laughed as though her words were all said in fun. "Don't fret over it."

"I didn't ensnare him." She looked up and down the main street at the other women who walked from shop to shop. Did they all think she was conniving? "I wish they wouldn't gossip about me."

"Forget I said anything. Quincy cares for you, and that's all that matters. He could have had these other women if he wanted them, but he didn't." Alice put a hand over her eyes, blocking the sun. "They're simply jealous because you've found such a good man and some of them haven't. But you can't feel guilty for finding love. Besides, you say you are old acquaintances, so you've known him longer than the women here anyway."

"We do share a bit of a past." Images of the broken man she saved from the birds filled her mind. What would the women of Longfield think if they'd seen him then? "I was always convinced he came into my life for a reason, but at the time I could not fathom what that reason was. There has always been something different about him. I think I have been smitten since the beginning."

"I've never been in love so I may be no help, but—"

"I was sure the reason you wanted independence so badly was because a man had hurt your heart." Norah could not keep the shock from her face.

"Men have hurt me." She shuddered. "But not in the way you're thinking. I never had a man court me." She pulled Norah down a small alley between two buildings. An unexpected urgency in her tread and her tone startled Norah. "I thought you and I were the same, but now I'm not certain. Did you not come here seeking a new start?"

"I . . . I did." She tripped over her words. "I was working at a saloon, the Whetted Whistle, before Quincy brought me here."

"The Whetted Whistle." Alice whispered the name. "You were one of Percy's girls." Her hand went over her mouth, and compassion and pity filled her eyes. "No, it can't be."

Norah had been able to bury her pain, cushioned by newer, sweeter memories, but now, here in this alleyway, she was going back to the sharp-edged pain.

"I did work there. He had plans to make me one of his girls." Norah swallowed. The words didn't want to come. Voicing such memories proved difficult. "I know about being hurt by men," she said at last in a hushed voice. "I know what their large fists and booted feet can do. It would have been worse, but Quincy came. Though I fear I will always be marked. Percy's girls, everyone knows . . ." She shook her head, but the memories were hard to shake away. "It seems like a lifetime ago. Here in Longfield with Quincy beside me, I feel like it was all just a bad dream."

"I'm glad he found you," Alice said. Norah looked away, unable for a moment to see anything but Warner Crossing and the Whetted Whistle. Alice's hand touched her arm, and her friend's soft voice brought her back to the present. "My parents died when I was fifteen. I went to live with an uncle I'd never met. He beat me, and then one night in a fit of rage he dropped me off at a brothel and told me it was time I made it on my own."

"Oh, Alice!" Norah stepped away from Alice and tried to catch her breath.

"I was there five years before I found a way to escape." She stood tall and proud. "I'm free of that now. We're both free."

"Does it ever come back? In your dreams, do you see the horrors?"

"Less often with every passing day. It seems every time someone speaks to me with respect or I am offered a piece of kindness, those nightmares lessen. When I talk to Sam, I cannot imagine him ever hurting another soul, and I find myself believing in the goodness of people again."

"I never had it so bad as you." Norah had still been in a loving home, although imperfect, full of kindness, at the age Alice was rejected and left to the mercy of others. "My injuries were not the same as yours. I was rescued before—"

"It doesn't matter," Alice said. "We don't have to compare the horrors we've seen. That's behind us now." Her eyes brightened. "Hearing you talk of Quincy makes me almost want to forgo Spinster Row myself."

"I think Alice Landon sounds rather nice." Norah squealed, her joy fuller as she imagined it shared with her friend. She'd felt a kinship with Alice from the start, but now knowing that they had both survived the darkness, she felt the bond of sisterhood grow stronger. "Sam would make a fine husband."

"Oh, Sam. I've never been so smitten by a man, but don't you go telling him that. It's ridiculous. I ask myself all the time, How can it be? How can I feel so utterly giddy over an ordinary man like Sam?" Alice tipped her head back and sighed. "Giddy or not, what would he do if he knew what I was? It's better to feel nothing."

"I believe he is a man with a heart big enough to see your true worth."

"Perhaps, or perhaps it's best I cling to my dreams of a small house and a kitchen of my own. There's less risk in that." She started back for the main street with Norah at her heels. "I can cook—that's a skill my mama gave me before passing. It's a good enough life, working at the café, being friends with you. What if I never told him?"

"It would never do," Norah said, wishing it weren't so. "Both parties have to be honest."

In silent reflection they walked together on the dusty streets, content with quietly sharing one another's burdens. A group of children skipped across the street, their lunch tins swinging and braids dancing as they went. At ease and unaware of the bumps that may one day riddle their path.

Norah's gaze lingered on them until they were out of sight. She looked toward the hotel, admiring once again the success Quincy had found. Her look of admiration was cut short. There ahead of her was a man walking toward them. He looked familiar. She stared harder, only to feel an acute sense of dread overtake her.

Alice stopped walking. "What is it?"

Norah grabbed her hand and pulled her behind a wagon. "I saw someone." She dared a look around the side of the wagon, hoping she was wrong and her mind was simply playing tricks on her because of their recent conversation about the past. But what she'd seen had not been her imagination. Her gaze locked with the tall man's, and recognition flared in his eyes. His lip curled into a wicked grin, and his long legs increased their pace.

"I have to get away!"

"Come on!" Alice pulled her across the street, into the café, and out the back door. "We'll lose him and then go into the hotel through the lean-to."

Norah tightened her grip on her friend's hand, looking behind her every few steps. Twice she thought she saw the man, but they moved quickly, cutting through shops and down alleys. Her heart beat faster with each step, but she didn't slow.

"I can't stay at the hotel," she said when they were near enough to the lean-to that they could smell the scent of lye soap. With her fears ignited, she could hear her heart thumping in her ears. "I could take the train." She kept her voice low. "I could go farther west. Montana or the Dakotas."

"Tell me who we are running from," Alice whispered back before pushing the door open and stepping into the hotel with Norah at her heels.

Norah closed the door behind her with more force than necessary, locked it, and leaned against it. They were safe, at least for a moment. "One of Percy's friends. He's here, and he saw me. The way he looked at me—" She shivered. "I don't want to leave here, but if Percy comes . . . he'll take me back." She pressed a hand to her forehead. This couldn't be happening. "Or he'll kill me."

Mrs. Dover stepped into the damp laundry room like a fox ahead of the hunt, quick and with purpose. Both girls jumped at the sound of her bustling in. "Nels said he saw you sneaking about town. He said you were white as a sheet." She shuffled across the floor to Norah and grabbed her hand. "Come on, let's go to the kitchen and you can tell me what's going on."

"We can talk here."

"I got knives and rolling pins in the kitchen, and I know enough to realize you're in trouble. Come on."

Norah followed, whispering about the man as they made their way to the kitchen. Mrs. Dover's eyes grew larger with each uttered word. After Norah described his looks,

Mrs. Dover put her hand on her heart and said, "Oh dear, I checked that man into the hotel earlier today. He's staying here. Said his name was Amos Pritchard. I didn't know a thing about him. I should have turned him away."

"It's not your fault." Norah put a hand on Mrs. Dover's arm. "Amos is not a good man. It's not safe for me here." Mrs. Dover's concerned face increased Norah's resolve. She had to go. She could not put her dear friends in danger. "I'll go, and then you'll be safe."

"If only Quincy were here," Mrs. Dover said, wringing her hands. "I told him I'd look after you."

"We don't have time to debate. He's in town, and he saw me. If he sees me with you, then you could all be in danger."

"He's already seen me," Alice said, her voice strong. "Most likely he's passing through. We can hide in Longfield somewhere, and all will be well in a few days."

"You could go to your room and stay there until Quincy is back," Mrs. Dover suggested. "I'd send meals."

"No." Norah flinched. "I will not be locked in a room again." She would never again cower in the corner. An idea formed, and with so little time to debate its merits, she spoke it. "We'll send Nels to get Sam. We'll ask him if he will help us. No one would suspect us of going out to his farm. You said it was out of town, and he drives such a large wagon, we can easily hide in the back. Do you think he'd help?"

Alice nodded. "He'll help. I know he will."

Nels agreed to find Sam, scampering off and promising to return as fast as he could. True to his word, he returned twenty minutes later. He stopped in the doorway and stared with furrowed brows at the women and the rolling pins in their hands. "You aiming to fight with those?"

"If we have to," Alice said. "Is he coming?"

Nels nodded, then he snuck to the ice box and pulled out a piece of cheese. He took a bite and licked his lips. "I think Mrs. Dover worries too much. But you're gonna be fine, right?"

"She worries because she cares," Norah said. She ran her hand over the smooth wood of the rolling pin. "I hope to be safe."

"I got bad men in my past too," he said, staring at the cheese in his hand. "I never worried they'd track me down. Besides, I've grown half a foot, so no one would even recognize me." He smiled at Norah. "You weren't very pretty when you came, but you look fine now. No one would recognize you either."

"Pretty or not, someone *did* recognize me." Norah looked at the door, her guard up, ready. "Where's Sam?"

"He had to hitch his wagon, but he's coming. He told me to hurry back and tell you he's on his way."

Alice stood by the window and pulled the curtain back ever so slightly.

Nels looked at her then back at Norah. "Seems like a long way to go chasing after somebody."

"He might not have come to town looking for me, but now he's seen me." Norah wanted to promise Nels that she'd be safe and life could go on as before, but that would have been a lie. Life had shown her that peace could be disrupted in an instant. What could she promise? "Nels." His eyes found hers. "I am not like your pa. I'm going away, but I'm going to do everything I can to come back and be with you."

"People are always leaving." His chin quivered, and her heart quivered with it.

"Don't worry about me."

"I will worry about you." He set down his cheese, wiped his hands on his pants, and came closer to her. She met him halfway and took him into her arms. Her stomach twisted into a knot. She did not want to leave this boy. "You need to stay with Mrs. Dover," she said in an urgent whisper. "Promise me that you will stay with her and then with Quincy when he comes back?"

He nodded. "I'd rather be with you."

"I want to be with you too." She bent down so she could look him right in the eye. She kept her hands on his shoulders, not wanting to let go just yet. "No matter what happens, you have to remember that you are smart and good. Promise me that you will keep working on your letters." The tears came then, racing down her face. She didn't bother to wipe them, since doing so would require her to let go of Nels and she wasn't ready.

"I promise." His big eyes held hers. "You will come back?"

"If it's safe to." She looked between Nels and Alice. Alice let go of the curtain and came closer. "I'm really sorry."

"They're the bad ones, not you," Alice said, her voice unwavering.

"I signed a contract," Norah said. "I agreed to work at the Whetted Whistle. No one cares that I signed because I was starving."

"I don't care what you signed," Alice said. "Don't blame yourself, you hear me."

Norah nodded, grateful to be fighting this fear with friends.

beside her. With kitchen tools in hand, they waited, Nels by her side like a chick to a mama hen.

Mrs. Dover returned from gathering a few of Norah's belongings. "I ought to send Quincy a telegram."

"Do you know where he is?" Norah asked.

"Blackwell." Mrs. Dover's eyes went wide. She gasped and covered her mouth. "Oh dear."

Norah stood. "Blackwell?"

Mrs. Dover's hand fluttered near her face. "He had other stops too. I could send a telegram to one of the hotels he said he might be at, but I'm not sure it'd do any good."

"Don't send word." Norah paced the wide plank floor. "Then Jim at the post office would know we were in trouble, and word could spread. It's better we keep this to ourselves."

"Why don't we tell the sheriff?" Nels asked. "Then you wouldn't have to go away from us, and he could lock up this man you're so afraid of."

"I wish it were that simple," Norah said. "But Amos hasn't done anything wrong yet. The judge can't lock up a man just because we're worried." To Mrs. Dover she said, "If Amos tries to track me down and starts asking questions around here, tell him you don't know where I ran off to. Tell him I'm flighty."

"I'm not one to lie, but I'll find a way to keep him from sniffing out your scent. You'll be safe, and Quincy will be back soon."

19

Mrs. Dover hugged Norah tight before leaving for the front desk so she could keep her eyes on all that was happening in the hotel. She dragged the resistant Nels along with her. He didn't want to go, but Norah felt better having him near Mrs. Dover, so he went.

"Don't worry," Alice said with her rolling pin still in hand.

"I worry I will always be looking over my shoulder, afraid Percy will come back."

Alice opened her mouth to speak, but Norah wasn't finished. "And how long before this town knows my past? Amos may go to the saloon tonight and tell everyone that I was one of Percy's girls. No one will care about the particulars. They'll look at me with scorn and refuse to sit by me at church. I know what gossiping tongues can do. I may have lost my chance at happiness in Longfield."

Alice did not argue. There would be no sense in it. "We will stay at Sam's until Quincy returns. You have to at least wait for him."

Norah nodded, hating the thought of leaving her new friends and the blossoming love she'd only just found.

Circumstances had torn them apart once. She didn't want to accept it, but it seemed inevitable that they would again, leaving her and Quincy moving in different directions, farther and farther from each other.

Norah and Alice waited in silence for Sam and his wagon. When he at last opened the door, he removed his hat and rushed inside. "I've brought my wagon. Tell me what's going on."

Alice took the liberty of telling a rushed and abbreviated version of all that had happened, beginning with Norah's past and finishing with her being recognized. Norah cringed as the gritty details were exposed. They ricocheted around the room, filling it with persistent looming. But they were the truth, and anyone willing to help needed to know. Alice finished the tale and they both waited, Norah silently hoping Sam would feel the heaviness in the air and be willing to aid them in their plight.

He rubbed the back of his neck and shook his head. "Oh my, Norah, I'm sorry you got all this trouble following you. You don't need to be running off though. We'll figure something out."

"We all hope she doesn't have to leave for good. But she may have to run and start over, all because some evil man decided to try to own her."

"But it's not her fault." Sam reached for Alice, laying a tentative hand on her shoulder. "Norah doesn't have to hide forever, just until we know she's safe. After that, we'll tell folks how bad it was, and they'll understand. Some of them will, at least."

"You don't understand," Alice whispered. "When people find out a woman has a past, they see her differently. If you found out a woman in town had a past as a tainted woman or some other unseemly profession, would it not change how you saw her?"

Norah held her breath, knowing what Sam said now was far more important than he knew.

Sam looked from Norah to Alice, gripping the hat in his hands tightly. "I suppose I'd want to know why, and I'd want to know if she was hurt or if she was wanting that life. I guess it'd change things, but not everything."

"Could you love a woman like that?" Alice asked, her pleading eyes never leaving his face.

Sam backed up, bumping into the wall. "Alice," he said in a hushed voice, "I don't love Norah. It's got nothing to do with what she's been through."

"Quincy loves Norah. We both know that," Alice snapped at Sam. She let out an exasperated sigh. "Forget I said anything. We need to get out of here."

Sam, now red in the face, nodded. "I got my wagon out there. Let's go."

The women crawled into the back and sat deep in the shadows where they could not be seen. Norah whispered, "You were rather forward."

"I don't know what came over me. Maybe it's because I'm not sure I want to live on Spinster Row." She grabbed Norah's arm. "Did you see him sweating?"

"Be careful or you'll scare him off." She laced her arm through her friend's and leaned back against the rough wooden boards as the wagon bounced over the bumpy road away from Longfield.

"I'm going to sleep in the barn," Sam said after they'd walked into the house. Norah had been mostly silent as he showed them around. "If you need something, let me know."

"Thank you," Norah said. He nodded, grabbed a blanket, and started to go, only to have Alice follow after him out onto the porch. Norah remained behind, hoping her friend would be able to coax the man from his shell so they could both find the happiness they were so near grasping.

While Norah waited for Alice to return, she inspected the house. It was well built and free of drafts despite the windy weather. The woodwork throughout testified of the owner's occupation and skills. Norah ran her hand along the smooth built-in shelving and the side table with its detailed inlays. The craftsmanship was exceptional, like the furniture Sam built for the hotel and the work he did on both the store and the café. He was certainly a man of detail, not so unlike Alice, who went to great lengths to make the café meals not only hearty but also rich and flavorful.

When Alice still did not return, Norah crept to the bed she'd been told was hers for the night and attempted to sleep, but her mind would not slow down enough for her to drift from consciousness to sleep. The thought of having to start over again without Quincy beside her . . . She shuddered. She did not want to leave him.

"Norah." Alice's voice roused her from her troubled thoughts. "I'm sorry I was gone so long."

Norah pushed herself up in the bed, curling her knees tight against herself. "I'm glad you were able to spend time with him." She yawned and said, "Sam has a fine house."

Alice sat on the edge of the bed and ran her hand over the quilted bedspread, pausing to pick at a loose thread. "I agree."

"Did he stay quiet the whole time you were out there? Or did you force the poor man to talk?"

"We were silent at first, but I didn't mind. Sometimes it's peaceful just sitting beside someone. But then I started thinking about how I liked sitting beside him, and I wanted to know if my past was going to make him turn tail and run." Alice fell back on the bed and looked up at the ceiling. "He kept starting to talk and then stopping. And I finally said, 'Sam, I want to court you and maybe even be the woman to stick around, but I have a past and it's an awful one.'"

"You said that?"

"I did. I figured if he threw me out, I could run off with you and we could go west and begin again. No doubt Oregon has enough land for us to form our Spinster Row."

"But he did listen to you." Norah smiled into the darkness. "You won't be living on Spinster Row, will you?"

"He said when I was ready, he'd like to hear about my life. Then he told me about the girl he loved when he was young. And about a woman he offered marriage to out in the Dakota Territory. She ended up marrying her childhood love instead of him." Alice sighed and turned toward Norah. "He threw himself into his work after that, afraid to try again. He's been a bit of a recluse ever since."

"It's hard to imagine him being turned down."

"He wasn't sad when he told me. He took my hand and held it. Then we sat like that, neither of us talking." She sat up, eyes sparkling in the dim moonlight that shone through the window. "I stood up to leave, and he stood too. He walked me to the door, and then he put his hand on my cheek. It was so gentle, nothing like the way men touched me before. I wasn't afraid of him, and then he said he was sorry I'd suffered."

"Oh my, how romantic, don't you think?"

"It wasn't even a kiss, but I could feel so much in his touch. I told him he was a good man. He told me he hoped I had a good night, and then I came inside." Alice sucked in her bottom lip before saying, "I don't like not knowing how it will end. I've been fighting for years so I could be in control of what happens in my life and be free of men. And now I'm afraid I've just invited one in. He could hurt me."

"I don't think he'd ever hurt you."

"Not with his hands, but he could break my heart. I've never been in love before." She groaned. "I'm afraid and excited all at the same time."

"There's a chance, though, that you won't get hurt. That you'll get to have a life with a very quiet carpenter. A man who will sit by you on the porch and look at the stars." Norah sighed. "I bet he'd plant lilacs right outside the front door if you asked him to."

"Nothing's settled yet. Sam only held my hand." She slid into bed and shoved the pillow under her head. "But I think I'll dream about it tonight."

Quincy stepped off the train platform with a sense of relief. Being back in Longfield, no matter what awaited him, felt like coming home. Four days away felt like far too long.

He decided to stop at the café and talk to Alice about Irene and see if there was a chance she could train a new server. He found the door locked. He cupped his hand and peered through the window. All was dark and quiet.

Confused, he headed to the hotel, anxious to see if Mrs. Dover could tell him why the café was closed. Nothing else alarming caught his eye as he made his way through Longfield, but alarms were going off in his head. Something was amiss . . . but what?

"Mrs. Dover," he said after cornering her in the hall. "The café is closed."

She put a hand to her lips and hissed for him to be quiet, grabbed his hand, and pulled him away from the main lobby. They stepped into his office, and she immediately began telling him the tragic tale that had transpired since his departure. "They've been at Sam's since. She's worried Percy will catch wind of where she is and come get her. I'm worried she'll run off. Nels is worried too."

"Where is this man?" Quincy said through gritted teeth. "Tell me where he is. I'll take care of this."

"You can't go back to fighting. Besides, he checked out this morning. He was still staggering from whatever he drank last night, but he took his bags. I say good riddance. I got a bad feeling whenever he was around."

"Did he say anything to you about Norah?"

"No, not a word. But it makes no difference. He saw her, and he may tell Percy."

"He might forget he ever saw her. She's nothing special to him."

"How will we know? She'll never be at peace if she's always worrying." Mrs. Dover sniffled loudly. "It's just not right. The two of you were going to be so happy."

He rubbed his jaw. He didn't want setbacks or Norah fleeing. He didn't even like the idea of her heading back to Blackwell, but at least then she was going home and not running to who-knew-where. "Keep an eye out for Amos. I need to know if he comes back." He moved for the door. "I'm going to ride out to Sam's and beg Norah to give us time before she does something irrational." He flexed his muscles as though a foe were about to swing at him. "She can't run forever. She needs to pick the future she wants and then face it."

"She can't."

"What do you mean? I'll find a way to end her worries over Percy." His voice was gruff and thick. "She told me long ago that anyone can have a fresh start. That includes her."

"She can't decide on a future when you've kept the details of the past from her."

He moved by her. "I'm going out to Sam's."

"Wait."

He stopped. "I don't have time to stand here and listen to the mistakes I made repeated over and over again. I'm doing what I can for her."

"For you. You're doing what you can for you. You don't want to lose her, but don't you understand that you'll never really have her if you don't tell her the truth? Tell her all of it. Tell her about the basement and about the money. Let there be no secrets."

"I can't," he said without looking at her. "Did the doctor see to Irene?"

"She's settled and recovering. Go see to Norah."

20

Norah slowed her walk and looked out at the farm-land, admiring the straight fence posts and well-kept bushes near the house. Sam's farm was small, with a garden and a chicken coop. Beside the house a large workshop provided the setting for his business. Sam's dog, Dakota, walked beside her, giving her a sense of security as she ventured the short distance on her own, leaving Alice and Sam to explore his woodshop together.

"Your master keeps his land up." She patted the dog's head. "I had land once. It was vast and golden."

He barked once and then again. Norah blocked the sun with her hand and tried to see what caught the dog's attention. A rider.

"Come on." She started back toward the house, urging the dog to follow. When he did not, she looked once more toward the still-distant man on horseback. Her racing heart skipped a beat as it switched from fear to relief. The rider was Quincy!

She switched directions and ran toward him on swift, un-wavering legs. They met at the edge of Sam's land with the sun beating on them and the wind blowing through her hair. Quincy slid from his horse. "You're still here. You didn't leave."

"I couldn't . . . not without seeing you."

He closed the distance, his smile spreading wider with each step. And then his hand was at her waist, his touch firm but kind as he wrapped his arms around her. "I was afraid." His voice cracked. "When Mrs. Dover told me—"

"I'm here." She brought a hand to his cheek before saying, "I couldn't leave you, not like that, but he may come back. I don't know what to do. Percy doesn't like losing."

His large body towered over her, strong like a pillar of protection, shrinking the fears that had gripped her so tightly since Amos had seen her. She leaned against his chest, savoring the feel of him. Leaving him would mean losing that comfort. She cringed and buried herself deeper in his arms.

Without letting her go, he said, "He can't have you."

"I signed a contract," she sobbed into his chest. "I left. I broke it."

"He was trying to break you." He pulled away from her and looked into her eyes. "He broke his own contract when he treated you like chattel."

"He's not good like you," she whispered. "He doesn't care about right and wrong. He's a liar who cares about profits and power, that's all."

"The law there—"

"The sheriff in Warner Crossing knows Percy, and he's never done anything about him." She looked past him, toward the distant horizon.

He pulled her close again and buried his head in her hair. "He's taken enough. He can't have any more."

"What then? I've thought it all through and can't think of a way to live free in Longfield." With her head against his chest, she could feel his heart thumping a rhythm so melodic, so enchanting, she wanted to forget the world and lose herself to the gentle beat.

"I will think of something. I promise you that. Until then, I'll stay close so you don't have to worry." His hold on her eased, and his heartbeat slowed. "Where is Sam?"

"He's in his workshop with Alice." She smiled then, her worries set aside as she thought of her friend's happiness. "So much has happened."

"Tell me."

"Alice is not a docile woman. You know this, of course. She acted boldly, and now the two of them are courting." She laughed, thinking again of all that had transpired between her fiercely independent friend and the good-natured Sam. "I suppose it's not very traditional, but I found it amusing. And, Quincy, it was beautiful."

"He knows about her past?" Quincy stilled, his face alarmed. "Did she tell him?"

"You know?"

He rubbed his face and walked a few steps from her, where he stooped to pet the dog. "I do."

"How?"

"I met Alice when she first came to town, and she told me what led her to Longfield. I didn't tell you because . . . well, for one, it wasn't my story to tell—"

"Why else?"

"I have rooms in the basement of the hotel. They aren't rented out to guests. I let her stay there for a while before she moved into Mrs. Dover's loft." He straightened and looked off at the horizon. "You took me in. You gave me a new start."

"And so you did that for Alice?"

"And others. Not often. But the word got out, and when someone comes needing a haven, I do what I can. I keep it quiet, letting them live free of the stain of whatever they are running from."

Warmth, sweet and comforting, filled her. Quincy's quiet charity touched her to her very core. He was a good man, she'd known it from the start, and this only further strengthened her belief that Quincy Barnes was a man of honor. "I feared you had a secret, but this . . . Well, it's a good secret. Thank you," she whispered, "for trusting me with it." She pressed her hand to her heart. "I won't speak of it to others, but I'm glad I know. I believed you were a good man, but truly, you are a man of honesty and charity."

He stepped away from her touch, grabbed the reins of his horse, and yanked on them. "Let's go and find Sam and Alice," he growled.

What had changed? Norah watched his back a moment before racing to catch up to him. When they stepped into the woodshop, her eyes struggled to adjust to the dim light. When at last they did, she smiled at Alice, who sat atop a workbench, seemingly relaxed and at home, with Sam nearby sanding the leg of a table.

Quincy broke the silence. "Thanks for keeping Norah safe while I was away."

Sam smiled at Alice and offered her a hand down from her perch. "It was my pleasure."

"And mine," Alice said. "Norah may have told you, but Sam and I are officially courting. He practically begged me."

Everyone laughed at her coy comment. Quincy slapped Sam on the back. "Glad you finally got brave enough to ask."

Sam shrugged. "Alice can be a hard woman to resist."

More laughter, and for several minutes the world felt right. She was in a room full of friends, her heart still swollen from happiness, knowing this man beside her was charitable in quiet, noble ways.

Despite his happiness for Sam and Alice, Quincy didn't want to stand around dwelling on it when there were big problems to solve and more confessions to make. He kicked himself for being an idiot and not laying it all on the table when he told Norah about Alice and his role in helping her get settled in Longfield. Telling her that hadn't been hard, not really. In fact, he hadn't thought of it as a secret at all. With so many of his basement guests coming from violent circumstances or bawdy houses, he'd gotten used to not speaking of it unless there was call to. The basement rooms had been vacant since she'd come, giving him no reason to discuss his philanthropy.

After offering a few congratulations to the newly courting couple, he told them Amos had checked out of the hotel and suggested they return to town. Alice and Sam seemed reluctant, but they nodded and went to ready the wagon. Norah was quieter and looked at him with pleading eyes.

"I'm sorry for earlier," he said when they were alone. "Knowing you feel afraid and have thought about leaving doesn't sit well with me."

"It's more than that," she said. "Something changed after you told me about the people you've helped. If you're worried that I'll tell others, I won't. I'd like to help you care for them if you'll let me."

"Let's get back to the hotel." He took her hand and led her away from the woodshop. "A woman named Irene came seeking help right before I left town. A preacher who knew I would help sent her to the hotel. We can see to her needs . . . together."

She squeezed her hand tightly around his. "I would like that."

21

An hour alone with Irene in the small basement bedroom was enough for Norah to be converted to Quincy's cause, for surely it was a cause that belonged to the Lord as well. She put a cool cloth on the woman's perspiring head and spoke words of assurance to her, promising that all would be well soon.

Quincy had left them alone together, returning later with news that eased both of their minds. The ticket master confirmed that Amos had indeed left town. For the moment they could relax. Quincy also brought the doctor back with him so he might evaluate Irene's health again. Norah and Quincy stood together in the hall, waiting to hear what the doctor would say about Irene's recent spiking fever and chills.

"How many people have you helped?" Norah asked in a hushed voice.

He scratched his head. "I don't know, maybe seven or eight. One night the preacher came and asked me if I would put a lost soul up in one of my rooms. I agreed, and we decided that it'd be easier if we let her recover quietly. After that, every couple of months someone else would show up."

"You took me in too—and Nels."

"That was different. You were not an act of charity. Taking you in . . . it was selfish. I wanted you to be near me not only so you could heal but also so I could spend time with you." He took her hand, then brought it to his lips and kissed it. "I wanted you here because everything is better with you nearby."

"I've a confession." She pulled their clasped hands to her lips and kissed his knuckles. "When I thought of leaving, I didn't want to go because you are the best friend I've ever had."

He shifted his weight, refusing to look her in the eyes. Why was a shadow looming over them in this perfect moment? She could see a hesitancy, a battle raging inside him, but she could not understand its origins. She kissed his hand again, willing him to feel the growing love she had for him, but he pulled away.

"Will you go to my office and get money for the doctor? It's in the bottom drawer. I'll wait here to talk to him."

"I'll hurry back."

"Thank you," he said as she scurried off, eager to help.

She stepped inside his large, well-furnished office and paused. She'd been inside this room several times before but never alone. She was always with Quincy. Without him here, she could take the room in with no distractions. He was organized, his correspondences stacked in neat piles. She picked up a few letters and fanned through them, amazed again that her once beaten and directionless friend had found himself in a position of importance.

She touched the top of the chair he so often sat in, then ran her hand along the desk, stopping her investigation of the tidy office only when she thought of Irene and the doctor and her promise to hurry. Forgetting which drawer he'd told her to look in, she opened the top one first.

A happy warmth seeped through her veins at the sight of her letter asking him to dance—he'd kept it. She picked it up, letting the memory of his hands around her and the kisses they'd shared come rushing back. Beneath it was an envelope. She looked over her shoulder, assuring herself she was alone, before she picked it up.

Norah Granger was written across the front in Quincy's crooked scrawl. She'd almost become Norah Granger. Could this missive be for her? Forgetting her need to rush, she sat back in the large office chair and studied the envelope in her hands.

It'd been opened before. She could tell by the broken seal. With access to it so easy, she pulled the contents out, only to have money fall in her lap. Shocked, she grabbed the money and quickly shoved it into the top drawer. With hungry eyes, she began reading the letter, hoping for answers to this new mystery.

Dear Norah,

It's been over a year since I walked away from your land. Bandaged by your hand, I was dressed in your father's clothes and determined to start over. I want you to know that I did begin my life again. I found honest work, I read my Bible, and I have tried to treat people with the same compassion you showed me. I'm not nearly as good-natured as you, so don't go thinking I've become some perfect gentleman. I am not, but I am a better man, and I have no one but you and the Lord to thank for that.

*One thing weighs on me. That is not true, many
things do, but one more than all others.*

Several words were crossed out. She held the paper closer
to her, wanting to know what he'd scratched out and why, but
she couldn't decipher what was written beneath the smeared
ink. She sighed, reminding herself it was not likely a confession of love since this letter was dated and written when
Quincy believed her to be a married woman. Giving up on
the scratched words, she read on.

*Nearly two weeks after walking away, I looked through
the bag you packed me. I should have done so earlier,
but I was caught up in healing and surviving. I worked
whatever day labor jobs I could find and tried to make
a plan for my life, but mostly I wandered. I regret not
looking sooner. Had I done so, perhaps so much could
have been different. Within the pocket of your father's
trousers, I found money. I pray you'll keep reading and
that somehow my words will help you know that I am
sorry. I used the money to begin again. I told myself you
would want that for me, that you were secure and your
needs met in your new marriage. I bought a business, and
then every penny I made was carefully saved or invested
until now. I am enclosing double the amount I found.*

Norah stopped reading. Her mind raced back over the
timeline he'd written of and the choices he'd made. Her
breath caught in her chest as the consequences of his actions
sunk in. All the pain, the mistreatment, the begging could
have been avoided.

Her father had likely taken that money with him to gamble. It was the only explanation she could think of for why she'd never known it existed. It took a concerted effort, but she read the rest of the letter, unsure if any words could right all that was wrong.

> *I beg you to forgive me. Use this money for your farm and your family. If this is not enough to make restitution, send word. I'm in Longfield, Iowa, and will send more at a moment's notice. I wronged you, and the burden weighs heavy on my conscience. I pray for your forgiveness.*
>
> > *With remorse,*
> > *Quincy*

One moment Norah wanted to tear the paper to shreds, but then the next she felt his anguish and only wished she could undo it all and save them both from the heartache they'd suffered.

Nels burst through the door. "You're back, and you didn't come find me!"

"Nels!" She shoved the letter in her dress pocket and went to him. "I'm sorry. I should have. I was helping Quincy with something, but the whole time I was wishing to see you. I kept thinking about you and hoping you stayed out of mischief while I was away."

"I did. Weren't easy though, with Mrs. Dover making me do all kinds of chores for her. What's wrong with you? You got that splotchy red face again."

"I think what I need," she said, spreading her arms, "is a hug from you."

He stepped into her arms and let her hold him. How good it felt to have this sweet, precocious child in her arms. She kissed his forehead before letting him go.

"I don't want you to go away again," he said, letting a sob escape.

She brought him back in and hugged him tighter.

He wriggled free of her grasp. "Quincy said to run up here and see what's taking you so long. He said the doctor's ready to leave."

"Oh," she groaned as she grabbed the money from the desk and handed it to him. "Take this to him. Tell him I'm not feeling well."

He cocked his head. "You don't look sick."

"Just tell him, will you?"

He agreed, looked her over once more, then shrugged and ran off with the money. Norah watched him go before carefully making her way through the hotel to her room, where she bolted her door and tried to make sense of the words she'd read.

"Here's the money." Nels thrust it into Quincy's waiting hand. "I'm supposed to tell you that Norah's not feeling well, and she's not coming back down here right now."

"She's sick?" Quincy turned to the doctor. "Did she seem sick to you?"

"She seemed fine to me. Perhaps it's a womanly problem." He took the money and put it in his pocket, unaffected by the turn of Norah's health. "I'll see myself out."

Quincy said goodbye to the doctor, then turned his attention to Nels. "Do you know what's wrong with Norah?"

"She was in your office when I got there. She did look like something was wrong, but she said it was missing me. I don't think that would make her sick though." He scratched his ear. "I did miss her too. I was worried when Mrs. Dover said Norah might go away."

Quincy put a hand on the boy's small shoulder. "You did a good job here while I was gone. No need to worry. I'll take care of things."

"But if she goes . . . I wanted things to stay good. But they never do."

"They will be good." He saw himself again in this child. He could remember the many nights he dreamed of happiness in his home and in his future. Over and over he'd hoped someone would promise him love and stability. Was Norah right? Did Nels need more than a job and a friend? Did he need a family? He put a hand under Nels's chin and with gentle force had the boy look into his eyes. "Nels, I don't want you to worry. When I invited you to the hotel to help and to sit by Norah, I thought it was just so you wouldn't be begging for your meals. But I think, if you're willing, it could be for something more."

"What do you mean?"

Quincy took a deep breath. "I'd like to be your pa. I want you to live here with me, go to school, and not worry again if there will be someone around to take care of you at the end of the day. I've never been a pa before, so we'd have to learn together, but, well, why don't you think on it."

Nels burst into tears, his tough demeanor gone. Sobbing, he fell into Quincy's arms. "You want to be my pa?"

"If you'll have me."

He didn't speak, but his head bobbed against Quincy's

shoulder. Quincy closed his eyes, wondering if this decision was foolhardy or as right as it felt.

"I'll have to talk to a judge and see what we have to do to make it official. Why don't you run and tell Mrs. Dover, and I'll check on Norah and tell her."

"Are you going to marry her so I'll have a pa and a ma?"

"I don't know," he said. "It would be nice to have a mama and papa, wouldn't it? But even if it's just you and me, we'll get by."

"We sure would, but I think you ought to ask Norah."

"Go on." He laughed. "Go find Mrs. Dover."

Nels scampered off, his step light and carefree like a boy's gait ought to be. He wondered what Mrs. Dover would say. She was forever worrying about the boy, but would she think Quincy a suitable answer to their many worries? And what would Norah think? He believed she'd be relieved. After all, she had been the first to realize how badly the boy needed a family of his own, but never once had she suggested it be him.

He knocked on her door, still not sure how he would tell her.

"Is that you, Quincy?" she said through the door. "I don't feel well."

"Open the door so I can see what's wrong and help." He smiled at a couple who walked nearby on the way to their room. "Norah, I can't talk to you through the door. Open up. I've got news."

"I really can't talk right now," she said again.

"The doctor said perhaps you were having women's troubles. Is that it?" he said in a loud voice so she could hear him through the door.

The door flew open. "Quincy, you can't go shouting something like that in the hallway for everyone to hear."

"I asked you to open the door."

She grabbed his arm and pulled him into her room, then slammed the door behind him. "You are the most infuriating man I've ever met."

Rather than offer a defense, he simply watched her pace the floor. Nothing about her seemed sickly. In fact, she paced with gusto.

"What in tarnation is wrong with you?" he said when she didn't stop. "You were perfectly happy in my arms less than an hour ago, and now you won't even look at me. And I need you to. I have news, and I think you'll want to hear it."

"About Irene?"

"No, she's been given something for her fever and is sleeping. It's about Nels."

At last she faced him. "What about Nels?"

"You told me he needed a family. I've found him one."

"Oh"—she stopped moving altogether and clutched her middle—"you did?"

"Yes. I think you were right. He was worried when we were gone, and he shouldn't have to worry about being deserted. He needs someone committed to him as he grows, someone willing to teach him and show him how to be a man."

"I do think he needs that," she whispered. "But I can't imagine him anywhere else." She tensed. "Oh, I don't know if I can bear it. Nels is so dear to me. If he leaves . . . But I suppose if I am gone too . . . But that's selfish of me. Of course I want him to have a family."

"You're making me nervous. You're rambling like a fretting old woman."

She glared at him. "You can't walk in and tell me you found a family for my boy and not expect me to fret. What if whoever takes him in doesn't care enough and he grows up a regular heathen?"

"I think he's bound to end up a tad vulgar and only half a gentleman, but I plan to do my best by the boy." Quincy grinned then. "I've asked him if I can be his pa."

"You?" Her hand went to her heart, and a muffled laugh escaped. "You're going to adopt Nels and be his father?"

"Laugh all you like, but I will do my best. I'll probably let him get away with too much mischief, and I might teach him how to throw punches just in case he ever needs to, but I also plan to teach him to care about others and to be honest."

"Honest . . ." Her laughter died away. Her hand that had once been fidgety now went to her pocket, crinkling something within the folds of her skirts. "Are you honest, Quincy?"

He took a step back, bumping into the wall. "I try to be. I didn't tell you about the ladies I helped in the basement, but I wasn't meaning to keep it from you."

"What about before that? Were you honest with me about everything else?"

"No. I haven't been perfectly honest." He shook his head, knowing the bond between them may be severed. He could feel her slipping away from him, and every beautiful dream he'd ever had would vanish. "I . . . I do have things I need to tell you. I tried before, but I was afraid. When I left your land two years ago, I found money—"

"I found this in your desk." Norah pulled the letter from her pocket and waved it in the air. "My family's money! How could you? How could you keep that from me?"

He pounded his fist against the wall. Mrs. Dover had been right. Having her learn of his error like this—could anything be worse? "I tried to mail that. It was lost and then returned. There's a letter somewhere . . . I'll find it. It says it went to the dead letter office before coming back to me. I didn't know . . ." His own anger against himself made his words come out terse. "I sent it. I tried to say I was wrong and sorry. It doesn't have to change anything."

"Get out," she said, shoving his shoulder. "Get out of here and let me think about all this. I'll decide if this changes anything."

"Norah," he begged, "let me explain it all."

"Not now." She turned away from him. "Please go."

22

For two days Quincy gave her the space she'd requested. He busied himself at his other businesses, spending time with Nels and meeting with the bank to discuss the deeds to his property and what selling them would entail. He looked for her every time he entered the hotel, hoping to see her and somehow find understanding in her eyes, but he caught no sight of her.

"You were right," he said to Mrs. Dover when she looked at him with sympathetic eyes. "I should have told her myself. I should have told her everything the very moment I found her."

"What's done is done." She sat beside him at the small table in the kitchen.

"Have you seen her?"

"I have. She's well in body, and I think her spirits are coming around." She nudged him with her elbow. "I think she's trying to make peace with what's happened. She believed herself in love with you."

"And now I've made a mess of it all." He put his head in his hands. "What can I do?"

"Just keep being the man you are. In time I believe she'll realize you're a man who can be trusted, and she'll be assured that you are not like the other men she's known."

"And if she doesn't?" He pinched the bridge of his nose. "What if she never forgives me?"

"You cannot force a woman to love you. If she won't have you, then you'll have to carry on without her by your side."

Quincy winced, each word a blow to his heart as he fought to accept that his future may be lonely and void of the bright presence Norah had become in his life. He wanted to bang on her door, plead for her forgiveness, and beg her to accept not only his remorse but also his hand. He smiled sadly at Mrs. Dover before going outside to find solace away from the walls of the hotel.

He walked Main Street, first on one side and then the other. His café was closed for the day. He peered inside anyway, wondering if a new owner would let it remain as quaint and hospitable as it had become under his care. The door opened, startling him.

"Can I get you something, Quincy?" Alice asked from the doorway. "I have some rolls left. I could butter you one if you're hungry."

"I'd like that." He stepped inside and took off his hat.

"Neither of us are good at skirting around what's happening," Alice said after he seated himself at an empty table near the kitchen. "Survival has made us callous and blunt."

"I'm afraid that's true."

"So, tell me, what do you plan to do for Norah? She says you are one of the reasons she lost her farm and her life went awry."

"What she says is true." Would the weight of it ever go

away? "Mrs. Dover says I need to give her time. I want to grant her the freedom to choose what she wants for herself. I won't be like the men in her past who tried to control her, but I wish she knew how sorry I am."

"Her cast is gone," Alice said matter-of-factly. "Her injuries are all healed. At least the ones to her body. You give her time, and she may leave. She was worried for Nels, but you've said you plan to keep the boy, and though she will miss him, she feels assured you'll look after him. I don't know if you have time to wait."

He'd planned to listen to Mrs. Dover's advice and move slowly and cautiously forward, but Alice was right. Circumstances as they were, there was no guarantee he would have a chance later. So much hinged on her forgiveness, or at least on them reconciling enough that he could help keep her safe. Her leaving would only put her in danger of meeting more men like Percy and Jake.

"I have to go." He stood up and looked around the café with a twinge of regret. "You've done well with this café."

"Because of this café and the repairs you had Sam do, I found myself a man unlike all the others. You were sitting at that table over there"—she pointed—"when you asked him to make me a cart."

"He doesn't have our blunt ways. He needed a push."

"She's scared. You're a good man, Quincy." Alice walked with him to the door.

"If I can't earn back her trust, I can at least keep her safe. She doesn't need to run." He pushed open the door. "I'll let her know she can go home."

"Quincy said to give this to you." Nels put the letter in Norah's hand. "He said you were mad at him and that you didn't want to see him, but he hoped you'd still read this. Why are you mad at him?"

"I'm not mad at him, not exactly." Norah took the letter from him but didn't open it. "I just have a lot to think about and decisions to make."

"You been thinking for a long time. Why not just talk to him? He always has lots of good ideas." Nels sat down, picked up his school slate, and drew on it while he waited. "Quincy said I should stay and tell him if you read his letter or not."

"He did, did he?"

"Yep, so no shooing me away this time. I'm going to sit right here until you're done reading." He set down his chalk and folded his arms.

Despite her melancholy, she laughed. "You're already rather loyal to him, aren't you?"

"He's going to be my pa. He wrote a letter to a judge asking what he'd have to do. I figure if he's my pa, then I best listen to him. Besides, I want to be like him."

"I wouldn't want to keep you from being a loyal son." She sat on the edge of her bed and opened the letter.

Dear Norah,

I am torn between following the advice of Mrs. Dover, who tells me to bide my time and simply wait for you to come to me, and the advice of Alice, who says that I am a rather outspoken man and should just bang on your door and tell you every thought and argument in my head. I've decided instead to follow your

Captain Wentworth and write a letter, hoping it'll both be bold and give you space.

Please, don't leave. I know your arm is healed and you may be tempted to catch a train and never look back at Longfield or at me, but I beg you to stay and consider other options. I've been thinking and have several offers to present. The first plan I propose for your consideration is the one I pray you choose.

You could stay, court me, and somehow find it in your heart to forgive me for my error. I made a mistake, one I tried to make right when I mailed the letter that never made it to you and one that I will try to make right again and again. If you stay, I promise my protection and friendship. I promise more than that. I promise to hold you when you cry (have I told you I love the feeling of you in my arms?). I will kiss you as often as you'll let me, and I'll dance with you. I will want to hear all your dreams, and I will do everything in my power to make them come true. We could be together here with Nels and Mrs. Dover and Sam and Alice. We could grow old in Longfield.

"Why you frowning?" Nels asked, interrupting her reading. "He'll want to know that too. He said to tell him how you looked while you were reading."

"I wasn't frowning." She forced a smile, but inside the frown remained. He'd offered a great deal with this first option, but his intentions were not entirely clear. Was he promising marriage or merely to court and spend each day making amends for the past? If he were asking for her hand, was it possible to accept it when he'd been the cause of so much anguish in her life, even if he'd never intended for her to lose her farm?

"I have more to read. Let me finish before you run off and tell him I was frowning."

Nels scratched at his ear impatiently but said nothing, so she returned her attention to Quincy's words.

If you cannot find it in your heart to stay, then I present another option. I went to Blackwell while I was away. I did spend time in the other town stores (that much was true), but my most important stop was to see Jake about buying your land back. I went in hopes that if I could give you back your beloved land, then my guilt would ease without me ever having to tell you the extent of my role in your misfortunes. I was wrong. You deserved the whole truth from the start, and if the clock were mine to turn back, I would. I can't undo my errors of judgment and pride, so I give you the truth now and the promise to be honest from this moment onward.

I asked Jake, and at first he rejected me. But every man has his price, and he has agreed to sell. Buying it will require some changes to the businesses I own, but if you choose to leave Longfield, at least you would have a home to go to and a creek to splash in. I cannot give you back the time you lost or remove the memories of the cruelty you suffered, but I can give you your land and the truth so you can choose your future.

Her land. She closed her eyes and recollected the picturesque setting—her childhood home, her creek, and even her bench were there for the taking. So many nights she'd dreamed of going home to her beloved bit of earth. But now, with it within her grasp, she felt no eagerness.

"You done reading?" Nels asked.

"Letters are not meant to be read quickly. Don't rush me." She shifted on the bed before devouring the rest.

Norah, for you I would sell all I have and start over again. If remaining here does not appeal to you, if Blackwell no longer calls to you, then tell me what it is you want and I will give it to you. The hotel, the café, and the store are all yours. I will be your servant if that is what you wish. Not only because I regret so deeply what has happened but also because I want nothing more than your happiness. Don't run from me. I am not Percy, who hurt you and threatens you still. I am not Jake, whose love of money dictated his decisions. Think, dear Norah, of all we've shared and ask yourself if I am a man you can forgive.

Out of respect for Mrs. Dover, I will not come pounding on your door, but if you are willing to discuss your future with me, I invite you to come to the café tonight. I'll be there waiting.

How does your Captain Wentworth put it? "I am half agony, half hope."

Quincy

"Now I am done," she said, folding the letter and putting it in her pocket, knowing that as soon as Nels left, she would read it again and ponder every word. Her heart, no doubt, would beat wildly as she pondered his every word.

An idea popped into her head, sprouting like a seed. "Tell Quincy . . . tell him I am not decided on whether to meet him or not."

"You ain't . . . er, you aren't? You must be *real* mad."

"Come here." She put her arms around him and kissed the top of his head. "A woman is allowed to steer the boat on occasion. Remember that."

"I'll try," he said with a look of confusion on his face. "Mrs. Dover has been talking 'bout what you'll do now. I think you should stay, and you should love Quincy."

"It's not always that simple."

"It don't got to be that hard either." He picked at a jagged fingernail on his left hand, working at the uneven edge. "I done lots of running, and then I came here, and well, I like staying better."

"You won't have to run again." She nudged him toward the door. "Go let Quincy know that you delivered your letter. And will you tell Alice I need to see her?"

23

"You better hurry," Alice said after peeking out the window. "I'm sure he'll be here any minute."

"Do you think I'm wrong?" Norah asked without stopping her stirring.

"No. I don't. To expect any man to be perfect would be wrong." She straightened the tablecloth she'd just laid out. "Sam's not perfect, but he sure tries hard. And heaven knows I'm not perfect."

"I keep asking myself, How do I know he's not going to somehow betray me? Trust is a finicky thing." Norah stirred too hard, sending her soup splattering. "Oh, I'm all jittery. I've been praying and thinking for two days, wondering what to do. But this . . . well, it seems awfully forward."

"No, it's not forward. It's honest." Alice looked in the pot. "And it's very green." Since officially courting Sam, she'd been nothing but smiles and laughter. "You could catch him completely off guard like I did with Sam. If I hadn't, we might have forever been two friends who walked home together and nothing more."

"I don't know that I could ever be as daring as you. But I'm happy for you."

"Well, whatever you decide to do and say, you better do it quick. He's here."

Norah stayed in the kitchen, her heart racing and her nerves threatening to send her running, but she stood her ground and listened as Alice greeted Quincy at the door.

"Hello, Alice."

Norah's chest tightened at the sound of his voice. He was here!

"I can't stay, but I do hope things go well for you," Alice said. "I've agreed to go with Sam to his parents' house. I'm nervous as can be."

"Don't be nervous," Quincy said. "I've no doubt they'll be over-the-moon excited that Sam is showing interest in you."

"He says the same. For years now he's been telling them he is content in his bachelor ways. It's a big night for both of us."

"Do you think she'll come?" Quincy asked. "I invited her, but she hasn't given me a firm commitment."

"Where would the fun in courtship be if everything was easy?"

Quincy guffawed. "You sound like Mrs. Dover. But you have a point. It'd be like fighting an opponent who was already on the ground."

"Courting is hardly a boxing match. Promise that you'll do what you can to keep her in town? I've long needed a friend just like her, and I would hate for her to go. Percy still worries me, but with you here, I believe she'll be safe. And I know you can make her happy."

"If she comes, I will plead my cause."

Alice wished him well, said goodbye, and the café became very quiet. Norah could only imagine that Quincy had sat at one of the small tables, where he waited for her. The moment of decision was upon her. She could retreat and sneak off through the back door of the café or go through with her plan. Mustering her bravery and reminding herself of all she knew of this man, she stepped out from the kitchen.

"I told you once—"

He flew from his chair and the sound of it crashing behind him interrupted her speech, but she didn't care. The grin on his flushed face brought a smile to her lips.

"You're here." He went to her and she felt certain he was going to take her in his arms, but he stopped a foot from her. "I wondered if you would come."

"I wondered too, but then I asked Alice if I could make you dinner."

"You cooked for me?" He gawked at her, his eyes hungrily roaming her face. She felt as though he was drinking her in, assuring himself that she was real. The relief on his face made her tentative heart soar.

She reached behind her back and with shaky hands attempted to untie her apron. "I was about to tell you that I made you pea soup. I told you once I'd make it for you, and I've decided tonight is the night."

He stepped behind her, and his hands went to her apron strings. Her breath caught in her chest as his knuckle brushed against her back. She swallowed but held still. He was only loosening the strings, but every time his hand touched her, she felt her mouth go dry and heat race through her. Nothing about his touch frightened her. It was quite the opposite, in fact—she found it intoxicating.

"Pea soup," he said with his hands at her back and his breath tickling the hairs on the nape of her neck. "I don't like pea soup."

"You said you'd tell me that you liked mine." She felt the strings of her apron fall loose, but he stayed near.

"I did tell you that," he said, standing at her back. "But I won't now."

She pivoted and faced him. "You won't?"

"I will tell you exactly how awful it is. I'll tell you it's the most disgusting green sludge I've ever had."

"Why?"

"Because I won't ever lie to you again." He inched closer, his eyes pleading with her. "Have you decided what you're going to do?"

"First, I'm going to serve you my soup." She stepped away from him, far enough that she could catch her breath before backing into the kitchen. All the while loving the way her body and mind celebrated his presence. She ladled the thick green soup into two bowls, making sure to fill his extra full. With bowls in hand, she hurried back to him. "There you are."

He took his bowl and waited for her to sit before diving in. "You are watching me like a hawk."

She took a seat, her eyes never leaving him. "I'm rather curious to know what you'll do."

"I told you, I'll tell you what I truly think of it." He swirled his spoon around in the soup before pulling a bite near his mouth and inspecting it. "I think it may be the color I find off-putting."

"There are plenty of green foods." She took a bite and sighed, grateful for the plethora of pleasant memories the taste evoked. This night would one day be a memory, one she felt certain she would recall with fondness. "My mother used to make this soup. I can almost feel her nearby now. She would have liked you. If she were here, she'd pull up a chair and insist you eat. She loved feeding everyone."

"Your stories are only going to make me feel worse when I tell you I don't like it." He moved the spoon closer to his face and scrunched his nose up in disgust. "I don't want you to take offense."

Norah took another bite, licked her lips, and made a sound of enjoyment. "You're stalling."

He shoved the bite into his mouth, made a face, and swallowed with dramatic effort. "I was right. It's awful stuff."

She let her spoon fall into her bowl, pushed it aside, and leaned across the table. "You never meant to hurt me when you kept that money. I know you didn't."

"You're right, but how did my dislike of your soup convince you?"

"I already knew it. I think I knew right away, but it was still hard for me, considering all that happened because of it. And I kept wondering what if it'd all played out differently. I wondered if when I saw you I would see nothing but a reminder of what I lost. But I find my fears were in vain. Seeing you with your big bowl of soup, hearing you tell me the truth about it, well, it only solidified what I've always believed—you are honest. Imperfect, flawed, callous at times, but good and trustworthy." She reached across the table, palms up, inviting him to take her hands.

With his hands around hers, she felt as though the storm that began blowing so many years ago was finally settling. And like the sun after a storm, the world seemed brighter—

better than it ever had. "You've given me the freedom to choose what I want. That was a beautiful gift." She leaned farther across the table and held his gaze. "Don't sell your businesses. I can't imagine anyone else owning this café or the store. The hotel must stay yours so you can continue helping the lost souls who cross your path—"

He ran his thumbs over the smooth pads of her palms. "Then I cannot buy you your land. I can give you money but not enough to convince Jake to sell."

"Forget Jake. He can have the land and do what he wishes with it. His conscience is not my concern. Let God judge his deeds. My father talked of a legacy, and for a very long time I believed the legacy was the land, but I don't think that's what he meant. Our legacy was the happiness in our home and the way we stuck together and kept going even when life was hard. Family was our legacy, and I do want to feel that again, but I think I can feel it anywhere if I have the right people near me." She looked toward the front windows of the café, out across Longfield. "I think a family with a young boy should own at least a small piece of land for him to roam, don't you think?"

"A family with a boy?"

She shrugged, suddenly afraid she was being too presumptuous. "I only meant someday I'd like to have land, even if it is not the land I grew up on."

"You said a family with a boy."

"Quincy, stop. I am not good at speaking my mind."

He scooted his chair around the table to be closer to her and took her hands again. "Then I will be direct. Tell me what you want to do now. We are at a crossroads. Do you intend to take the money I owe you and leave?"

"No." She held his gaze.

"You say you do not want me to buy your old land back. Is that true?"

"I don't think Blackwell is my home any longer. I used to cling to that dream, but now I realize it is only land and my heart is no longer there. My legacy is not in the soil."

He gripped her hands with more urgency. "Are you to stay in Longfield? Tell me, I beg you."

"I still fear Percy, but this is where I want to be. Does your offer to court me still stand?" she asked, feeling emboldened by the touch of his large hands on hers and the longing in his eyes.

"Yes, of course it does. If you can truly forgive me?"

"I do." She pressed her eyes closed, searching inside herself to ensure she spoke the truth. She found no hardened feelings toward him, only growing affection for who he truly was and gratitude that their lives had once again crossed. "I forgive you," she said when she opened her eyes. "And I am proud of the man you are." She let go of his hands and touched his face, letting her hand rest against his cheek. "I believe Providence may very well have brought you to me all those years ago, and now we have been brought together again."

He put his hand over hers, cradling it against his face. "There is one promise I have not kept."

"You kept them all. You even ate my soup, though you did not pretend to like it, which I think only adds to your charm." She kissed his cheek and was tickled by his end-of-day stubble.

With their heads close together, he said, "I promised to find a girl, discover her dreams, and make them all come true." He paused, staring at her with intensity. "I wanted to keep my word, but I could not. It was always you. You are the only one whose dreams I want to know."

"I dream," she whispered, well aware of the risk she took, "that a reformed former boxer will kiss me. Does that sound terribly—"

His lips met hers, cutting off her rambling chatter. One large, gentle hand worked itself into her hair, the other went to her cheek. His lips moved against hers with sweet desire. When he pulled away, he laughed. "Tell me your dreams anytime you wish, and I will oblige you."

She laughed with him, her spirits light and jovial. Her heart soared, and her lips begged for more of his touch.

"Go on, wish for whatever you want." He ran a hand over her once-broken forearm.

"Very well." She leaned against his shoulder. "I wish for . . . more afternoons spent discussing books."

"That's too easy. I complain a bit, but you know I enjoy it."

"I dream that I'll see you hit a baseball out of the field."

His chest shook when he laughed, but she continued to lean against him, feeling safe and content. "There's a game already scheduled, so that dream will not have to wait long. Tell me another."

"I dream I'll be able to walk through town and not worry that Percy is going to come and try to take me back." She shuddered at the very thought. "I dream of living without fear."

"I'll find a way."

As she leaned against his solid chest, listening to the gentle pounding of his heart, she wanted to believe it was possible. That Providence could weave their lives together, offering security and relief from the tight grip of fear.

24

Nels sat beside Norah and Quincy on the back lawn of the hotel. The day felt like any other, except now Quincy made sure to hold Norah's hand when they strolled, and if Nels wasn't looking, he snuck a kiss from her.

"Have you heard from the judge?" Nels asked as he pulled up the green grass and piled it on his lap. "You said you wrote him."

"I heard back only early today. He says we ought to post an announcement in a paper in case you have a parent looking for you. After that, making it official won't be hard. They'll be able to grant it on grounds of desertion."

"My pa isn't looking for me, and my ma's been gone for years." He pushed the grass off his lap and turned toward Quincy, a smile on his face. "It won't be long, and you'll be my pa."

"You're a blessed boy." Norah's smile was bright, but Quincy felt certain she was holding something back. "I'm glad you'll have an official family."

"The judge answered some other questions I had too,"

Quincy said. He quickly clamped his mouth shut—he hadn't planned to bring it up now. This wasn't the right time, so he shifted the conversation in a new direction. "I wrote to Jake too. I told him you were the most forgiving woman I'd ever met and you had decided to let him keep the land. I thought of calling him a few choice words before mailing my letter off, but for your sake I did not."

"I'm amazed by your restraint *and* very glad to have that matter settled. How strange it is to think I yearned for that land for years, and now I don't feel sad at all that I won't be going back."

Nels, losing interest in the adult conversation, stood to go play.

"Enjoy these afternoons in the sun," Quincy said before he got very far. "When school starts back up, I'll be enrolling you."

"Real school!" Nels clapped his hands. "You were a fine teacher, Norah, but I've dreamed of going to school my whole life."

"Your soon-to-be papa loves making dreams come true." She took Quincy's hand but kept her eyes on Nels. "I think you'll do very well in school."

"Thanks to your teaching." Nels smiled as he ran off.

"I'll miss him," she confessed, her eyes still on his retreating figure. "We've had such fun together."

"He needs to be around other children. Life made him grow up too quickly." Quincy yawned and lay back in the grass. "If I fall asleep, will you wake me before my baseball game? The other men will taunt me for ages if I'm late."

"I'd be sorry too. You've promised me quite the show today."

He put his hands over his eyes, blocking the sun. "Be sure and wake me then. I'd hate to disappoint you."

With the warm sun beating against him and the woman he loved beside him, he felt peace. If there was a way to freeze time, he would choose a moment like this one to linger in.

Earlier in the day he'd walked with Norah to the edge of town. They'd looked at land, never broaching the subject of marriage as they took in the countryside. She'd insisted they take off their shoes when they found a small, nearly dried up creek. "I think this is the piece of land you should buy," she'd said as she slipped her feet into the shallow water and sighed.

He'd stood beside her, barefooted and content. When she'd asked if he was embarrassed by her flippant ways, he'd taken her in his arms and kissed her. "No," he'd said, and meant it. "I think you ought to go barefoot whenever you wish. Be as brazen as you want."

He watched her now, drinking in the landscape and smiling in the bright sun. The road they'd taken to each other had been riddled with bumps, but the ruts and bends all felt trivial now. They were together, and he'd never felt so calm.

"What will the town think when they see you wasting a perfectly good afternoon just lying around?" Mrs. Dover's voice startled him from his comfortable state.

"Let them think what they want." He waved a hand in the air. "I've had too much on my mind to sleep well, so I'm sleeping now."

Norah laughed from her seated position near him. "Better wake up," she whispered. "Mrs. Dover has her hands on her hips like a mother about to give a scolding."

"Very well." He rolled to his side and propped himself up on one elbow.

"The train was just here," Mrs. Dover said. "Some men were asking after you. I told them you were out for the afternoon and you would not be back until late because of the baseball game."

"Why didn't you fetch me?" Quincy sat all the way up. Something was wrong. They had guests coming and going every day, and he was rarely alerted. "What is it?"

"Well, I'm not rightly sure. I had a sinking feeling, that's all."

He stood and went to his protective housekeeper. "Tell me what it was about these men that set you ill at ease. It'd be best if you just spit it out. I've been busy, and my brain feels too addled to decipher anything cryptic."

"You have been rather distracted. But for good reasons. It does make my heart happy to see you and Norah together."

" I've never been so pleasantly distracted in my entire life. I will gladly tell you all the ways she's changed my life for the better, but first, tell us, what has you worried?" He brushed away the grass on his trousers, trying to look presentable in case he was to meet with strangers.

"I could be wrong, but they seemed angry about something. And when I asked if I could leave you a message, they scowled." She threw her hands out to her sides. "I told you I was probably worrying for nothing."

"We don't want you worrying." He offered a hand to Norah and pulled her up from her spot on the grass. "I met a few shopkeepers on my last trip. Could be one of them. I'll walk Norah to her room and then ask around a bit before the game."

Mrs. Dover sighed. "Hurry and take her to her room. I'll

feel better knowing you two aren't out here staring at each other."

"We don't stare," Norah said, already stepping toward the hotel.

"I've seen you staring at me," Quincy said, bringing an alluring blush to her face. "And I openly confess to admiring you whenever I can. Is that wrong?" he asked Mrs. Dover. "Tell me, Mrs. Dover, is it right for a man who is smitten to have eyes for only one?"

"You're hopeless." Mrs. Dover laughed, making her chin jiggle and her eyes dance. "I think any woman would be flattered to have the man they're courting look at them the way you look at our Norah. Now, go on. I could be wrong, but I didn't like these men." Mrs. Dover waved again at Nels. "Come help me."

Quincy took Norah's arm. "I'll be back before the game begins."

"Do you think we are safe at the hotel?"

"We'll be perfectly safe. Mrs. Dover is likely extra worried. If something is amiss, I'll find out." He opened the back door of the hotel, and they walked quietly up the steep and narrow staff staircase. "I do wish I could spend the rest of the afternoon with you."

"You survived most of your life without me," she said. "I think you can manage another hour."

"I'm not sure I can." He put his hand on his heart and made a pained face. "Everything inside me hurts when you're not there."

"You poor dear," she said with mock concern. "I could send for a doctor."

"No, no doctor." He winked before going on, his voice full

of pleading. "You've nursed me before. If I need anything, I'll trust my care to you."

She giggled as she slid by him. He skipped a step, bringing himself back near her.

He may have been jesting on the stairs, but there was truth in his words. When she wasn't near him, he missed her. At her door he looked down the hall in both directions—they were alone. He stole a kiss and promised to return.

———————

Norah tapped her foot against the floor while she waited impatiently for the time to pass and for Quincy to knock on the door and escort her to the game. She'd tried reading, the diversion that normally provided calm to her frenzied mind, but even reading did not prove an adequate distraction. She wondered if other women were equally single-minded while courting. So much of her day was spent thinking of Quincy and eagerly waiting for the next time she'd see him. When with him, she hung on his every word. Jake had certainly not had this powerful effect on her. She'd dreaded her time with him, always grasping for words. With Quincy . . . She exhaled and leaned against the wall, her hand clasped against her heart. It was different with him.

When they were looking at land, she'd been tempted to jump up and down and exclaim that she wanted this to be their land, not his alone. His presence often liberated her tongue, but she'd bitten back the thought, practicing restraint and the patience Mrs. Dover so often talked about.

Here in her room with no audience, she let all restraint go. "Norah Barnes," she whispered aloud, letting herself dream once again.

25

Donned in his green-and-white jersey, Quincy knocked softly on Norah's door, careful to not draw attention to himself. The hallway was empty, like it so often was in the late afternoon, but he still checked over his shoulder an extra time to be sure.

"I'm coming," he heard her say before she opened the door. When she did, she smiled, evoking one of his own.

He put a hand on her waist, leaned in, and kissed her cheek. "I missed you."

"It *was* a long hour," she said, grabbing his hand and pulling him toward the back stairway. "Did you discover anything?"

"I asked the other hotel staff if they've seen the men Mrs. Dover described. One of them said they checked in two men that matched their descriptions earlier today. We checked the logbook, only to discover names we did not recognize. Mrs. Dover may have been being extra cautious, is all."

"I'm glad to hear it." She took his arm. "I can hardly wait to watch you play."

"Nels and Mrs. Dover have agreed to come. They said for us to go on ahead, but they'll be there before long."

"Nels will want to see his pa playing." She grew more serious. "Does it make you nervous, becoming his papa?"

"I want to do it right. I think of all the things I wanted in a pa that I never had." Buying the hotel and agreeing to fix it up and run it had been a big undertaking. Raising Nels felt far more important, and in truth, he was ill-prepared for such an endeavor, but his heart was willing. "I worry I'll fail, but it feels right. And a family is what he needs. You said so yourself, so why not me?"

"I can think of no one better to raise him." She sighed. "I am jealous though. You'll see more of him than I will."

He grunted and opened the back door. "I don't think he'll let a day go by without seeing you. He's always talking about you."

Quincy looked over at Norah. She walked tall and proud like this was her hometown. No longer a stranger, she waved as she passed people she knew. And when she saw Alice, she greeted her like a sister.

"I need to go be with my team," he said to her once they stepped onto the field. "I don't think there is anything to worry about, but—"

"I won't leave without you. I'll be safe here with everyone around me." She squeezed his arm. "I want to see you play."

He left her to visit with Alice and joined his team. His teammates laughed, slapped him on the back, and soon were tossing warm-up throws.

Sam held the ball in his hand after Quincy threw it. "I think the ladies are whispering about us."

Quincy looked toward Alice's cart and sure enough, Norah and Alice were giggling about something.

"I wouldn't worry." Quincy waved when Norah's eye

caught his. She grinned, then whispered something else to Alice that he had no way of hearing. "Norah tells me Alice is beyond happy. I think you've made her believe there are good men in the world."

"She's made me hope that maybe, someday, I could be a woman's first choice and not their castoff." He smiled. "You and Norah already act like an old married couple."

He laughed at the truth in his words. It seems they had always been comfortable with each other. "You're right, though there are some things married people do that will have to wait."

Sam's eyes crinkled in the corners. They were grown men, but the women in their lives had them downright giddy.

"We spend every afternoon together, doing things most would find dull, but I've had plenty of adventure in my life. I think I'd be content to read books and stroll through gardens until the day I die."

"Funny, isn't it, how life changes us?" Sam's eyes were on Alice. "When I look at Alice, I realize she's my first choice too. I would go through everything I've been through again if it led me here."

"Let's play ball and show our first choices that we're who they want to be cheering for. We can't impress them much if we are both standing around like a couple of lovestruck fools."

Nels arrived five minutes into the game and ran right for Norah. "Mrs. Dover started talking about maybe mopping the floors." He caught his breath. "But I told her I needed to see my pa play. I had to drag her the entire way here."

"You haven't missed a thing," Norah said. "The score is still zero to zero. I am sure by the end of the game she'll be glad she came."

"I suppose. Got any extra cookies?" Nels asked Alice.

Alice grinned. "You're a regular little beggar."

"Not anymore." He held out a penny. "I been earning wages."

"Keep it." She handed him a cookie, then raised her hand to block the sun from her eyes. "Who do you suppose those men are?"

Norah followed her gaze to the edge of the field where two men lumbered across it, heading toward the crowd. They came closer, each step causing the easiness of the day to fade. A sickening tension formed in her abdomen. Her head swam, and her breath came shallow.

"Oh no," she whispered.

"What is it?"

"That's him. That's Percy. He must have checked into the hotel using a different name." The old feelings of dread and panic took over, causing her palms to sweat and tremble. Nels was beside her, staring up at her face. She had to be strong and think clearly so this boy she loved could be safe from harm. She knelt in front of him, grabbed his arm, and spoke with more force than ever before. "Go to Mrs. Dover and stay there. Don't go anywhere alone, and whatever you do, stay away from those men."

"Why?"

"Because . . ." She could find no words. How did she tell this child that something horrible might happen to her? She pulled him close, kissed his cheek, and nudged him toward Mrs. Dover. "Stay by her. I'll explain later."

Norah looked around frantically. There had to be a way to escape. Her eyes bounced from one person to the next. She knew so many faces now. Longfield had become her town and these her people. She grabbed Alice's arm. "I can't let him win. He's taken too much already." Wind whipped through her hair. She could follow the wind, ride out of here, and disappear out West, but she didn't want to. There had to be another way.

"Everyone will stand by you," Alice said. "You're not alone."

Norah's eyes landed on Quincy. Oh, how badly she wanted a life with him. She straightened her spine and forced her breath to come evenly. This was her home, her life, and she would not let this beast take anything else from her. But how could she stop him?

"I won't hide," she said to Alice, growing bolder and stronger with each uttered word.

She stepped from behind the cart, walked with a purposeful stride over to the stands with their many spectators, and met Percy eye to eye. He spat on the ground when he saw her and moved closer. A few eyes left the game and went to the unusual exchange, but Norah gave them no heed.

"What do you want?" she challenged him.

"I came for you." He threw her a wry smile. "It's time for you to come home with me."

"I was never home with you." She forced her spine to stay straight, refusing to let even her posture succumb to this man.

"Everything alright, Norah?" an older man who frequented the café and knew both her and Alice asked.

"It will be when this man realizes that women are not chattel." She glared at Percy. "And when he leaves."

Aware that others were listening, he sneered at her. "You signed a contract." Then louder, he said, "She signed a contract to work for me. I am here to see that she honors it."

A hand came around her shoulder, and without turning, she knew it was Quincy. His presence steadied her, adding to her strength. "I will not," she said loud enough for anyone witnessing the scene to hear.

Percy took a half step backward. She knew it was Quincy who alarmed him, not her words, but she still felt strong. Empowered and ready to say everything the weaker Norah could not, she went on. "You need to leave."

"Let's talk somewhere else," Percy said in a sickly-sweet voice. "We don't need to interrupt anyone else's fun. Let's sort this out in private."

"No," Quincy said. "Whatever it is you have to say can be said here. This is her town and her people."

The game had ceased when Quincy walked from the field. The crowd sat silent, watching, everyone waiting to hear what would happen next. Percy and the man beside him glared at Norah, but she didn't tremble. Norah met Percy's gaze, knowing she'd caught him off guard when she approached him instead of running. The men faltered, looking at each other. Surely they'd planned to scare her off and advance when she retreated, but they didn't know the stronger Norah, the one supported by friends.

"She has a contract," Percy said again. "I had her sign it when she came begging for work. All of you are looking at me like I'm a villain, but she was desperate when she came to me. I took her in. I fed her when no one wanted her."

A low murmur rose from the crowd as they considered his comment. Someone spoke up, asking, "Is it true?"

"Yes." She nodded. "I lost my land, and I could not find work. In a moment of hunger and fear, I signed a contract, believing I would only be doing menial work in his establishment. It said I'd work for this man for two years. I left before my time was up."

"What sort of work?" a balding man in the back of the crowd shouted. Her heart plummeted, knowing the crowd would demand she relive it all and then together they'd decide her fate.

"You don't have to answer that," Quincy said before she could speak.

"She was one of my girls." Percy smirked. "Ever heard of Percy's girls?"

People gasped.

"If this is to be my public trial, then so be it." She looked at this cluster of people she'd so badly wanted to belong to.

"You don't deserve a trial," Quincy said. "You took care of yourself when you were down on your luck, and no one needs an explanation."

"Look at their faces," Percy said. She followed his gaze, her heart sinking at the sight of the crowd. They didn't know what to make of her. Some were even leaving, turning their backs against her.

"They want to know what sort of a person you are." Percy sneered at her. "Go on. Tell them what it was like working at the Whetted Whistle. See if they want you here then. Coming back with me might be your only option. You know I take care of my girls."

Her resolve teetered, losing its strength one moment and rising up again the next. It was Nels's eyes that she found, large and searching. She clung to them. "We all have a past," she said. "We run from it, pretend it away, and bury it. I could stand here and tell you every detail. I could try to prove my innocence, but what difference would it make? Every Sunday I listen to sermons on forgiveness, redemption, and grace."

More murmuring.

"You weren't innocent," Percy said. "Come back with me and stop embarrassing yourself. These people don't want a tainted woman sitting in their midst."

"How many of you," she said to the crowd, "saw me when I first arrived? My arm was broken, I was bruised and beaten." She pointed to Percy. "It was by his hand."

"No," Percy said. "That bloke behind you is the one who sent you down the stairs."

"He was rescuing me," she said through gritted teeth. "Saving me from you."

"If she's a tainted woman," a man she'd rarely seen before began, then scowled as though the whole matter was inconsequential, "let us watch the game we came here for."

Several others nodded, eager to be done with the distraction or too uncomfortable to speak up. A knot formed in her stomach. They may as well have been casting stones, their looks hurt so deeply.

"See, Norah, no one wants a girl like you here. They're ready to turn you over to me. Make this easy and come along. When your contract's fulfilled, you can be on your way."

She opened her mouth to defend herself again, but Quincy spoke first. "You say that no one wants someone with a past. I say you're wrong." He pursed his lips as he paused and looked at the crowd. He had their attention. "I've got a past. Before coming to this town, I boxed in back alleyways for money. You think I'm unrefined now, you should have seen me then." She took his hand, squeezing her fingers around his. He'd tried so hard to leave his past behind, but now, for her, he unveiled it all. "We can have a fresh start, thanks to the good Lord and people who are willing to look beyond our mistakes. Or in Norah's case, her desperation."

"You're talking nonsense," Percy said. "Blast you, woman, you're coming with me."

"No, she's not." Quincy looked around, making eye contact with anyone willing to look his way. "Everyone here is different from what they used to be."

A middle-aged woman stood up and nodded. "I've never worked in a saloon or anyplace like that, but Mr. Barnes is right. We are all changing all the time."

Alice stepped forward and stood beside Norah, taking her other hand. "I was left at a bawdy house when I was not yet sixteen. I don't like talking about it, but it did happen. Judge me if you wish, but that's not who I am, and Norah's not one of Percy's girls. She's part of our town."

Sam stepped beside Alice and offered her a gentle smile—one that screamed of his acceptance—and then he turned to Percy. "You can't have Norah. We want her here."

Mrs. Dover stood up, with Nels beside her. "She's family. She stays."

The preacher stood, Sam's sisters stood, and then slowly one by one the rest of the crowd rose to their feet. Tears streamed down Norah's face at the breathtaking sight. A few others told their stories of arriving in town looking for a haven to begin again. Several mentioned Quincy and his role in helping them. Stories that had long been stifled by fear were shared, uniting these silent refugees.

"You all talk pretty," Percy said. "But she has a contract with me."

Quincy grinned then, surprising Norah. "It's no good."

"Says who?"

"Says Judge Windgate."

Norah's mouth fell open, unsure what he was talking about but hopeful his words were true.

"I met him a year or so back when he stayed at the hotel. I sent him a letter about another matter and asked what it would take for a woman working for a worthless man like yourself to break her contract—"

Percy took a large step forward, rage burning in his countenance. Two men grabbed him and pulled him back, holding his arms. He brushed them off, swearing. "It's a bunch of lies."

Longfield's sheriff arrived then, led by one of Sam's sisters. He was a large man who was armed and, from what Alice had told Norah, eager to keep the peace. With Percy still surrounded by men ready to hold him back if necessary, the story was retold once again, only now the crowd was not listening to choose a side. Instead, they seemed eager to defend Norah.

"And what does Judge Windgate say you need to do?" the sheriff asked Quincy as he glared at Percy. "I'm not saying I think that contract's valid."

"Contracts are hard to hold up. But we all know our word should be our bond," Quincy said. "But the work Percy offered was anything but honorable, and his character here today and what I saw in Warner Crossing have proven it to me. Having said that, it is almost impossible to force a married woman to uphold a working contract."

Norah's head jerked to him. What was he saying? She wasn't married. "I'm not—"

"You could be." He grabbed her hand. "We could marry, and the contract of marriage would trump the other."

Marriage. Night after night she'd dreamed of marrying Quincy and never having to leave him. Not once had she pictured it like this, him offering his hand to rescue her. She searched his face, wanting to know why he'd asked. Was it only to keep her from the serpent Percy? Or were his words motivated by love?

"There are other ways to put this behind us too, if that's what you wish. We could hire a lawyer and fight." He shifted on his feet. "I wasn't keeping this from you. Not really. I just wasn't sure how to tell you."

Heat rose to her face, and she put a hand to her cheek as she struggled for words. Everyone around her stared, eager to hear her answer. "Quincy," she whispered when she found her voice, "you don't have to marry me."

"I know."

"Why . . . ?"

"Norah"—his eyes never left her as he moved closer, creating a circle of intimacy despite the watching crowd—"my dream, the one I've had since the day you saved me from the birds, has been to live with you as my wife. I planned to court you properly and be patient like Mrs. Dover is always telling me to be. I would have waited as long as it took, but here we are. You are free to choose."

Percy turned, shoved the man nearest him, and with his friend beside him stomped out of the park like an angry child, swearing and staggering as he went. The sheriff's eyes followed them. "I'll keep an eye on those two until they leave town."

Quincy thanked him, and Norah wanted to, but all she could think about was Quincy's proposal.

"Marry me, Norah, and we'll buy that land with the creek that you liked, and we'll build a house. We'll fill it with memories and children. Let me spend my life making your dreams come true."

Norah dared a glance at the crowd. So many eyes were on her. She'd faced Percy, the man who'd haunted her dreams, so she could face the eyes of these good people. Grinning, she turned back to Quincy. "Yes! My answer is yes."

Whooping and shouting burst out all around her, and then Quincy's powerful arms swept her up, spinning her in the air. When he set her down, she sighed, knowing they'd very soon be married and she could be in his arms anytime she liked.

The baseball game resumed, and Norah sat beside Mrs. Dover. Nels was on her other side, leaning his head against her shoulder and every few minutes smiling up at her and telling her how excited he was for her to be his ma. Mrs. Dover wiped at her eyes throughout the game, proclaiming herself happy beyond words—a description Norah could have easily used to describe her own feelings. Never before had she felt stronger, freer, or more hopeful. What an unexpected path her life had taken, but it was a road that had led her to all of this, and she had no room inside for anything but gratitude.

26

Every time Quincy walked next to any member of his team, they patted him on the back and congratulated him on his upcoming marriage. Only one player quietly asked him about Norah's past, showing some concern over it, but even he seemed to understand once Quincy told him how he felt. The atmosphere at the field was always lighthearted and warm, but today, with all that had transpired, there was an extra level of excitement.

When he stood with his bat in hand, ready to swing at the ball, Quincy couldn't help but first steal a glance at Norah. Everything felt more than right, having her there cheering him on and knowing that soon he'd be going home with her to the same room, not merely the same hotel. He'd never again have to worry about being separated from her.

The first pitch went wild, so he didn't swing. He tapped his bat on the ground, impatient to connect the bat with the ball and be on with the game. When the next pitch came right down the middle of the plate, he stepped into it, swung, and sent the ball soaring high into the air. He threw his bat down and ran.

He made it halfway around the field before stopping on second base. Two batters later and he had a chance to get home. He ran full speed ahead, sliding into home plate just before the catcher caught the ball. Declared safe, he jumped from the ground and found Norah in the crowd. She was on her feet, cheering louder than anyone.

The North was losing, but he felt like he'd already won to have such a woman rooting for him. It took great patience for him to sit through the rest of the game without going to her. Stolen glances were no longer enough. He wanted to hold her, kiss her, and celebrate their now-public love.

Sam sat beside him near the end of the game. "You're a brave man."

"For standing up to Percy?" He laughed. "I'm not scared of him."

"You're bigger than Percy, and I was sure you could take him. But you talked about everything people try too hard to hide. Folks don't like talking about things like that. I know Alice was worried she'd be thrown out. I think she always would have worried if today hadn't happened."

Quincy nodded. "I don't know if I was brave or just tired of seeing fear in the eyes of people I care about." He slapped Sam's back. "Can you believe it? I'm getting married."

"Best news I've heard in a long time."

"It'll be your chance next. I hear the girls used to laugh about ending up on Spinster Row." He shook his head, laughing at the turn of events. "We'll have to change the name to Married Row. Look at us—sitting here talking about women in the middle of a baseball game. We're just a couple of fools, aren't we?"

"We are indeed."

Marriage and Norah were all he could think about as the game went on. When at last the South was declared victorious, he left his moaning teammates and went to her, eager to steal her away and tell her again what a happy man she'd made him.

"You were wonderful!" she said. "I'm sorry you lost. Perhaps next time . . ."

"It doesn't matter." He took her hand in his and pulled her closer. "I feel like I've already won today. Let's leave this field behind and go for a walk."

Her small hand wrapped around his arm, fitting perfectly. "I was so afraid when I saw Percy."

"You didn't look it."

"I kept looking at you and Nels and everyone else. I didn't want to lose any of it." A wide smile filled her face. "But now even with Percy still so near, all I can think about is how happy I am."

"I'm sorry I had to ask you like that."

"I don't mind. Nothing in my life has gone how I thought it would, but it's all getting me to where I want to be. I'd live it all again. It was my road to you."

They were away from the crowd, alone to finally bask in their love and make whatever plans they wished for the future.

"How long do you want to wait?" Quincy asked as they stepped behind the hotel to the gardens they'd spent so much time together in. Benches, pathways, and vibrant plants provided a beautiful backdrop.

"I have no family to plan around or home to ready." She ran her hand over his forearm. "I feel like we've already been waiting forever. I think we should marry soon."

"A week?" he said before bending and kissing her forehead, then her cheek and the tip of her nose.

"Yes," she said, stepping into his embrace. "And then the contract, that worthless piece of paper, will mean nothing."

"Forget the paper." He kissed her lips, wishing they could marry that very moment. When he pulled back, he said, "I'm not marrying you because of Percy. I'm marrying you because I love you."

They stayed in the garden until late in the evening, making plans and confessing the dreams of their hearts to each other. They reminisced about the past, marveling at the sequence of events that had brought them together—not once but twice.

When duty beckoned them to go in, they at last left the seclusion of the grounds.

"Where have you been?" Mrs. Dover asked when they stepped into the lobby. "The sheriff's been here looking for you. He says he lost track of Percy and his friend. The sheriff used the hotel keys and checked the rooms, but they aren't there."

"Are their belongings still there?" Quincy asked.

"Yes, the sheriff believes they're still in town."

"They probably went to the saloon." Quincy gripped Norah's hand tightly, trying to ease whatever worries she may have. "They'll leave soon enough."

"He has an evil look about him." Mrs. Dover shuddered. "Best stay close. No more sneaking off and kissing in the garden."

"I'm a changed man," Quincy said, "but I will never stop looking for chances to steal a kiss or two from Norah."

"It's a good thing you're getting married soon." Mrs. Dover clicked her tongue and smiled.

"One week," Norah said. "I wish it were today."

"Oh my, a week!" She rubbed her hands together like she was ready to go to work making plans that very moment. "There's so much to be done before then."

"You two stay together," Quincy said. "I'm going to find the sheriff and see what he knows."

Mrs. Dover and Norah both made him promise to be careful, and he complied. He had no desire to seek out trouble. Those days were long gone for him, and he didn't miss a thing about them. He wanted Percy gone for good so he could have a quiet life with his bride.

Quincy found the sheriff leaning against the wall outside the small jail, looking out at the town he oversaw. His hand went in the air when he saw Quincy approaching. "I wired Warner Crossing asking about Percy."

"Did you hear back?"

"Not much. He owes taxes and has fights break out at his place pretty often. I can't kick him out of town for anything like that."

"Norah said the sheriff in Warner Crossing is friends with Percy. I don't expect we'll get much help from him. So what do we do? Just keep our guard up until they get tired of being here?" He scowled. That would put a damper on their wedding week. "I can kick them out of my hotel."

"You have every right to," he said. "There aren't many places for them to stay. They might lose interest fast."

"I can throw punches and handle a gun, but there are two of them. Do you mind going with me to track them down and get them out of my building?"

"It'd be my pleasure. I've never had time for men who treat women the way Norah's been treated."

"There's no room for men like that in this town."

The sheriff shook his head. "There's not room for them anywhere. Let's find them."

There were two saloons in town—one near the hotel, which Percy wasn't at, and one on the edge of town. They stepped through the doors, only to be attacked by stale, smoky air. Through the haze Quincy easily spotted Percy. He and the sheriff stood back, silently assessing the situation. Percy sat bent over the bar, a drink in his hands and an expression of disgust on his face. He was armed but so were they, and they had the advantage of spotting him first.

Quincy stepped closer. "I came to let you know you won't be able to stay at the Mission Hotel," he said matter-of-factly. "You'll have to get your belongings and go."

Percy set down his glass with enough force that the dark liquid splashed over the rim and onto the bar. He grunted like a wild animal before turning in his seat and pulling a gun on Quincy. "I've had about enough of you," he said with a slur. "I came here to get what belongs to me. She's my girl. Get out of my way."

He staggered to his feet, swayed, and nearly fell, but the gun never left his hand. He clung tightly to it, pointing it at Quincy as he inched closer.

"Put the gun down," the sheriff said, but Percy didn't listen. He twirled it on his finger and laughed like a man out of his head. Percy was outnumbered by guns. Quincy had one, the sheriff had one, and so did most every man in the room. Under normal circumstances, overpowering Percy would be easy. The threat of death was enough for any sane man to submit, but he wasn't sane. Overthrowing an unpredictable man who seemed to care little for life was dangerous. He could fire his gun at any moment, taking an innocent life.

"Put it down and go," Quincy said. "Forget about Norah. She lives here now, and she's going to marry me."

"Shut your trap." Percy's wicked smile never left his mouth. "She's mine."

"No." Quincy felt the blood in his body go hot. He wished he were in the ring and they were fighting with fists. He'd take this man down in a hurry. "You're scum, and you know it. Leave this town. Don't make us fight you, just go."

"You and your perfect town." Percy spat on the wooden floor. "You think you're better than everyone else."

"People here, they're trying. That's all." Quincy kept his voice level, hoping to talk the man down despite his burning desire to see him flat on his back. "You could go and have a new life too."

Percy smirked before waving his gun in the air like a fool. Then without aiming, he fired.

Quincy fell backward, knocked to the floor by pain. He heard noise, more shots, but he could see none of it, and then he heard nothing.

Norah was still up, making wedding plans with Mrs. Dover in the lobby, when the doors of the hotel burst open and a group of men hurried inside.

"He's hurt!" one of the men hollered as they carried someone.

She left her seat, racing to them. Her hand went to her heart as fear crept in. In their arms was Quincy. Her Quincy.

"No!" She sprang to action. "Take him to room number two. It's empty. Has the doctor been called for?"

"He'll be here soon." A gray-haired townsman pushed open room number two. "We were going to keep him at the saloon, but Quincy woke up for a few minutes and said we had to bring him here. He was adamant."

"I'm glad," she said. "What happened?"

The youngest-looking man in the group told her about Percy while they settled him on the bed. "He was drunk and raging mad. There was no stopping him. He fired his gun even with the sheriff and most every man at the saloon aiming their guns at him. He wouldn't back down. Drunken fool."

"What happened then?" Norah reached for Quincy's hand.

"The sheriff shot him." The younger man grimaced. "He's over at the jail. He'll live, but he'll be behind bars for a good long time. You don't have to worry about him."

"I don't care about Percy," she said, ready to put Percy forever behind her. "Thank you for bringing Quincy. I'll take care of him until the doctor gets here."

"Yes, ma'am."

They stood watching a moment before backing out of the room.

Norah closed her eyes, silently praying for strength, and then turned her full attention on Quincy. Blood stained his left shoulder. She put a hand on the wound and could feel the bullet hole through the fabric. She ran and retrieved a pair of scissors and made quick work of cutting off his green-and-white jersey. She pressed the torn cloth against his wound, doing her best to stop the bleeding. His skin, normally bronze from sunlight, was ashen. She couldn't lose him. Already she'd mourned this man once, and she wasn't ready to do so again.

"Tell the vultures they can't have you," she said in a low but urgent whisper. "Tell them you're mine and I need you. Tell them I have dreams you have to make come true. Tell them I love you."

He groaned then opened his eyes a sliver, giving her hope.

"Where's my shirt?" he said in a hoarse voice. "You're always taking it."

No one should laugh at an injured man, but Norah could not help herself. "I've cut it off you."

"Again?"

"Yes. You get well, and then you can tease me about it all you want. Just promise you'll get better." She ran her free hand through his hair. "Promise me."

He lifted his hand and set it on hers, his grip on her strong despite his obvious pain. "I'll get better. I'm marrying you in a week."

"One week, even if you have to be carried to the church." A tear ran down her face and dripped onto the pillow beside Quincy. "And then we'll buy our land, and we'll live on it with Nels." She swallowed, fighting to stay strong. "You have to live and make it all come true. You are the dream I want."

"And you . . . you are my dream." He opened his eyes wider despite his weakness and looked her right in the eye. "The vultures, they can't have me. Only you can."

A week of rest was enough for Quincy to get back on his feet. He wasn't about to spend another minute on his back when there was so much to be done. Norah fussed over him, asking him daily if he was pushing himself too hard and if he needed to rest. So rarely in his life had he been worried over, and he decided he rather liked it.

She was a vision of compassion and happiness as the week crept by and their wedding approached. "Are you sure you'll be well enough?"

"I'm certain," he reassured her time and again. "Do you think your Captain Wentworth would have waited a moment longer to marry his Anne?"

"I don't recall Captain Wentworth being shot."

"Perhaps you should read it again to be sure." He reached into his pocket and pulled out a package. "This is for you."

"For me?" She took it and, using great care, removed the paper. A book. She turned it over in her hand, then pulled it to her heart. "How?"

"When I wrote Jake and told him I wasn't going to be buying his land, I asked if he still had your old copy of *Persuasion*. I paid him for it, and it arrived yesterday. I wish I could give you everything back."

"This . . . it's perfect." She opened the front cover of the book. "Look here." She held it up for him to see. "'For Norah: May you find a man as faithful as Captain Wentworth. Love, Mother.'" She darted her eyes heavenward. "I did," she whispered. "Quincy, I love this. I love you!"

"I promise you, Norah King, soon to be Barnes, I will love you every day of my life. Tell me"—he took her hand—"have you finished your list?"

She tilted her head toward him and smiled playfully. "I have, but you can't see it yet. Not until we're married."

"Why not?"

"Because some of my dreams are for my husband's eyes only." She blushed. "There I go being brazen again."

"This old ruffian loves it." He brought her hand to his lips. "I told you when we first met and you were about to marry that cad, marriage isn't supposed to be feared."

"I find I have none of the same jitters about being married to you," she said. "I'm thoroughly excited for it all."

Epilogue

ONE YEAR LATER

Quincy unfolded the list of dreams Norah had gifted him on their wedding day and crossed out the third item—"bring a baby into this world that has your dimples." He looked over at the elegant cradle, a gift from Sam, and marveled at the tiny baby girl it held. Their little girl, swaddled in blankets made by Mrs. Dover, often watched over by her brother Nels, and adored by her parents.

"Sam and Alice will be here soon to see our little Anne." Norah crept quietly into the room and put a hand on his shoulder. "Whenever I can't find you, I come here."

"I can't seem to stop watching her."

"She's the most beautiful baby," Norah said with her eyes on their peaceful infant. "I fear she'll be a very doted-on little girl."

"I don't think she can have too much love."

"She'll have just the right amount." Norah leaned in and kissed his cheek. "You've got the list out?"

"I was crossing off line three." He turned the faded paper toward her. "I'll find a way to get them all crossed off."

"You have certainly kept your word. We have a baby, a home, and you've even taught me to throw a punch. I might have to make you another list. This one is half crossed off already."

He put his hands on her waist and eased her close. "Make me as many lists as you want." He kissed her cheek, then the tip of her nose. "Make me a list a thousand lines long."

"A thousand lines long." She leaned against his shoulder and let her head rest against him. "I'll set right to work on it. Line one, I dream—"

"Ma!" Nels's voice startled them both.

"Shhh!" They both rushed to the bedroom door. "You'll wake your sister."

"I'm sorry." Nels set down his lunch tin, quieted his voice, and said, "I had to tell you, I got fifth place in the spelling bee."

Norah clapped her hands. "I'm so proud."

He grinned. "I ran all the way home so I could tell you."

"I'm glad you did." Quincy put a hand on his boy's shoulder and patted it. "News like that deserves to be celebrated."

"I told Sam and Alice on my way home. They're headed here but walking awful slow."

"Expecting a baby slows a woman's gait." Norah sighed. "She's so happy. I'm sure she would tell you it was worth every ache."

"Sam's been grinning ever since he married Alice," Quincy said. "I'd say we all ended up exactly where we ought to be."

"On Married Row." Norah laughed before intertwining her fingers with his and leading him to the front porch of their newly built home to watch for their friends. The sound of the small creek gurgled beside them, and Nels ran for the swing that hung from the lowest branch of an old oak.

Quincy's throat grew tight, and his chest swelled. This life filled with love, in a town that felt like home—it was the finest dream.

Discussion Questions

1. Quincy is found injured on Norah's land. She makes the choice to bring him into her home and nurse him back to health. If you were in a similar situation, would you have taken him in? Was there a better option?

2. Norah is engaged to Jake for practical reasons. Was she wrong to accept his engagement?

3. Quincy is penniless and unable to help Norah keep her land. Was it the noble thing for him to walk away when he did? Was there a way the two of them could have been together early in the book?

4. Two years later, we discover that Quincy is thriving in Longfield. He justified using the money he found in the clothes Norah gave him and started his life over. Have you ever justified something, only to regret it later?

5. Quincy wrote a letter trying to make amends. Was there more he could have done?

6. When Quincy discovers that Norah's life has fallen apart because of him, he goes after her, ready to set things right, but he doesn't tell her about his role in her misfortune. Was he wrong to withhold the information while she recovered?

7. Norah finds a friend in Alice. They have suffered different but similar struggles in their pasts. Do you find it easier to connect with people who have led a life similar to your own?

8. Quincy uses his basement rooms to help people trying to start over. Do you think he does this out of benevolence or because of his guilt? If done out of guilt, does that diminish the goodness he is doing?

9. Norah lives in fear that Percy will come looking for her. How can someone move past their fears?

10. When Quincy's secret is revealed, Norah takes time to think about it but ultimately forgives him. Why is she able to make peace with his error so quickly?

11. When Percy returns, Norah is able to stand up to him. What changed?

12. Quincy and Norah are engaged at the end of the book and married in the epilogue. Do you think they will have a happy marriage? What makes you think so?

Author's Note

When I pitched the idea for this story, I said I wanted to write *Les Misérables* meets the Midwest, with a hefty sprinkling of romance. As you can see, I did not follow that masterpiece very closely. But I did like the idea of someone's life changing overnight and the consequences, both good and bad, that follow.

I hope that as you read Quincy and Norah's story, you felt the challenges and celebrated the victories these two faced, and finished the last page with a happy sigh.

This novel was written at the beginning of the COVID-19 pandemic. My husband was home from work, my children were home from school, and we were all wondering what the future held. Obstacles and questions were not simply something in the novel I was writing, but they were part of our lives as well. Like Norah and Quincy, we had to choose to make the best of the circumstances we found ourselves in.

Even though life was strange and unpredictable, so many people helped me make this novel a reality. Mom, Leah,

Stephanie, Anna, Amy J., Rachel, Emily, Katie, Heidi, Jill, Julia, Leslie, and Amy P. all read early copies and offered feedback that helped me shape this story into one worth reading. My husband built a barn and got the kids working beside him nearly every day so I could write. At night he asked me how far I'd gotten and listened to me hash out the plot and gave feedback on different sections.

My editor, Rachel McRae (who also loves *Persuasion*), championed this book all along. I am grateful to have such an enthusiastic and all-around sweet person beside me. I love everyone at Revell. Brianne, Karen, Erin, Michelle, Amy, and the rest of the gaggle—you make publishing fun!

I'm grateful for the creativity God has gifted me with and the ability to finish what I start (even when I am so tired). I know that in him, I am strengthened.

And thank you, readers, for picking up my books, sharing them, reviewing them, and encouraging me. You make the journey rewarding.

Remember that when life is hard, the vultures can't have you! Keep fighting the good fight.

Turn the page to start reading
another heartwarming story
from Rachel Fordham

1

AMHERST, NEW YORK, 1898

"Have you worked as a lady in attendance before?"

Hazel forced her eyes to remain on the man opposite her and made herself appear confident and at ease. It was no easy task, considering how long it had been since she'd been in such close proximity to a man who wasn't a guard. Nothing about Doctor Watts was overly intimidating, yet her heart raced as she searched for an adequate response.

Her eyes betrayed her and darted away, landing on a painting above his head. A lush, green landscape. Peaceful, serene, calm. Something her life hadn't been in a long time, not since before—

"I wish I could tell you I had years of experience, but the truth is that I've never spent one day, not even one moment, as a lady in attendance. From what I understand, not many women have." She sighed, worried her chances at a dignified job were over with the confession. Since leaving the reformatory, she'd already faced a slew of rejections and disappointments. Leaning forward, she said, "I have spent time in the medical field and know how to care for patients."

She winced, knowing she was stretching the truth—a habit she'd fought to leave behind. Her uncle *was* a doctor, and she had spent a summer in his home. That counted toward medical exposure, did it not?

"You're correct. It's quite new." His soft but steady voice interrupted her thoughts. "I try to keep up on what's working in dentistry, and there has been much success found in hiring help. It will not be long before it is the normal way of doing things." His words came slowly, as though speaking to her made him uneasy. Even his posture screamed of nervousness—his long fingers wringing together in his lap and the way he shifted about in his seat. "You say you've been involved in the medical community. That will help." He nodded his head, a small smile pulling at the corners of his mouth, and with it her hope grew. "I don't see the need to interview anyone else. Nursing experience is better than nothing at all. You may begin tomorrow."

Thrilled by his words, she grinned. A real, legitimate job— her first!

"Thank you," she said, rising from her seat so quickly the chair nearly overturned. "You won't be sorry. I can learn quickly, and I'll work hard. I'll work so hard. Oh, thank you. To work here is more than I could have hoped for."

"Just one more thing." His cheeks took on a slight pink hue similar to the shade of dress she'd often worn as a girl. The uneasiness she'd sensed in him multiplied tenfold.

"Yes?"

He shook his head and turned away. "Never mind. It's nothing. I look forward to having your help."

"Do you have a concern?"

"Well, yes. I suppose I do." He stood on his long legs and paced behind his desk. "I've never worked with anyone other than my father before he died. Since then, it's just been me and my patients. I . . . well, I'm not sure how exactly to go about it. We'll be in close proximity and . . ."

"Yes?" she said when he paused, unsure what it was he was afraid of. She'd given him no reason to suspect she had a shameful past, had she? "What is it?"

"It's just . . . I don't want things to get uncomfortable. That's all." From the looks of it, he was already distressed over the matter. He cleared his throat. "I see the advantages of hiring help, but I've heard stories. I need not go into what I've heard, but . . . there are potential problems with having a woman in the office."

"Problems?"

Sweat beaded on his forehead. He pulled a handkerchief from his pocket and wiped it. "There will be no . . . no extra affection given to patients . . . you know what I'm saying, what I mean?"

"I understand, and I assure you it won't be a problem."

"And . . . and, well, my father told me that . . . he said I ought to always be honest from the start." The pink in his cheeks deepened. "I feel it important to say that I have every intention of remaining unattached. We will be professional in our relationship, keeping firm boundaries. Never overstepping the lines of propriety." He wiped again at his perspiring forehead. "I apologize for my bluntness."

Hazel bit hard on her bottom lip so she wouldn't laugh. She needed this job and couldn't lose it on account of one ill-timed guffaw. Little did he know she was the last person he needed to worry about. All the romantic ambitions she'd held long ago had been put to rest and replaced by much simpler dreams. Now she craved a future unblemished by the past, enough bread to eat, and to be reconciled with her family. Beyond that, she dared not hope.

She politely put her hand out to him. It dangled in the air only a moment before he took it, his large hand enveloping her much smaller one. "You needn't worry on that account. I have no motives other than working."

He seemed to relax. "I'm sorry, it's just I've had a whole slew of ladies stopping in about the position, and most of them are young. The way they spoke and giggled unnerved me. Some even had mothers with them asking after my personal affairs. It has left me with my guard up."

"Please, be at ease." Hazel smiled, still delighted with the prospect of real work. "I'm twenty-five, well past my youthful years." She swallowed, knowing she ought to say so much more about her past, but voicing it was not an option. Her past, her identity, and especially her years behind those iron gates could not be mentioned, not if she wanted to remain employed and off the streets. "I assure you, ours will be a most proper arrangement."

"I believe we'll work well together," he said in his soft way. "Let me show you around the office."

"What shall I call you?" she asked before they'd gotten very far. "Should I call you Doctor Watts at all times?"

He ran a hand through his dark hair. "I suppose you could call me Gilbert when it's just the two of us. First names wouldn't be crossing any lines, considering we will be colleagues in a sense. But *Doctor Watts* would be more appropriate when we are working around patients. Does that suit you?"

"Any name will do. I simply wondered what you would prefer." *Gilbert*, she said in her mind. They were hardly acquainted, yet she already felt that his name fit him. It seemed like a gentle, friendly name.

"And I will introduce you as my lady in attendance, Miss McDowell."

She flinched at the pseudonym, looked toward the door, and for a moment thought of running away from the shame she felt, hating herself for the lie. Regret once again swept over her, churning inside until she feared she would be sick. Life outside the reformatory walls was supposed to be fresh and new, but already she'd soiled it with a falsehood. She blinked quickly, trying to still the rush of emotion. She'd lied, it was true, but what options did she have? In two other towns she'd asked after work and been swiftly rejected when she told them her story. "Call me Hazel whenever you'd like. I prefer it."

"Very well, Hazel. Here is where our patients come in and wait if we are busy." He motioned around the small front room that consisted of four wooden chairs set against a scuffed cream-colored wall. In truth, the room would have been forgettable if not for the vibrant paintings that added luscious colors, warm and rich, to the small space.

Without intending to, Hazel sighed. "I was so nervous waiting to meet with you that I didn't notice the paintings before. They're exquisite."

Gilbert looked from Hazel to the paintings. "Thank you. I'm glad you find them pleasing." He motioned for her to follow. "You'll greet our patients, and when I am ready, you'll bring them back." They stepped past the front counter and walked to the back of the office. "I have one chair here that reclines, and it's where we do our actual work. In this next room, I have a cot, so if someone needs time to recover before leaving, they may rest there. Your job will be seeing to patients before and after they come to me. I like to help everyone be comfortable, but I'll work faster if you can help me with that. You'll also hand me instruments as necessary."

"I can do all that." She pointed toward a door. "What's down the hall?"

"That's the room where I make bridges and dentures. I call it my art room." His gaze stayed on the door at the end of the hall, giving her a moment to study him. He reminded her of someone, but she couldn't peg down who. She'd guess he was thirty, give or take a year or two. He was tall, much taller than she was, with a lean build and long arms and legs. His rich dark hair was in need of a cut and his clothes were in need of ironing, but even with him being slightly disheveled, she still found him a handsome man who was shy and unsuspecting.

Why was he a dentist? Teeth and mouths were far from exciting. In her case, the work was a necessity, and being a woman, her options were limited, but he could have been anything. A commanding lawyer or a dashing doctor. She pushed the thought aside, realizing it was a tad early to judge his motives.

"Is there anything else I should know?" Hazel asked, breaking the silence.

"Most of it I'll teach you as we go. But, well, I do want you to know that my patients—ours, now—matter a great deal to me. I want them to have the best care."

She stepped a little closer to him and with genuine conviction said, "Then that is what I will give them."

He held her gaze and nodded. "I believe you will. We discussed the particulars when you first arrived. I'll show you tomorrow where we clean the instruments and how to keep notes. If you have no questions, then I think it is settled. I appreciate your help."

Glancing once more around the room, she admired other paintings that hung throughout the simple but comfortable building. Working with him did not seem daunting, and neither did filling her days attending to the patients' needs. She could do this. There had been a time in her life when it would have been an ill fit, but now, she felt immense gratitude. The patients did not scare her, and the teeth, well, she'd manage. Perhaps Providence had led her down Front Street on the very day Gilbert Watts was interviewing for a reason. A pleasant warmth filled her heart, and for a moment she felt less alone and less afraid.

Grinning, she said, "I'm very thankful. I'll be here tomorrow."

Gilbert Watts watched Hazel leave. She'd said she was twenty-five, and he'd believed it when she walked in. She'd been so prim and proper, not a bit silly like the younger female interviewees had been. But now, seeing her skip away, he didn't think she seemed all that different.

No matter her demeanor, he'd given her his word, so there'd be no changing his mind—at least not until after he gave her a chance. Ladies in attendance, once a novel idea, were on course to become the norm. And he saw the benefits. With a lady in the office, his young female patients could come more freely rather than having to find a chaperone.

With good help, he knew he could work faster. And with the demand for his services so high, he'd be able to help additional patients.

Despite the obvious rewards of having help, he worried. He'd mulled the decision over in his mind for many weeks before putting up the "Help Wanted" sign. Somehow he'd become a creature of habit, comfortable in his bachelor-dentist ways. Hazel may wish to prattle aimlessly about everything and nothing all at the same time. Or worse, she may cry at the sight of someone in pain or be too delicate to handle the bloodier side of dentistry, and he had no experience with tears or with prattle.

Looking out the front window again, he caught one more glimpse of Hazel before she turned the corner. He'd thought her hair was brown, but now with the sun shining on it, the color looked nearly red.

In dental school, the other men called redheads *spitfires*, and they swore they had tempers that matched the hue of their hair. The thought of a hot-tempered woman working for him made his palms sweat. He wiped his hands on his pants, turned away from the window, and retreated to the art room, where he threw his nervous energy into Rebecca Weidel's bridgework. He'd been working extra hard on this one and wanted it to be perfect. Poor Rebecca had lost both of her front teeth as a youth, and now she was about to marry her sweetheart. The teeth, the wedding. He knew it was all expensive and important. These teeth would be a work of art that Rebecca and her future husband would never regret spending their savings on.

Rachel Fordham is the author of *The Hope of Azure Springs*, *Yours Truly, Thomas*, *A Life Once Dreamed*, and *A Lady in Attendance*. She started writing when her children began begging her for stories at night. She'd pull a book from the shelf, but they'd insist she make one up. Finally, she paired her love of good stories with her love of writing and hasn't stopped since. She lives with her husband and children on an island in the state of Washington.

"Fordham brings new depth to her signature charm as her characters grapple with questions of self-worth, accountability, and justice."

–Booklist

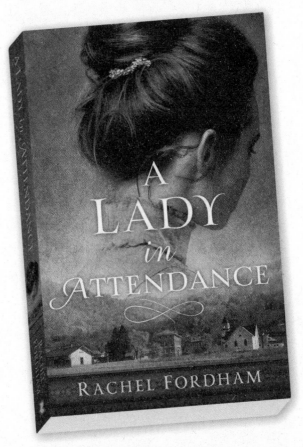

After spending five years in a New York state reformatory serving an unjust sentence, all Hazel wants to do is secure a job so she can begin clearing her name. Assisting dentist Gilbert Watts offers her that chance—and more. But can her hopes for the future ever expunge the shame of her past?

"Fordham delivers another winning inspirational romance in this lavishly detailed tale set in the Wild West."

—*Publishers Weekly*

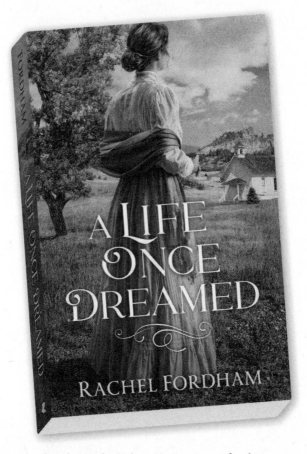

A schoolteacher in the Dakota Territory must face her past—and her shameful secret—when a familiar doctor arrives in town and threatens to unlock the heart she's guarded so tightly.

Head to Azure Springs, Iowa, for Stories of Hope, Love, and New Beginnings

Meet
Rachel Fordham

RachelFordham.com